PRAISE *for* DOUGLAS CLEGG
and MORDRED: BASTARD SON

"Clegg maintains a nice balance between the human and mythic dimensions of his characters, portraying the familiar elements of their story from refreshingly original angles."

—*Publishers Weekly*

"Douglas Clegg's *Mordred, Bastard Son* will inspire and refresh. Clegg has spun a modern portrayal of sexual awakening, coming out, and being separated from society's mainstream. Gay readers will recognize an alternative Arthurian reality here, one that resonates on a personal as well as mythical level."

—*The Advocate*

"Douglas Clegg writes of…nightmares with such clarity and passion you don't end up reading it; you end up drinking them in."

—Christopher Rice, author of *A Destiny of Souls*

"Riveting. Clegg puts an inspired wrinkle in the hoary tale of Arthur and the grail by casting Arthur's kindred enemy, Mordred, as a gay man. How excellent."

—*Booklist,* starred review

"Douglas Clegg is the future of dark fantasy."

—Sherrilyn Kenyon, author of the Dark-Hunter novels

"A nifty way of making an oft-told tale fresh again. This new direction in storytelling augurs well for fans of fiction imbued with myth, magic, and man-on-man adventure."

—*Seattle Gay News*

"Well-crafted. Written in lyrical prose with colorful characters and historical depth. Lovers of both history and fantasy will discover within an enchanting read."

—*Edge Boston*

Mordred, Bastard Son

Book One
of the Mordred Trilogy

by Douglas Clegg

alyson books
NEW YORK

MANUFACTURED IN THE UNITED STATES OF AMERICA.

THIS TRADE PAPERBACK IS PUBLISHED BY ALYSON BOOKS,
P.O. BOX 1253, OLD CHELSEA STATION, NEW YORK, NY 10113-1251.
DISTRIBUTION IN THE UNITED KINGDOM BY TURNAROUND PUBLISHER SERVICES LTD.,
UNIT 3, OLYMPIA TRADING ESTATE, COBURG ROAD, WOOD GREEN,
LONDON N22 6TZ ENGLAND.

FIRST EDITION (HARDCOVER): JANUARY 2006
FIRST PAPERBACK EDITION: JANUARY 2007

LIBRARY OF CONGRESS CATALOGING-IN-PUBLICATION DATA
  CLEGG, DOUGLAS, 1958-
    MORDRED, BASTARD SON / BY DOUGLAS CLEGG.—1ST ED.
    P. CM.--(MORDRED TRILOGY; BK. 1)
    ISBN 1-55583-987-8; ISBN-13 978-1-55583-987-1 (PBK.)
    ISBN 1-55583-899-5; ISBN-13 1-55583-899-7 (HARDCOVER)
    1. MORDRED (LEGENDARY CHARACTER)—FICTION. 2. ILLEGITIMATE CHILDREN OF
    ROYALTY—FICTION. 3. ARTHURIAN ROMANCES—ADAPTATIONS. 4. GAY MEN—
    FICTION. I. TITLE.
  PS3553.L3918 M67 2006
  813'.54—DC22

                         2005053069

07 08 09 10 a 10 9 8 7 6 5 4 3 2 1

ISBN 1-55583-987-8
ISBN-13 1-55583-987-1

For Raul

With thanks for being as much a partner on this novel
as you are with every novel I write.

Acknowledgments

Thanks to my agent, Simon Lipskar. A special thank-you to Dan Cullinane, a friend and colleague who first heard of Mordred's true story and saw the possibilities. Additional thanks go to Jeff Funk; M. J. Rose; Thomas Malory; Chrétien de Troyes; Marie de France; Alfred, Lord Tennyson; Geoffrey of Monmouth; and Taliesin. To my editors and the folks at Alyson, gratitude and thanks: Nick Street and Angela Brown, Matt Sams, and Greg Constante.

Preface

A note on the tale contained herein:

With all the research done on the historical Arthur and Mordred, and the understanding in the twenty-first century of the Dark Ages in which this story takes place, it would've been fashionable and proper to stick with the wood forts and the unmythical kingdom of the Britons. But I love a legend. I'm returning to the romances of Brittany and Cornwall and Wales, to the high chivalry and magick, and to Marie de France and Chrétien de Troyes and Thomas Malory and Tennyson with "many-tower'd Camelot," yet Mordred's is a twist in the tale.

I decided that this trilogy of novels, of which *Mordred, Bastard Son* is the first, should take the form of fantasy and legend—fiction, if you will—rather than a vague history of that moment when the Dark Ages had begun.

I think I owe the legends at least this much: to find them again, within the myth itself, and to tell a new tale of the Arthurian legend. The legends of Arthur and Mordred vary, but in the earliest ones, Mordred was not the villain but the hero. As with all things, I think the truth lies in the middle. The addition of Mordred being a gay man is my own.

Mordred, Bastard Son is the opening tale of a trilogy of Mordred's life, his confessions, and his quest.

Chapter One

1

The long wooden boat, its sails lowered, glided along the marshy shoals at the inlet from the mist-shrouded sea.

Standing at the boat's prow, a cloaked figure guided the boatman between the rocks, toward the strand, as if knowing the place by heart.

2

These were the days after the fall of the kingdoms of Arthur, King of the Britons, whose sovereignty had run from Cornwall to Wales to England to the west of Gaul, called by some Armorica; by others, Britannia. The Romans threatened battle to the east; the Saxons and the men of the North had launched boats upon the southern kingdoms, and it was rumored that an attack on the coast was imminent. The omens of the last days emerged through the mist of smoke and ash that touched the stone-gray sea. Great dark fish of the deep flung themselves onto the sand, as if the water itself had been poisoned. In the air, flocks of ravens flew swift along the twisting roads at the edge of the marshy strand that led to the great rock island, the Dragon's Mount, that jutted out from a strand of the southern Armorica coast called Cornouaille by the Celtic tribes. The priests and bishops called out for the heathens to be hunted down, for they had brought ruin to the crops and kept the land unholy and allowed the Saxons and the men of the North to destroy the holy sites. But those who had known the Days of the Kings and of the Druid priests had remembered the Roman captivity, calling out for Merlin in the old tongue, hoping that the ancient mage might save them from the devastation.

Atop the peak of the Dragon's Mount, where the rocks flattened like great altars, soldiers stood vigil lest those who had lost faith during the fortnight might risk the quicksand marshes and ascend the rocky stair to the ancient place of pagan worship.

The year of war and fire lay dying, and the cauldron of Rebirth, called by some the Grail, had been lost. The isles of Avalon in the brackish summer sea had turned to haze, and even the finest boatmen could not find them. Those who worshipped the heathen gods went underground; those of Christendom sought sanctuary in the ruins of abbeys and monasteries and nunneries and the Roman villas, which had become property of either church or warlord; the wars continued, even after the great castles of Arthur, pen-Dragon had fallen and lay in ruin.

All of it, so it was said, could be laid at the feet of one man whose infamy had spread throughout the kingdoms and whose name had quickly come to mean, simply, "traitor." That name was Mordred.

"Mordred" curved upon the lips of those men who sought the source for the unraveling of the world as if the word "Mordred" were an eel that wriggled and slithered along the tongue. Many grimaced as the name was spoken. He was known to be unnatural, a demon, a spirit of malevolence rising from the miasma. Some believed him to be a creature of the night, drinking the blood of youths; still others remembered his mother and how she had turned to darkness and raised her son in shadow. A great price of gold and silver had been set upon the head of this bastard heathen as well as upon the sword he had stolen from the greatest of kings of the Britons.

And yet, few could recognize the face of this man. By legend, he was a hideous, deformed creature, with the horns of the bull-god upon his forehead and the stench of the grave about him.

The villagers expected a phantom in the form of a man.

It was to this craggy shore that a stranger arrived, cloaked and masked.

3

He paid his fee to the boatman with a sack of gold, and none questioned him, though rumors spread as fast as fire across a field of drying hay.

A soldier under Bedevere's command, standing with his comrades along the Roman wall, found the boatman soon after his landing. After he and his crew were threatened with death, the boatman confessed that the masked stranger had first come to him with blood on his hands, blood on his gold, and had only washed in the sea when the stranger had noticed the boatman's glare. "He wears a mask of gold and silver, as I have seen the heathens wear for their infernal celebrations," the boatman said.

The soldier struck the old man hard, and the boatman fell to the earth. "You are heathen yourself. I see the markings upon your wrist, old man. You brought this murderer to our land to escape his fate among Arthur's knights."

Then, he took the gold from the boatman. Passing it to his companions, the soldier told them to arrest the boatman until a confession was had as to the whereabouts of "that bastard Mordred who shall not live to see another dawn."

4

And yet, for one long day and night, the stranger traveled inland, finding the narrow byways off the main coastal roads, avoiding the trade routes and the endless run of horsemen and soldiers.

The nameless days of December passed, the days without sun following the solstice; the hours since the song of swords had last been sung; many nights since the last cry had been heard on the battlefields, beyond the gentle slope of land. The fires had come, and then the silence. The dead remained unburied where they had fallen; the living had retreated from the sea to the forest and the inland villages. Smoke plumed at a great distance from the still-burning towers along the seawall. The sky above, at twilight, ran crimson through thatched gray clouds, and the local folk who lived along the marshlands and the fields beyond the ruined castle of the dead warlord Hoel felt this was a sign that Arthur had begun his journey to the Otherworld, through the isles of Avalon.

The forest by the roadside grew dark too fast. Omens and auguries were read by the priests of old in secret places, and predictions of the coming year mingled with prophecies of the immortal king. Whispers rode the wind across the wolf-scavenged battlefield at the plain beyond the woods. At the far end of the torn castle wall, near the abbey and the old Roman road, it was whispered that all that had been found was lost, and all that had been dreamed, disturbed.

Into this approaching dusk came that dark-hued stranger, a man of shadows, like the spirit of one long dead now raised to complete a task. That phantom, masked and shrouded, carrying a staff that looked as if it had once been a spear of war.

5

He wore a heavy, ragged cloak, as a beggar might, and some folk grew afraid that he brought a plague with him as he skulked beneath the fallen towers, still blackened and smoldering; his face covered by that jeweled mask placed as if hiding a war scar.

He grasped his staff, trudging up the dirt road with its markers of pikes with the heads of traitors upon them. In a time of plenty, he might be judged a wanderer, but in these dangerous times after the wars, fear had spread across the land. Strangers brought with them dread. The kindest among the folk in the village whispered in doorways that this might be a hermit come to the forests, having retreated from the world of men in order to fight the demons of temptation. Those of the old beliefs, those who still kept the antler headdress hidden beneath their straw mats or went to beg the Lady of the Wood for herbs and salves, felt that he might be one of their Druids, perhaps even the sacred Merlin disguised as a wanderer.

Those who held to fearful beliefs thought it might be one of the undead of the battlegrounds, called the Wandering Ones. These spirits had not been invited into the Otherworld for crimes they had committed and debts they owed.

This cloaked man went along, unmolested, unharmed, and as twilight grew near, he stopped along the rotting wood and crumbling stone of an old Roman villa that had but one standing wall left to it.

Here, he slept, curled nearly into a ball, against the cold stone.

6

He awoke shivering. Above him, a boy of no more than nine or ten, standing in a peasant shift, pointing down at him. Beyond the boy, two monks watched his slow movements as he sat up.

"The soldiers came. Three nights' past," the little boy said. "Sir Bedevere's, they told me. Looking for a stranger, they told me. They promised my father and brothers gold should any of us find him."

"That warlord's army might have more pressing things to do than raid these villages and search for one man," the elder monk said, resting his hand upon the boy's shoulder briefly as if for comfort. "Do not be afraid of these things, child. And if gold is to be had, you shall have it, I'm certain." His voice carried with it a wheeze and a cough, and the young monk with him touched the edge of his hand as if to steady him.

The young monk moved closer to the stranger, raising his russet robe slightly as he got down on one knee beside him.

"Is it the devil?" the boy asked. "They say he has the jaws of a wolf."

The monk lifted the stranger's hood so that he could better see his face. The monk reached up to the mask that covered the stranger's eyes, and drew it from him. He recognized the mask as one used many years before in the heathen ceremonies, and it was the face of Cernunnos, the Lord of the Forest. A pagan god's face, etched into the gold and silver mask. Around the eyes, amber and garnet stone.

The hunter and the hunted one.

Beneath the mask, a face sharply handsome, yet worn as if all his energies had been spent.

The stranger's eyes opened and closed as if he believed himself dreaming rather than waking.

When the stranger opened them again, the elder monk said, "He has been hurt much. I dread what will become of him. Yet, we must take him. If not us, the soldiers. Or the wolves."

The stranger's eyes were warm and a brown-green shade.

Then, the young monk turned back to the boy and his companion, "This may be the one who has been sought these many days."

7

The stranger did not resist the monks as they took him at the elbows and prodded him along; for the stranger, despite his youthful appearance, no more it seemed than a man in his late twenties, yet showed infirmity of limb and fell once or twice before reaching the monastery gate. The little boy trotted after the monks alongside the dirt road, and now and then reminded the elder monk that his father would want the gold "if the good Sir Bedevere keeps his promises."

Watching the monks from a distance, some of the villagers came to the edge of the winter fields to ask after this prisoner. The boy's father came too, and drew his son back, "for the plague may be with him, and demons upon his robe." And then, his father shouted after the monks, "I will not forget what is owed me from this! What my son is owed!"

The elder monk glanced back at the shouting man and shook his head when he saw the folk who had gathered to watch them. He said to the young monk who shouldered the burden of their captive, "They will want blood. It is all anyone wants, these days. More so than gold."

The other monk remained silent, while the strange man leaned against him for support as they walked.

At the north gate into the monastery, which led first to the gardens, the elder monk said to the younger, "Bedevere will come soon enough for this man. We must keep him here overnight before the soldiers force their way to him. I do not want an innocent man murdered in a time like this. Too much murder has gone on. Too much greed. You will find what he seeks. Why he is here. If he is the traitor, we shall pass him to the knight's men. But if he is not, we shall give him sanctuary."

8

Inside, they took the stranger to a room of straw and dirt, and after a while, in the dark, he slept again, the heavy-gated door closed and locked. Though it was a prison cell, the place held a bit of warmth in the earth, and when he awoke briefly before falling back to the deepest sleep of his life, he found a bowl of fresh water near him as well as a trencher of bread soaked with milk.

Sometime in the night, the young monk entered his cell, a slow-burning lamp in his hand.

9

The stranger sat up in the straw, stretching his arms over his head as he woke. "Thank you for the water," he said, sleepily. "It revived me much."

"You have great need of sleep."

"I have need of that sleep from which one does not wake," the man said. Then, when he tried to move again, he groaned slightly, reaching down to touch his side. When he noticed the monk's eyes upon his hand, he said, "Do not trouble yourself with my pain."

"You are wounded?"

"I am healed," the man said.

"I want to see your wounds," the monk insisted. "They may need tending."

The captive lay back on clumps of straw and drew back the fabric of his cloak, but slightly. Then, he smiled, but did not say a word. He reached to the stays along his cloak and undid them, up to his throat, and drew out the curved silver pin that held it in place.

When it opened at his neck, the monk noticed the torque that encircled his neck. He had seen torques in his childhood, but they had been outlawed by the church and the king as symbols of the heathens. It was a twist of beautiful gold, a collar band that did not seem too tight against the muscled cords of the man's throat.

"It was given me by one whom I loved much," the captive said, fingering the torque, like a slave collar. "It cannot be removed, though I have tried. But you are after wounds, my friend. I offer them to you."

Drawing back his cloak completely, the man reached up with his hands and tore the thin fabric of his shirt open to his waist. Between the jagged tears of the cloth, the curves of a lean physique, well-defined muscles, with a chest that was thick and broad despite his body's overall slender build. Upon his smooth flesh, small tattoos of the type that adorned the pagan priests—markings in the ancient tongue that could not be deciphered without risk of heresy. The small image of the sun itself lay just above the curve of his left nipple and of the crescent moon at his right. Three small markings had been etched just below his navel, with what looked like the welt of a healing wound that rose from the thin strip of leather at his thigh. He had no tufts of hair there, as was the old ritual of the forest priests to remove the body hair of initiates into certain forbidden mysteries and damnations.

"Yes," the man said, watching the young monk. "Are they not beautiful? It is hard to take your eyes from this art, for it is said that it holds a glamour for men to look upon it."

The monk, transfixed by the body art, his fingers gliding lightly along the captive's ridged and taut stomach to his navel, and felt the slight welt of scar where the tattoos had been made just above his loins. The man shivered slightly at his touch.

"You are a most unusual monk," the captive said, softly, his eyes warming to the monk's face. "Would you like to inspect the rest of me before I am throttled by soldiers? I could step from these trousers that you might see more of this magickal art."

His skin shone with oil and sweat, and when the man drew open the strip of leather binding at his trousers and parted the opening, he grinned. "I have lain with monks before, so if that allows me escape from this place, then we may know each other freely." He brought his hand to the monk's sleeve and tugged it. "Is this what you wish?"

The monk drew his arm back and returned his gaze to the captive's face.

His eyes seemed like shiny black stones now where they had seemed warm and bright beneath the sun, and although the man remained smiling, his lips thick and curved, he radiated fury.

"I do not wish to..." the young monk said, his throat dry. "I want only to know."

"To know? Is that why you keep me here? Or is it to sell my head to the highest bidder?"

"No. But you are hunted like the forest stag. You are safer here than out in the cold fields where Bedevere's men might find you. You are the one who betrayed the king. And the knight Lancelot. And the Queen of the Britons, Guinevere."

"All those?" the man said. "You know this?"

"I have heard. And worst of all, to the people of these lands, from here to the islands, you murdered King Arthur, the greatest leader of the Britons."

"My father."

"You are truly Mordred, son of Morgan le Fay?"

"Yes. I am Mordred. I could lay claim to the family pen-Dragon, but I do not wish to do so. I am a prince of the Wastelands and of the isles of Glass and of Avalon and a priest of the sacred Grove. And only son of the king."

"Why do you return here? We had heard you would escape to the Saxon lands, if alive. But..."

"You heard I had died, on the field. So here I am, a ghost."

"Some reports were of your death, some not. I never believed you were dead."

"Who are you not to believe in my death? You seem young to doubt me. How old can you be?"

"I am old enough," the monk said. "I am nearly into my nineteenth year."

"A dangerous age to bury yourself in a monastery, little brother monk," Mordred said. "Your beauty is like a young stag in springtime. You should be out in the field dances, or riding a wild horse along the banks of a river. Chasing nymphs. Or men. The monastery is meant for old men, but the wilderness is meant for you. Your life has been shackled."

"My life has been pure," the monk said. "For I was born of sin and must atone."

"All the world, according to monks, born from sin," Mordred laughed. "Tell me, pure one, why have you come to me so late? To see my wounds? To cut off my head as I lay sleeping?"

"No." The monk's face reddened. "I would tend to your wounds, yes. But they seem healed. I would ask of you that you tell me of your life."

"Why?"

Then the monk said in a voice that was both nervous and hopeful, "That I might understand all of this." In his eyes, a glistening of tears, yet he did not wipe them. "I cannot tell you more, for if I did, I would have to leave you to your fate. I have been raised among the gardens and cells of this abbey. My mother died before I reached a full year, and I have not experienced the world at all. The monastery has been my lot this whole life."

"So tales of my crimes will please you?" Mordred asked.

The monk nodded.

"So that when you are on that hard wood bed, in your itchy shirt, after your evening prayers, you may lie there and think of the great and evil Mordred to whom you are superior?"

"No, my lord. Not in any way. But they say the world has unraveled, and the great knights and the king have passed. And you are the only witness who has come here who has known these noble knights and ladies of whom...of whom I speak. I wish for truth, good sir. I wish..." But the monk's voice faded, and a troubling look came into his eyes. "I wish to know."

"I will tell you what truth I know," Mordred said. "If, with each tale, you allow me one freedom."

"I cannot promise freedom."

"I do not mean the freedom from this cell. I mean, the freedom with you that I desire."

"I have heard of your desires," the monk said.

"And I know the desires of one kept among monks his whole life, one of such beauty and longing and purity," Mordred said. "But I need one freedom to begin and another when I have finished."

"Tell me," the young monk said.

"For a kiss," Mordred smiled, his gaze steady upon the youth, who leaned forward while Mordred rose to meet it and pressed his lips against the monk's. The young monk withdrew after too long a moment, his face flush red in the lamplight.

"Thank you," Mordred sighed. "I have not felt so refreshed in days. And now, where shall I begin? Shall it be when I brought the queen into the light of day? Or when, as a boy, I learned of the secrets of the earth and the lakes? Or of my training with Merlin in the Eastern arts of necromancy and of war? I owe you my life tonight, my friend. I will tell you what you wish to know."

"All of it," the monk said, a slight rise in tone to his voice, as if he were angry now for having given the kiss. "I want to know of Arthur and his knights. I want to know of meek and beautiful Guinevere and that shining knight Lancelot and the Lady of Astolat. I want to know of that terrible witch, Morgan le Fay and of her ogre-sister, Morgause, and of..."

"The lies that you've heard, secondhand, in your monk's cage," Mordred said, his eyes seeming to sadden a bit, "they are not true. Morgan and Morgause were not ogresses, neither were they terrible. In fact, many men believed them to be the most beautiful and powerful women of their time. If I tell you the truth, the truth as I know it from my own memory, tonight, will you help me escape this place?"

Without hesitation, the monk nodded his head, keeping his eyes on Mordred's. "I will. Tell me of your mother. I have heard she was a great sorceress and spoke with the spirits of the dead."

Mordred began his tale. "The king would one day call my mother the Witch-Queen, and she bore that title as if it were the greatest in all the world. And that is how I think of her, as the Queen of Witches, of the Faerie, of Broceliande and of Tintagel and of the Wastelands. But mostly, I think of her as Queen of the Britons. She was heavy with me in her belly when first she learned that Arthur, the king, but seventeen years of age, meant to murder her."

Part One

The Witch-Queen

Chapter Two

1

In those days, the world was different from now: the forest, wilder, the rivers, deeper. The waters between Cornwall and the shores of Armorica were not so wide nor so deep, and you might send a white raven as a messenger from Tintagel's small windows at dawn and by midday it would reach the stone trees of the Dragon's Mount. To even think back on it is to remember the scent of sirus blossom, like honey and thick incense in the air on a summer's twilight, and to taste the white brana berries from the twisted brambles along shores of the Lyonesse, the bittersweet flavor on the tongue, like a memory of the Otherworld; the gambol of the horses when they escaped the paddock at the villa, and the horse-herd boys who chased them across the marshy land and into the woodland path; the sound of laughter in the hills; and the way the deer ran along the edge of the field when dawn struck the earth with her holy light before all this smoke and mist that obscured the living from the dead and the dead from the living, before even I came into this life.

But my mother had remembered it all for me, and through a forbidden art she had stolen from Merlin, she raveled her life into mine.

She taught me the art of raveling. It is the backward glance within the soul, and the sharing of the visions from one to another. The raveling was a torment and cannot be done lightly. It may burn the recipient from within if not performed in the exact ritual; it may cause bleeding from the one who offers to unravel into the other. It was meant to be done only at dying before the soul passes to the next life. But my mother brought this into me that I might understand all that could not be understood by mere words. The raveling brought with it deep sorrow, but also great understanding. It was like pulling at threads of a magnificent tapestry, and in the torn places, another tapestry forms, and in this, in the raveling, one could see into the past of another and the other could see into you.

Raveling can be shared by people if they lay close and hold each other in such a way that the souls might merge, from the eyes into the eyes, breath into breath, skin into skin, and blood to blood. I was a boy when she raveled into me, and I became sick with fever for several nights afterward, while she took to her bed for a full moon, exhausted from the effort.

She brought the vision of her past memory into my soul that I might understand the world better and the echoes of one life to another.

What I saw within her memory, within that raveling, was her home of Tintagel, of Merlin, and of my father, the king.

2

King Arthur had not yet fought in the wars, and he had only just grown his first beard. His advisers had played up the boy king's fears, and the prophecies of Merlin were repeated again and again to him until, it was said, he could not sleep for remembering what was foretold by that great mage—Myrddin, son of Morfryn: Merlin, the Immortal.

You must know the way of Merlin. He is born, like a phoenix from ashes, into a new sacred vessel of flesh with each death of the previous Merlin. He is the wisest of the wise, though sometimes he spoke in riddles and confusions. Whereas all other men, when reborn into life, forget our previous lives and lose much of the knowledge of our flesh, Merlin's wisdom and memory continue in each incarnation as if he had never died and been reborn. He possessed secrets and arts that no other man living held and few women knew of; he taught me the ritual of the shifting, which is the way of becoming a creature of shadow in the dark of night. He taught me to see through the mist of the marshes and to watch out for the shimmering ones, "elementals" he called them, energies of deception within the rock and water.

Merlin in my lifetime was a big man, stout and thick of arm and leg, as large as a Norseman, but with a gentle demeanor unless he was in a fury, and then he was like a thunderbolt. His head was shaved, a ritual of the one called Merlin, and half his body was painted with images of the grove and of the Druids. He had a penchant for torques and rings, and a taste for mead and Roman wine as well as whores. He cursed like the worst Roman soldier, but his various verbal arrows stung less for the colorful way they'd been adorned. He wore the old robes of the Druid priests, though never the crown of the high-priest, though he was more than priest himself. It was said that he brought the great stones to the kingdoms and that in his thousands of years of incarnation, he had wandered the entire world from his earliest days in the land of Egypt and Troy.

Some thought him a terrible evil; others believed he brought blessings from the Otherworld.

To my knowledge, he was both a curse and a blessing, but I could not have loved life half so much—nor understood it—without his wisdom. His wood-spirit was the bear, and he was, as I remember him, a great bear of a man. He roared when he spoke, or he growled when he whispered; his eyes sparkled with mischief when the lusts of spring had him in their thrall, and he loved many women, though none so much, I think, as my mother, though she did only think of him as a kind of father and guardian to her. Still, he treated me as if I were his own son, and in the raveling time, I learned more of this remarkable being who was said to be the son of the stars and of the wind, who had been born within the dust of the earth on a night of fire and terror, long before our people had even come into being, long before the forests and rivers ran, before even the kingdoms of men had grown from the fertile valleys.

Merlin existed to carry the wisdom through the generations—as a living scroll that the high-priests and priestesses might read, and from whom Kings would learn much. He was said to have been with the pharoahs in Egypt and had crossed the river beneath those deserts into the Otherworld, and had come back with knowledge that had cursed him from ever returning to the country of spirits. His soul had been vesseled by both male and female, and he had been both priest and priestess in his incarnations, always bringing the memories fresh into his new body. The raveling had been his way of keeping the memories of our folk alive when the great and small among us lay dying, when the priests and priestesses drew themselves back into the arms of the goddess.

He was a terror and a wonder, but I cannot speak badly of him, for his understanding of the world was greater than that of any other woman or man, and his reasons for his actions are beyond my own wisdom.

Merlin who came into my life, the one who raised my father, who is known to you as King Arthur, pen-Dragon of the Britons, had four visions of what will be, and each carried the weight of the world upon them. These would affect all our lives, whether the visions were meant to be or not.

His first vision, which came to him within burning incense and a drug known to the Druids as stag thistle upon his tongue, was that Arthur should be the greatest king of the seven kingdoms of the Britons and would unite again the warlords and their lands.

The second vision, brought about when Merlin slept against the standing stones of the ancients on the winter solstice in the forest of Broceliande, was that Arthur would bear the sword of power all his days, though it would heap disaster upon him as well as victory.

The third vision, which Merlin claimed the ravens of the towers had whispered to him during his time imprisoned, was that the king would marry a Roman, which would bring peace to the lands held to the east.

And the final vision that Merlin had for King Arthur was that if he brought no bastards into the world, his kingdom would never be destroyed.

I am that the one of whom Merlin foretold. Born bastard and heathen and child of an incestuous mingling of the bloodline pen-Dragon
and the bloodline of the Fay, who are called the Faerie Folk, for we still
worship the grove and our gods and goddesses who bless us and teach
us the secret wisdom. I am a pagan prince of the Wastelands and of
North-galis and of the isles of Avalon. I am a priest of the grove and of
the mysteries of Namtareth, and I am the lover of men, as some fear in
this world who know not of love.

And by my birthright, I am the heir to the thrones that were stolen
from my mother.

The first was of the Castle Tintagel itself.

3

It was not the greatest of castles, nor did it hold the finest palace
on the islands, and yet it was, to my mother, the most wonderful and
magical place she knew of in all of the isles. It had been the seat of the
pagan queens of the Wastelands, with my grandmother Ygraine, who
was both high-priestess and queen of the three lands surrounding it.
She said that the stones, which had come from the isles of Avalon, had
once been a great invading army that was turned to rock when their
leader had stolen apples from the garden of the Lord of the Sun. These
stones, quarried from that rock, were brought over on great barges
along the sea coast during a time of impending war, and that though
the stones were heavy, still they did not sink into the deep, for they had
the blessings of the isles within them. After it was built, Tintagel had
many attackers, though few got beyond the cliffs themselves. The sea
itself had tried to bring down the lower balconies more than once, but
the stones had held. My mother told me that the doorways were tall and
arched, and looked out over the turquoise sea and the islands, and that
in summer, the seabirds would cry like children along its cliffside.

She pined for Tintagel most of her life, but would never again return to it after that night she dreamed my name, her belly full with child, and awoke to news that put dread in her heart.

4

The name she dreamed was not meant for a son.

I was named for the goddess of motherhood, for my own mother, feeling the goddess so much within her, in her dreams, wished to bless me with the name Modron. My mother had a dream that I would not be a boy at all, and she wished to honor the patroness of her own birthplace with a daughter of that name. She masculinized the name after my birth to Mordred.

She had seen Modron in dreams many nights—the goddess with three faces, of the Moon, of the Sun, and of the Sea itself. The Eternal Mother who sought out her lost children now that the Christian kings had taken hold of the Britons. "My dreams," she told me, "when I was heavy with you, were of cavernous palaces and groves of oaks so thick and tall that to climb them would be to reach the stars. I knew this place well, for it was Broceliande, and I had spent much of my childhood there with my sister, for your grandmother feared that Uther, while alive, would not ensure our protection."

She told me, "I returned to Cornwall, after Uther's passing, and tended my sick mother knowing full well that she would not live to see another midsummer's night, not a year before Arthur claimed the sword and the allegiance of all Britons. But how I loved it, the rough-hewn stairs that led down to the boats, and the May days upon the sea-cracked stones. The winter solstice upon the sea, among the many coves and islands—the smells of brine and salt air, and the scent of the wildflowers upon in the meadows above the cliffs come spring. It was to this castle that you were meant to be born to the world. I could dream of the mother goddess as I thought of my unborn child and of my sweet mother who had been so wronged in her lifetime."

"Why?" I would ask her when I was older but still too young to understand the world and its politics. "Why had she sent you? Why?"

"A queen of great lands must think first of the people of those lands. The crown of government is heavy for the one who must wear it, for upon it rests the fate of many. Had she refused Uther and the pen-Dragon claim to her and to Cornwall, her people would have suffered further war and pestilence, and these warlords had pillaged and burned much once the Romans began leaving those shores. Her husband—my father—was dead, and so were my brothers. What more sorrow could that lovely woman face and still call herself queen of her people? She had to do what she did. And it did, for a handful of years, bring about a peace of sorts. But those are old times, long gone. In her last year, I kept her mind from her treacherous son, that new-crowned king who, a mere boy of fifteen, had grown drunk with power."

My mother, in those days of my childhood, would tell me no more of this sorrow. She spared me for many years the shame of my birth, and so, as a boy, I did not learn of that crime that my father committed upon my mother. But I knew that it had changed her. Fundamentally it had turned her toward the dark edge of the goddess.

Caring for my sick grandmother then—as a young maiden of twenty who had determined for herself that she would never hand-fast with a man, nor offer herself to the pleasures of the body after what had been done to her—she had begun speaking to the dead and fallen, among the burial mounds of heroes, that she might learn the secrets of the Otherworld from them.

5

With me not six months in my mother's womb, and my mother overshadowed by fear as she thought of all that had been taken from her, her sister, Morgause, brought news to her. "The rumors are spreading, and you must heed them. Already, blood has been shed in Wales, and the boatmen of Mor, our retainers, have been slaughtered in the harbors to the south." Morgause had overheard, through use of magick, a conversation that her husband had when she had visited him with their son Gawain in the summer months in Orkney. "He spoke in whispers," Morgause said, "but I have spies within my own house, those of the grove who pretend to this foreign religion in order to survive. Our brother is scared of that prophecy of Merlin's, now that he knows you carry a child within you. Would that a raven might fly down and bite off his tongue that he would prophesy no more."

"Merlin is wiser than any," my mother told her. "If he offered his visions to Arthur, he cannot be blamed if the king brings dishonor and the murder of children upon his own head."

Because my cousin Gawain had been born just a few weeks earlier, Morgause feared for her child's life as well. She believed that the king's influence would spread to Orkney, and if that happened, he might see her as an enemy as well. "For we know full well that brothers and sisters are threats to kings who claim what is not theirs by right. Take my son for a season, although I will long for the touch of his small hands and the smell of his scalp in the morning when he nurses," Morgause said. "This madness may pass when the boy king and that traitor knight of his have seen many battles. In the summer, I will come to you at the Lake, and see him again and my nephew. But I will not let our children suffer under these men and their ambitions. They turn to bishops and abbots for their counsel, and Christendom does not look kindly on our wisdom."

"Surely I do not need to leave my dying mother. This must be a momentary madness of Arthur's."

"You know what these pen-Dragons are capable of," she told my mother. "He knows you carry the child whom he fears most. He knows that you are the rightful heir to the throne. Our grandmother was a warrior queen, and fought the Romans to a man, keeping them from our lands, and our great-grandmother led ten thousand soldiers to the Irish coast to fight the Norsemen—and when she lay wounded, defeated, she called to the goddess, and a great dragon came in great burning ashes from the sky, on a clear day, and so terrified the invaders that they surrendered and were slaughtered rather than fight the fire from the heavens.

"No dragon has come to defend us. No army can we raise. But the fears of our blood still remain with him whose fear of us, his sisters, will never die. He could not press you into a marriage with one of his warlord kings, as he did me. I was never meant to wear the crown of the kingdoms as you were meant, and as was prophesied. You are dangerous to him. So is what grows inside you. Already, foreign princes and kings entreat him with their young daughters that he should marry one day. When he takes a bride, prophecy or no, he will not want your child to live, who has our blood in his veins and a greater claim on the Britons of these lands than even he can claim. He has stolen the ancient sword. Would you have him also steal the cauldron?"

My mother's heart grew heavy, as she had to leave her dear mother, who had but months to live. Nuns had gathered around my grandmother Ygrain as my mother and her sister left their childhood home. The road along the sea was not safe, but Merlin knew how to navigate the caves until they could leave by the bay of the White Raven's Mount, a rock outcropping much like the Dragon's Mount here.

My mother, with me inside her, and with my cousin Gawain in her arms, bid farewell to her beloved sister at that sacred island. Morgause wept bitter tears as they parted, and kissed her boy several times over before she could let him from her grasp.

"Take care of our mother," Morgan said.

"As I can, I shall," Morgause promised. "But too soon shall I have to return to Orkney and to that life, and if she will not go with me, or is too frail, I will ensure that she has care. In the summer, I will return for you and for our children. Both of our children, Morgan, and I will see my beloved sister again, and our aunt, who is our protectoress in all things."

They pressed against each other, and whispered the blessings of the wind before a boat loaded with provisions came to take my mother and my cousin Gawain across the water to Armorica.

Less than an hour after they'd departed, an army of soldiers, led by a knight much beloved of the King, arrived at Tintagel to arrest my mother for treason, though some had orders to kill her on sight.

Chapter Three

1

In the boat with Morgan le Fay, besides six servants of the grove, and eight loyal and strong oarsmen who were Iceni descendants, was that prophet-wanderer, Merlin, who had guided my father in his own youth, and had despaired of the pain he had wrought in bringing the boy king to his birthright and the beginning of the shining kingdom.

He told me once, when I was past the age of nine, "Your father has a good heart, my boy, but the sword holds as slave him who bears it. This was true when Excalibur was raised over the battlements of Troy, and when a great Macedonian prince stole it briefly that he might conquer the world, and when those Caesars and tyrants held it, they too know of power and glory, but also of its terror. It is a sword of power but also of destruction, and I warned him against its use. Bury it, again, I told him. Make it safe but within your reach. But the sword calls to its handler, and if it is not well sheathed, it will sing too much in the mind of slaughter and possession. All the gold in the tombs of the East will not satisfy the one who wields the sword. I held it but once, and even I felt its promise of glory and dominion. It took me two lifetimes to shake off its vibrating hum. But he carries it always, and it speaks within his mind. He has the sacred tools of the greatest of kings, but even for a great man, these tools will become chains."

"But," I asked him, "is he a bad man?" For my mother had certainly made me believe so.

"He is both bad and good," Merlin told me. "As are all great men. He wants his people to have their freedom and their justice. He has brought peace in uniting the Briton warlord kings and raising the greatest of them to his circle of counselors. But even great men make bad decisions. The sword is meant to keep peace but is meant to remain buried in rock. But it attracts those who seek power. It brings war into the midst of men, for the sword itself has a spirit dwelling in its hilt and blade, and this daemon delights in slaughter."

"And yet, there has been much peace."

"You are young. When you are older, you will understand that there is no peace among men for long without threat of war, and much of peace is at the cost of others. Your mother's religion speaks of the mother goddess and her bounty, but even the gods war with each other, and even the forest hides wickedness in poisoned berries and its spiders devour the beautiful moths that gather at twilight. We live in a time where war is all that men live for. Soon…" he said. "Soon those knights will want to expand their lands and increase their stores of gold and grain and cattle. And Excalibur will sing to Arthur, and its song will be one of heroes and attack. But…" And then, it was as if a cloud had come from behind the sun, for his mood seemed to lift. "But I'm sure your father will continue to keep the peace as long as he resists these things. He loves his people."

"Would he love me?" I asked.

Merlin smiled. He had a large jovial smile that showed magnificently yellowed teeth. "Of course. If he knew you. But I will tell you, for now, my cave bat, you must not seek him out until the time is right."

"When will that be?"

"When it is, you will not need to ask 'when?'—you will know."

I loved Merlin as if he were my own father, though he had furies and tantrums as any who walked the earth. I suppose having knowledge of all his past lives must have made him impatient with the rest of us, who only could recall the experience of the present life. He had been born Myrddin but was "Merlin," which meant for our people of the grove that he was of higher rank than even the high priest and even the kings. And when he accompanied my mother on her escape from my father's assassins, his anger and his protection both kept her safe.

2

Beneath the outcroppings of rock islands and cliffs, they moved slowly, staying as close to the cliff face as possible and among the arched coves of the coastline so as to avoid detection should the high cliff-dwelling watchers of the king see them and report back of their escape. It took them until nightfall to reach the promontory of rock and sand that extended out from Lyonesse, undetected by those who held that castle built upon the low-water flatlands. But they saw the torches lit upon the bay within the finger islands of Lyonesse, and Merlin warned my mother that if she should be caught, she should not resist. "We must trust that no matter what happens, the goddess who protects you would not allow the death of your child in this manner."

"No goddess protects me," my mother said, bitterly. "Too much has been taken from me." She had drunk much of that noxious seaweed called cow-root, blended in a milk tea that morning, which was meant to be good for sea voyages as well as for those with child, but it had the curious side effect of short-temperedness. "Why should I leave my home? He has torn too much from me, and now he wishes to kill me? Let him have at me then, but should I see him, I will scrape the flesh from his damn face before I die. Let the gods curse me, let them. I will take from him all that he has taken from me, and may all my lifetimes be ransomed for this one."

At this, Merlin slapped her face, and she cried out with its sting. His sudden rages, like the storms of the coast, were legendary, and he never hesitated in slapping and hitting someone if he felt it was the only way to get their attention. My mother hated him for it. He said, "Your lot is to not despair or whine, nor were you meant to rule at Tintagel, as you knew from your own visions, stolen from me when you cheated from me the raveling and the Art, which you were not meant to have."

My mother held back her fury and pressed her hands against her belly, thinking only of me. Though neither king nor Druid, Merlin was of higher rank than both to our people, for he knew of the Days Before, and had kept our histories within his soul and brought them into each incarnation, fresh and remembered.

She muttered, "I stole nothing from you but what you were meant to pass to me. You aided that robber-king Uther; you persuaded my poor mother of this Fate you speak of as if it is written in stone when it is merely written in your blood." She spat the words as if they were poison drawn from a snakebite. "This is my child within me. His child. His bastard. My shame. And you would have us flee into the woods rather than turn and fight."

"A woman of six months may fight an army," he said. "But not fight well enough to win. If it is winning that you seek and not annihilation."

"I seek retribution. I seek *justice*," she said from between nearly clenched teeth. "You men who run this new world do not care for justice. And if the goddess has abandoned her country and her people, then I will go to that darkest part of the Otherworld to find my new goddess. To find the power to unravel this king and his false kingdom. And the gods be damned."

"Your anger will be your undoing, Morgan," he said. "What you send, you bring forth. Have you learned nothing from the sacred rites? We will do—all of us—what can be done to keep you safe on this journey. You must think of the child within you. Do not blaspheme those you profess to worship and adore. Do not forget to whom you speak."

"You may be wise and you may be strong. You have the memories of all your pasts wound into your skull, Merlin," she said. "But you are nearly as guilty as he for what has come to pass. You are the one who showed him the Lake and that sword. If you were not the instrument of this tragic tune, then you surely plucked its harp strings that it might play. And if you ever so much as touch me like that again, I will tear you limb from limb like those ancient Furies who did not allow men to cross their paths. And I will fervently pray that you never return to this life again, and would sacrifice the life of this child growing within me to ensure that some unknown god of darkness hear my prayer."

Merlin said nothing in reply to this but moved to the helmsman's seat, to watch the movement of the torches along the cliffs until the boat was well beyond the Lyonesse harbor.

3

By then my mother could only look back and imagine that she saw the towers of Tintagel far behind them, for the mists had come in and covered much of the coastline and all was a haze. She had great fear and anger within her, and she had begun to despise Merlin for his cruelty and superior air. She told me years later that she thought of nothing but my welfare and my little cousin's, but she dreamed in that boat of vengeance against the ones who had put them there. She fought within her own nature, for she had not grown up an angry child or an unhappy one, despite the sorrows of her life. But being hunted like a dog by her half brother who had stolen the sword and the thrones of the kingdoms from her—it had pushed her over the edge until she could no longer sleep nights thinking of all that had been torn from her. She wept into the little cap that Gawain wore upon his head, and dried her tears against her sleeve.

4

Merlin knew the stars well and was the first to see the fires lit along the eastern Dragon's Mount to help guide the slender, longboat into the harbor by the strand.

"Do you see?" Merlin said to her, as he drew the hood down from his shaved head and pointed to the west, back toward the water.

When my mother looked back, she saw distant green lights on the horizon, as of the eyes of wolves in a dark wood.

"Boats."

"Following us?"

"At least ten of them."

"I did not think he would launch so many."

"I am surprised it is not a thousand ships," Merlin said, and my mother, finally, had to smile at this. "He is afraid of his own future, Morgan. That is why you must not fear that which is to come. You have seen your death, have you not?"

"From scrying, yes," she said.

"I have shown him his, and he knows. He knows that if this child grows to manhood, his dreams will become nightmares." Merlin nodded. "He is afraid of you. He was taken with madness in that night that he possessed you. This is the evil of the sword. There is good to that precious blade, but it has its price for him who bears it. It does not belong to any man. It is cursed, and I should have understood what it would bring. When he came to me, to gaze into the Well of Sulis, I saw the future he feared. And he wishes to avert it."

"There is no future that cannot be altered," she replied, and whispered, "Forgive me for cursing our patron goddess and our Lords of the Earth."

"Forgiven," he said. "And forgive me for the slap upon your face. It was the fury in me."

"As it was within me," she said, nodding. "If anything should befall me, Merlin, I wish for you to raise this child. Do you understand? As you did Arthur, I wish for you to teach him the languages and the knowledge. He must know of the Otherworld and of the scrying. I want him initiated into the Groves as well, though you no longer dwell within them. Because he will have many trials and torments from those who serve his father, he must have the darkest knowledge as well as the shining wisdom. He must be greater than other men that he may live long enough to see our kingdom restored."

"As I can, so I shall," he promised her. Then, he kissed her fondly upon her forehead. They had a bond, which was both miserable and grand, and they fought like badgers at times, but they did not stay angry long.

But this sweet moment would not last long, for my mother kept watch at the helm, back to the west. The boats that pursued them were fast, with many oarsmen working at them and full sails to the winds. The small crew that piloted the craft in which my mother sat could not possibly outrace them, nor did they have the weapons to overpower the boats that swiftly approached across the midnight sea.

My mother's heart began beating too rapidly in her chest. Again, her head pounded as if stones were smashing down upon her, and she could not control her anger and fear. She clutched that boy close to her as if she could bring him beneath her skin for protection, and she watched the wavering lights of the boats pursuing them. "I have seen the High-Priestess of Epona call the brothers of the sea for aid. Might you not now do this?"

He nodded, but a grave expression had come upon him in the moon-lit dark. "I might once call up that which sleeps in the water, but if I did, my lady, it might harm us as much as those who follow us."

"Please," she begged. "For these children that we bring with us. Is there not something?"

"I trust we will make the shore," he said.

"And will they then not find us? Will the earth itself hide us? Will we sleep beneath the marsh waters?"

"You must believe that you are meant to live, Morgan. You must believe that I would not have even had the vision if your child was meant to die. Visions are not to bring action but acceptance."

"I trust in the goddess, and in the sisters of the wind and the brothers of the sea," she whispered. "But even so, I was not protected from a drunken boy who had become King, son of my mother as I was, but of a brutal father, possessed by some hatred of himself, coming to me with brutal swiftness at the moment when I could fight him least...where was the Lady then? For I was in my bath, and she did not rise from it to protect me. And now, for this act, which he forced upon me, I and the innocent child within me must die? And my sister's child as well? Where is that goddess? Where is she who protects and rewards?"

"If you could but remember your lives before this one, you might understand all. But know this: You are blessed, whether in this life or the next."

"You speak as my mother did," she said, her fury returning. "Queen Ygrain who lay with Uther, all the while knowing that he had engineered the murder of my father and my brothers just so he might part her thighs and take her lands. And still she spoke of blessing and acceptance. I might allow Arthur to push his hand between my legs when I could not slice his throat, but I will never let him touch a hair on my child's head. And if the Lady of the Sea and Sky and the Lord of the Deep will not hear your prayer, perhaps they will answer mine." She began to shout into the night a terrible chant for the death of those who followed. Finally, she exhausted herself and seemed on the verge of sobbing but did not.

"You are strong as the white raven who is your guide in this lifetime also is strong and free, and must fly when the storm comes but only for a little while," he whispered into her ear once she had calmed. "You may not entreat those aspects of shadow that bring pain into the world, Morgan. For every pain you inflict, you bring three upon your own head, and for every sorrow caused, ninefold shall be yours. Should you be reborn, this debt will follow you. Do not trade on your soul for this. Do not wish for others to die that you might live. Wish instead for the life of your child within you and for Gawain beside you and that your child's father will love him one day as well. Wish for your crown to be returned to you, and for justice to be done. Wish goodness upon our boatmen and servants, that they might have long life, and allow the sea and the sky and the wind to bless you. It is all that can be done. It is all that will be done. For what is cursed here may be commanded in that Otherworld but not as we would want it to be. Do you understand?"

"Do not blame me for desiring the death of him who seeks to murder me and my unborn child. You brought him to the sword within the sacred caverns of the womb of the Lady. You inflicted this upon him when both the sword and cauldron were meant to be mine."

"Aye," he said. "And I pay in torment for this. But this is not the moment to take this risk. Even death is not worth that price. There is a game that will not end this night."

"We are not chess pieces for you to move about as you wish. I do not think you care if we live or die."

"Though I have loved you and your sister and mother all these years, you believe that?" he asked. Merlin's dark eyes flashed with anger, and he muttered, "You cannot tamper with what must come to pass, Morgan. You swore an oath to the grove. I saw you take the blade upon your shoulder and drink from the golden chalice of Avalon when you were but fifteen years, and you swore on your life and upon your soul's journey. You understood the hardships that were required of you. You even then understood that you would bear a child of a terrible union. You saw this in the cup that was offered to you, and you did not then refuse that bitter draught. Are you now a rebel to your own kind? Do you believe the Lady of the Lake has forsaken you, even while she sends her winds to bring you into her embrace? Do not forget who protected you in your time of peril. Do not forget who stood before Uther pen-Dragon and stayed his hand from murdering the daughters of Gorlois."

My mother went silent and watched the lights in the dark behind us.

Merlin pointed up to the sky and said to my little cousin Gawain, "Do you see it? How the clouds gather? This is the blessing of rain, and it comes to us so that the grove might flourish and the rivers fill."

I looked too, for I could see within this memory. I can only say what I saw in the raveling, when my mother brought these visions into my mind, but soon, the moon became shadowed with clouds, and then a light rain began to fall upon the sea, and the wind grew until the rain became a storm and lightning crackled along the sky and at the edge of the horizon, lighting up the sea and the pursuing boats' sails, with the cross and dragon upon a field of white.

The torches that had been lit along the king's boats died out in the torrent, and the oarsmen seemed to have lost their senses of direction and floundered as they sought the coastline through a heavy fog that descended as the storm passed.

5

My mother carried little Gawain across the plank onto the shore. She uttered words of prayer to the daughters of the marshes who lived among the shifting sands at the edge of the strand to grant them safe passage.

And she prayed for the deaths of those who wished to kill her unborn child.

6

By the time they reached the inner marshland beyond the sea, others from Broceliande had come to meet my mother and her companions, for the raven messengers had flown the previous nightfall with the news of Merlin's impending arrival. Three men and six women of the Lake rode up on horseback, those tall and slender horse masters called Eponi, the old servants of the goddess Epona, as well as two white-garbed Druids—one male and one female—upon whose shoulders perched goshawks that then flew up into the sky to watch for the approaching enemy. Behind them, came charioteers, half naked and muscular, their loins wrapped in wolf fur, with the iron torques upon their necks that could not be broken after they had escaped their slavery, and the thick bracelets upon their forearms—these were Roman slaves of the provinces who had come willingly to the Lake of Glass and who knew the ways of their former masters too well. They guided their chariots over to the path to carry my mother and cousin and servants from the shifting sands down the hundred-league road. The storm had run its course in the sky, the fog along the water had begun fading, and a distant purple light of dawn played above the topmost branches of the trees, the rose-yellow halo of the sun barely visible.

"We must reach the Lake before the sun rises, or they will find us!" Merlin said and called out to the Druidess, "We are followed by cutthroats!"

The Druidess nodded, glancing toward her male companion. The Druid, whose beard was long and dark, lifted up his staff, and called out in the old tongue of Nimue to the taranis crows, which bring the omens of storms upon their wings, to fly from the tallest branches that we might be hidden on our journey.

My mother drew Gawain up with her into a chariot and crouched down, holding the boy tightly to her. She glanced up at the charioteer, whose long yellow hair seemed as if it were spun from gold. He turned to look at her as well, as if he had heard her thoughts. "Do not worry, my queen. My horses have outraced the chariot of Apollo himself and have not been singed by his fire. We will be home before the king's men reach the marshes."

On horseback and chariot they went down the labyrinthine path of Broceliande, that ancient highway that was like a spiderweb between the trees and moss-covered stones. My mother glanced back again as the chariot she rode raced through the great hall of oaks. The trees themselves seemed to bend and bow so that the assassins would find no good entrance into the Broceliande wood. Their branches reached across the road to those of another tree, and soon all she saw behind her was the forest itself.

She hadn't seen the Lake of Glass or its isle since she had been a little girl, and although she had not loved its rough ways and its isolation from the world beyond Broceliande, she now prayed that it was as she remembered.

And so they went, my mother, my young cousin, with Merlin and the two Druids guiding them, the horsemen, and the charioteers, under cover of the forest, into the kingdom of the Lady of the Lake, which lay beneath the ground.

A few months later, I came into this life during the Beltane fires.

Chapter Four

1

Fair monk, you were born, no doubt, after the celebrations of the spring were outlawed or were married to the Easter Mass by law. But in those days, the music of pipe and drum barely drowned the sounds of laughter and the clapping of hands and stomping of feet upon the earth. The fires and the dancing went on through the May nights with the sweet scent of wildflowers in the air, the arbors of the groves full of leaf and fruit, and the calls and cries of animal lust among the rising meadows.

I saw her sister, my aunt Morgause, and my great-aunt Viviane gathered around me soon after my birth, casting their prayers to the will of life. Morgause looked nearly like the mirror image of my mother, though she was years older. She had the long red-black hair, and when she grew it long, one would often mistake them at least for twins. Viviane was called Crone by one and all, for she had outlived nearly all the men of her time and many of the women. She was pale as a dove, and her hair, which she kept long and unbraided, seemed like the mane of a snow-white horse. Her skin was not so wrinkled, despite her advanced age, and it was only in her withered legs that she seemed to have lost vitality.

Through Viviane, the Great Lady of the Lake offered a blessing of her own to my newborn incarnation, and as my great-aunt parted her lips, the ancient language spilled forth from her tongue, a confusion of voices, yet the blessings of that nameless goddess were unmistakable. The Lady showed herself as a tower of yellow and orange butterflies swirling in beauty before us. She was like the wisp of light that carried the morning's dew, and she tickled my small ear with her blessing and her gifts that she gave to all the newborn children of her followers. Other elemental spirits came, too, although most were not seen by eyes, but felt with their presence. This was what others called the Fay, for these elementals were spirits of the wood and of the rock unseen by many but for those who felt their vibrations. They touched my skin and whispered to me, and through my mother's eyes, I sensed their benevolent prayers for me.

When the Beltane fires had died, my aunts washed me and returned with me and my mother to the stone chambers that were both palace and self-imposed prison of exile.

2

There are seven doors upon the lands of the Britons that lead to Annwn, the Otherworld. The greatest of these doors, and the last to remain open, is on the isle of Avalon, though this isle is not often found but by ritual and sacrifice and the blessing of the mother goddess and the father god of the tribes. There is a door in Glastonbury; another lies in Iona, along the ashen cliffs of the Wastelands; still another doorway exists, though it smolders; still another in the caves at Lyonesse; but the doorway into the Otherworld that I knew then was near the caverns of the Lady of the Lake.

Though there was an entrance through burning water at the lower point of the Lake itself, there was a door, though few could ever find it—a cave within the caverns, they said, that did not reveal itself to the living but the dead, where the black swans of Annwn hid during the long winters and from which the Annwn hounds escaped to quarry the dead. This doorway was unknown to me as I grew up, but the caverns themselves would be the home of my childhood, and it was this connection to the Otherworld that brought us the blessings of the Lady and even of the Lord of Death, King Arawn, who hunted the world each night for souls of the dead to bring into his kingdom.

I once found the beginnings of the entryway that might lead to that door to the land of the dead. Along a rock-encrusted ledge, an hour's boat travel from the isle, there was a low opening between rocks. A guard lived there, though few of the lake would ever chance going through the opening except at the designated night of the year. The guard was called Maponus, and he lived along those rocks, never leaving them. He was a criminal, though his crime was unknown to me. His atonement for it, however, was that he would guard the ledge and this opening so that none should pass until the midsummer rites. These were rites of manhood and were forbidden to all but the priests and the youths who would become men through ritual at the year chosen for them. No one was to ever talk about going into that place, though by the time I was a boy, I had heard that it led into a deep labyrinth of cavernous pathways, and that the ancient rites of the Bull and the Stag took place there.

There were other doorways into caves, some explored, some that had once been settlements, others that led to deep pits where one might fall to his death and never be found.

It was the sacred—and secret—place of our people, and the kings of the many lands knew to never search for any who had found sanctuary within it, for the curses of the gods would be upon them.

The Caverns of Glass had been an ancestral home to the Iceni, from whom our tribe descended. This network of caves and passageways was hidden at a break in the forest, with bramble thickets rising up and a slender waterfall that dropped across them like long wild hair. The entry was narrow, almost like an eyelid in the rock, opening up into a crevice. Another entrance to the caverns was farther into the forest, nearly a day's ride on horseback. But at the cliffside caverns, a child of ten or so could easily enter standing up, but most had to crawl in through the rock edge, just behind the waterfall and among brambles and damp moss. Inside, the crevice widened almost immediately, and within twenty feet even the tallest of men could stand and not touch the ceiling of the cave. With a torch in the hand, one could see the drawings that our ancestors had made here. It had always been a sacred place, a source of life for our tribes. The paintings using the charred ends of burnt wood and a red dye from the earth to depict the great hunters and heroes as they chased down the wild bulls and boars that had once dominated Broceliande's woods. In another section of the caverns were the chambers of the dead. Like catacombs, they were filled with skulls and bones of those priests and priestesses who had hidden here during the first Roman occupation centuries before. The Druids of my childhood had been hunted nearly into extinction for many hundreds of years, but those who sought refuge in the Glass caverns had remained there, and the chambers had been maintained for the Druid dead as a reminder to us all of those terrible persecutions of our leaders and chieftains.

Then, the torches might be extinguished in daylight; for a light, as of the will-o'-the-wisp of marshes, came up as the caverns deepened. The trickle of a stream broke through rock and warmed the cavern, for it was from the fires of Arawn and the place called Annwn, the Otherworld, beneath the earth heated the water that fed into the Lake. Within the stream was the residue of some substance that came from deep within the stone from which the stream and poured could also be rubbed on the skin to make the body shine even in darkness—we called it the Lady's Lamp, for it lit our way in dark places. You followed that stream along a narrow path that went down the stone corridor, and then the area widened, and even greater light came up, as if it were twilight here at all hours. The stream had grown in size so that one could not cross it without a leap. Far above, sunlight or moonlight would break through the rock ceiling in small holes that had been made by our ancestors to help the escape of the smoke from their fires so that they might dwell here, away from all others.

Here, the cavern took form: stonecutters had carved out steps down along the rock wall, which curved and descended and then rose again, this time above the stream. And here, then, you would come upon the Lake of Glass and the great island along it. Hot springs from above and below the rock warmed the cavern but fed into the Lake, which had a cooling effect so that the temperature here was always mild as if it were May most of the year. Flowering vines hung down from the chasm in the earth far above the Lake, and where the Lake came to the isle at its center, it narrowed into easily crossed streams. The Lake of Glass truly was like a mirror, for it reflected silver and gray from the rock ceiling, just before the cave ceiling broke apart completely, a great gap in the earth above it, though it was sheltered by trees that had begun to grow nearly vertically across it, perhaps two hundred feet above your head. It was like some ancient hidden world, and it was the wonderland in which I grew up.

The lake was wide, and on either side of it a sedge grew, and the horses, which had been bred from the original Iceni horse from distant lands to the northeast those hundreds of years ago, which were stocky and heavily muscled in the thigh and with a white fur about the fetlock, wandered along the paddocks that had been built for them. Upon this Lake, the black swans glided along the surface, having found the Lake of Glass even through the thick tree canopy above. Just beyond the far shore were the entrances to homes that had been built between the earth and rock, and the stone stairs that led from the doorways below to the doorways above. The ancients had carved entryways down a rough-hewn avenue, into the sides of the earth and rock itself. Though humble and mean in aspect from the outside, within these homes, deep chambers had been made. The hot springs that ran beneath, which fed into the Lake, warmed the homes in the winter. In the summer, they were often too warm for sleeping, and so many took to climbing up the steps along the clifflike abodes, toward the break in land above, and sleeping beneath the sky in the clearing above.

This other entrance to the Isle of Glass was where the horsemen and the chariots came. An old temple made of rounded rock and tall standing stone was here, and the entrance to the sacred grove where the Druids lived and prophesied. Finding this other entryway into the Lake and the isle had been made nearly impossible, both by the thousand-year trees that grew to hide it, planted by Arawn before he entered the Otherworld to rule the spirits who had not yet returned to the land, and by the thickest and cruelest of thorny trees and brambles. Only the Iceni horses could travel through them and be unharmed, for both the horsemen and the animals knew the avenues of the thorns that would not cut into them. It was said that any strangers to the grove who tried to enter would be blinded by the piercing thorns or by the white ravens of the goddess that stood sentry among the gnarled branches.

It was a world of magick and of great wisdom, and it is the abode of that sacred Lady who is the rightful keeper of both the cauldron of Rebirth and that sword of power and darkness called Excalibur. These were two of the twelve sacred objects of the Celtic tribes, and though these tribes were spread out from Iberia to Macedonia—even, some said, to the northernmost lands of ice and to the legendary lands far to the west of the Hebrides—these two, the cauldron and Excalibur, had provided protection and secrets to the Lake of Glass for many years. Even with the sword of power now within my father's kingdom, our protection remained, and the last of the Druids were safe in their worship of the grove, and those exiles and misfits of the tribes whose lives might be in danger in the lands could come and seek sanctuary here and know that no Briton king would find them.

If you can imagine its great curved stone steps, and the hanging red flowers that seemed like small trumpets, where the honey birds would fly about like faeries to catch nectar from within the summer blossoms and where the horses would be led down the trails from above with great spectacle, for the Eponi loved their animals as much as their children and felt the horses were their ancestors come back from the dead, by choice, into the bodies of their sacred animals. The black swans, rising all at once with a great noise, as they moved across the Lake to return to the world above: They mainly came in winter when the warm waters of the Lake called to them. And the festivals of winter and summer, the Lugos harvest that the Eponi celebrated, the wonders of Samhain, and Beltane, with its fires. One hundred folk lived among the cliff-wall chambers, and more lived above, and these were the last of our tribes in Broceliande, for the world beyond the forest had been taken by others. We knew of Druids who still lived in isolated places of Britain, but here, in Armorica, this place within Broceliande, were the last refuge of our kind.

The houses on the Isle of Glass, though carved from that deep, rich earth and stone of the caverns, was not rude or barbaric. The floors of our homes were made from beautifully painted tiles that the artisans had crafted, and the inner walls had a white plaster to them and looked finer than many a turf-and-thatch hut. The houses were a series of chambers carved back into the inner cavern cliffs, and a series of curved copper pipes that ran through holes at the corners of the chambers, from one home up through the other. These carried the steamy water from the hottest of the Lady's heated pools. Around the base of each pipe, as it entered the floor, porous black stones brought from the coast were heated and then placed at the foot of each bed, beneath the wool blanket, for additional warmth on a winter's night. This had been designed two lifetimes before by Merlin, who had stolen the copper cylinders from Roman baths that had been abandoned in past wars. My mother told me that she had never lived in such comfort, for the castles of Britain were all drafty and damp all year 'round. We had tables carved from blessed oak that had fallen after centuries in the forest, and flat stones for chairs, or stools made from the fir trees. Our kitchens were open and near the doorways; the hearths themselves were just outside each door, at a wide ledge that was like a balcony, and above the hearth the opening of the Lady's caverns to the sky above so that the smoke from our many fires would drift upward, though when summer was upon us, we cooked meals above the caverns to keep the air of our underground kingdom clear and clean.

The secret of my existence was kept by a handful of folk, including my mother's family, who lived here as well as the Druids and charioteers, and those who knew were sworn to secrecy of my true father. It was said that Merlin was my father, and that was enough to give me a special place in this world, but being a child of Merlin was better than being the son of a king.

My cousin Gawain stayed for a year, and then his mother, Morgause, came for him and took him to the Orkney Isles, only to bring him back a few years later with his brothers Agravain and Gareth, once King Arthur's hunt for Morgan's offspring had ended. They visited often in the summers, but my cousins and I rarely got along as I grew up. Gawain was the first to detect that I was different from other boys, that I had a sensitivity and some unspoken secret that he and his brothers did not share. Though we got along well enough, once Gawain turned thirteen or so, he ignored me completely, and some summers, Morgause came alone to Broceliande because her boys, she told me, "were training in the arts of war, in the style of the Romans." She did not say this with much happiness, and she mentioned often that she didn't like the way her husband, Lot, raised them "as if they are Roman soldiers." She always looked to my mother, her older sister, for approval and for guidance in matters of the heart and spirit, and once I overheard Morgause tell my mother that she had raised boys that she found she did not like at all.

Late at night, when I could not sleep, I would take the stone steps up to the world above where my mother and her younger sister often sat, playing a game called Ogham-lay. It was a game that had small bone chips with markings on it and I never properly learned it, but I loved lying on the summer grass, near them, listening to them talk about the old times of their childhood. Of Gorlois and their brothers, whom they barely remembered but kept alive through these evenings; of their mother, Ygrain, and the army of a thousand spirits she had once raised from the Otherworld in order to keep the longboats of the Norsemen off the shores of Cornwall. As they spoke, I nearly imagined my mother and my aunt as one person, for their voices were so similar. Where Morgause had warmth and summer in her throat, my mother had cool hollow in her tone, and together it was like music to a very little boy who loved the world he had been born into.

The caverns of the Lady of the Lake and its island were the whole world I knew, and though I heard of castles and kings and distant monsters of both human and otherworldly form, it seemed like a pleasant tale within a sanctuary of the goddess and god of the earth. This was my kingdom, my mother was its queen, my aunt its princess, and I was its prince.

But my mother had begun to move into shadow here, in this beautiful paradise, though she had once loved the sunlight.

3

My mother was cursed with a Celtic beauty. Some of the Broceliande road and its byways said that she was the most exquisite creature of her time. Morgause, nearly her twin in feature, also had beauty, but it is often the beauty within the soul that shines brightest, and Morgause's family life in Orkney had tarnished that a bit. Although the same could be said of my mother, Morgan le Fay, she seemed to have what the Druids called "the shining soul." But she scarred that soul and its light as her life continued, for the terrible act that my father had brought to her, and the unspeakable outrages with which Arthur's father had cursed her family, continued to haunt her throughout her life. But in those days, she was as beautiful as the underground Lake that was our passage from the caverns through the forest: brilliant and unfathomable. She had the dark almond eyes of her tribal sisters and skin that was olive. Her dark hair had been kept shiny with herbs that gave it a slightly reddish cast. When I was young, she allowed her hair to grow long and to fall along her arms like a cloak, with gentle curls. She looked like one meant to live always in the wilderness, and the curve of her hips seemed like a cauldron itself, and her longer fingers like the branches of a tree. Her body was like those of the athletic goddess who hunts the forest, and it is from her that I gained my love of athletics and competition—she told me that she had studied much with the wise of the southern countries, and she taught me the movements and ways to always retain health no matter the prison. She did not love anything more than a fresh clean spring and the sacred groves, but I saw early her love for handsome men and women of a striking beauty.

"All men are the god when love is within them, and all women the goddess," she told me as she prepared my herbal bath at night, as she had from the time I could remember. "Even among the many young men who seek me out, I see the god in their eyes."

"Which god?" I asked, being all of nine years and too inquisitive.

"The hunter," she said. "Cernunnos, who is the stag and the one who hunts the stag. The older Romans called him Sylvanus, for he is of the forest and of lust, as is the nature of men."

"In women, the goddess is there?"

"Yes," she said. "In some boys, as well. I see her in you. Do you know those soldier-mages who love one another?"

I nodded, for I had seen the men who coupled in hand-fasting, though they often left the Lake and isle, for many men left to go live among the towns and villas and castles.

"You are like them," she said. "In the kingdoms of men, they do not often understand this. But in the old days, when all the tribes were one, it was a blessing to have men like those who love each other, as it is to have women who hand-fast together. I saw it in you when you were but a few years old, as did your great-aunt, and Merlin too. You are blessed with love, Mordred. No matter what comes later in this life, nor what you hear from others, do not forget your blessings from the goddess and from Lord Cernunnos who walks among the stags of the wood."

I didn't then understand her, nor would I for several more years. All I knew was that my mother was beautiful, her words were full of promise and understanding. I was nearly jealous of her for the way she attracted men, although she considered this her curse and not her blessing. She had taken lovers, including the charioteer called Danil, who had first brought her to the Isle when she was pregnant with me. I saw him the most of any man whom she loved, and he let me tug at his long yellow hair when I was a boy. But she would not hand-fast with any man, and when I asked her of this, she told me that she had lost all love for men but for me and Merlin. "And even Merlin has his deceptions. Men cannot be trusted, and it is better to live a little lonely than to marry a man who cannot be trusted."

She rocked me to sleep at night with such words, and I had begun to form opinions of the world of men beyond our caverns well before I came of age. I was a funny, strange little boy: chubby until my twelfth year and with dark hair that always seemed to be dirty to me no matter how many times it was washed. When I saw my reflection in the mirror bowls, I did not think I was pleasing to look at. My nose seemed wrong, and my lips were too thick, and my eyes seemed more like the doe than the stag.

I was not the boy I wished to be, and when I watched my friend Lukat, who was born just a month before I had come into the world, I wanted to be him more than I wanted to be Mordred.

4

Lukat was the son of an Eponi horseman whose mother had died at his birth, and so we had something in common between us—or so I was told to say. I had been taught, once I was old enough to understand, that I must never tell anyone of my father, though it was known that he was my uncle. The shame and fury that my mother carried had to be passed to me, and instead, the tale was told that my father had died in some distant battle before my birth. The elders, of course, knew more than this, but this secret was well kept in order that should any of the young people leave to go seek their fortune in the world, it would never be known that the bastard son of King Arthur had survived.

The truth had been hidden, even from Lukat, to whom I told many secrets. And so I had been born without a father, and he had lost his mother at his birth. I shared my mother with him whenever he needed her guiding hand, and he his father when I wished to ride out into the forest with the other boys and play at war and hunting. Lukat had the glow of a god within him even as a child, and his eyes were sharp and he could lift up a great bow and shoot its arrow far across the Lake when I could not even lift it. He would take me riding with him on his horse called Lugos, and from him I learned of the poisoners who lived near the old well, itself poisoned by them, almost to the villas and castles beyond the forest, those three Roman women who called themselves Strega, and who knew the lore of the berries that kill and the red flower of fire with seeds that burned the throat until madness followed. It was rumored these Strega were three sisters with but one soul between them, and they grappled for dominion of it constantly and tried to steal the soul from others. Through Lukat's father, Anyon, I got to know the horse folk and the charioteers; through me, Lukat became closer to Merlin, who taught us both to read the ancient scrolls of Alexandria that he had salvaged from a fire. We learned of the Greek conqueror Alexander and of the friends Damon and Pythias, and of the legends of the gods of that world so far away from us, where Merlin said our ancestors had once lived. From the elders we learned of the dangerous creatures of the woods: the gryphons that lived in the hills and the dragons of the eastern caverns as well as those spirits that took the form of a beast in order to terrify all.

"Like the Boars of Moccus," Viviane told us by the fires one night.

"What's Moccus?"

"Who," she said. "The Moccus were deceitful kings and queens of the world, reborn as these ravaging pigs. Boars are sacred to Arawn, so even these demonic creatures serve him. They wander the desolate lands between the forest and the marshes, and there they have lived and bred for hundreds of years, perhaps thousands. But these are not our forest pigs. They barely resemble boars but seem like a mating of wolf and hyena, though in other ways, they have the boar's markings and behavior. The Moccus can grow nearly as large as an Eponi horse, and their tusks are curved like crescent blades and sharp as wolf's teeth. With six thick tusks; small, stupid eyes that glow red at sunset; and spiny hairs that can impale a boy if he gets too close, these are the most dangerous of the beasts of our countryside. In the olden days, the ignorant would sacrifice young virgins to the boars of Moccus by burying them up to their necks that the boars should come and tear them apart."

As she spoke, I was sure my knees shook and my eyes went wide.

We had gathered around, our wool and flax blankets at our shoulders to keep warm, all the children of the isle gathered in a circle with the priestess of the Lake telling us of her encounters.

"It is how I lost my legs," she said, drawing smoke from her pipe. Viviane liked to smoke with a long clay pipe full of the yellow-white virago leaf, which was forbidden to children, for it brought with it bad dreams. Sometimes, just breathing in the smoke, which always reminded me of the crisp air of autumn, brought me nightmares afterward.

"I was a young woman, not yet a priestess, and I had gone out with my bow to hunt deer for the Samhain feast nights. I had prayed to the Roman goddess Diana for the blessing of her ability and to Cernunnos for one of his stags. But as I went through the woods at twilight, I saw what I thought was simply a boar. And so, I pursued it, believing I'd been doubly blessed, for the boar would feed us for many nights. I chased it deep among the yellow-leafed wood, and it headed toward the cliffs that overlook the Valley of No Return. I thought I had him now, this great wild pig. But as I ran toward it and then crouched to aim my arrow, I realized that this boar was a monstrous spirit. It was larger than any creature I had ever before seen in the forest, and its tusks were like the teeth of dragons. One of the Moccus, I knew. I entreated the god of these creatures, Arawn of the Otherworld, for mercy, though he does not often hear the cries of the living for all those departed spirits who entreat him for rebirth. And I had been mistaken; this was a she-boar, and her full belly told me she had babes within her. There is nothing worse than a she-boar protecting her offspring, and this was as true for the Moccus as for any living creature. Smoke came from the she-boar's nostrils, and fire traveled on her breath. Soon, I was the one being pursued, for though I let two arrows fly, they did not pierce the creature's tough hide. I had to run along the cliffs, and other boars of its kind came to its war cry. These, its mates, were even larger and thicker than the Moccus bitch. I stood at the edge of the cliff, with three of the great boar beasts surrounding me and looked behind me: I was but a few steps away from a great drop into the fields below. You see, this was part of the Moccuses's training, for it had been how their ancestors had fought armies of men, by chasing them to the cliffs until they either had torn those men limb from limb or forced the men to take their own lives by jumping over the edge. I could try to fight the beasts, though they were nearly larger than I. They advanced closer to me. Closer. I prayed to the goddess and to Cernunnos for relief, and to Arawn, hoping he could hear me...but I knew what I had to do."

"Did the boar-bitch bite you?" I asked, and everyone around me laughed as I asked this.

"No," she said. "The goddess told me she would bring my breath back to me, but that I would have to give up my long beautiful legs if I wished to return to the Lake. And so—"

"You *jumped*?" Lukat asked, and we all went quiet, watching Viviane as she puffed at her pipe and looked each of us in the eyes before answering, the flickering firelight dancing across her face.

"I would not call it jumping," she said, a smile broadening on her face. "But the boars of Moccus certainly leapt toward me. The largest male nearly tore my throat, but I stepped backward, and he rolled with me over the edge of that cliff."

I felt the air suck out of my lungs as she said this, as if I were right there with her and the beast, falling into the Valley of No Return, where many had gone lost forever.

"And is that how you lost your legs?" I asked.

"I would've kept their use if that damn animal hadn't landed right on my knees," she said. "I landed far below but upon a soft bed of thick grass that had a swampy stream beside it. The boar weighed as much as a horse, and so my legs were of no more use. It was four days before anyone found me."

"How did you live?" another child asked.

"The blessings of our sacred Lady. The stream, and a bit of wild pig for supper." She laughed as she finished the tale. I am still not sure to this day what of it was truth and what was not. But tales of the dangerous creatures like the boars of Moccus, which terrorized villages far from our caverns and had even left deer and horses dead at times, were not to be ignored. The forest, I learned, was not always a safe place, and I grew frightened as a child if I found myself too far away from others in the woods above the caves.

5

Once, when I was ten, and went to gather wood for the evening's fires, I found myself lost along a streambed, unsure of which direction home might be.

I did not panic at first but followed the water, hoping that the caverns and meadows would appear to me through a break among rock and tree. After several hours, I began to call out, but my voice echoed in the last of the sunlight and my cries went unanswered. I continued to follow the stream until I came upon a fountain in the earth and near it an earthen home with a thatched roof that hung about it like a farmer's hat. Thinking that whoever lived there would be one of our tribe, I went in through the low, open doorway, but the long room was empty. In a corner, some furs, as if for a bed. And the strangest thing, to me, for I had never before seen it: a shiny metal shirt, hanging along the table of the kitchen, and beside it, a shield as well as a helmet that I would one day learn was that of a knight. Something about the place frightened me. It was not like my own home, and when I saw a sword in its sheath, although I wanted to go draw it out, I imagined the owner of this place to be some ogre, and I did not want to be caught like a thief in his hovel.

I swiftly left the little house, and when I finally found my direction home, I asked Viviane about the strange house and the one who lived there by the fountain. "It is a sacred place, called Bel-Nementon," she said. "It is watched over by a hermit who has taken a vow of isolation and meditation. Hermits often are in the woods—surely you've seen others? They live apart from us, though they come in the winter for warmth and food, or they act as messengers if the times are dangerous. But you must not return there, ever. Not to him. He is...a good man... I think. But he has many sorrows. Do you understand? He is sworn to protect the fountain with his life, do you see?"

"Why? What does the fountain do?"

"It speaks to him," she said. "The way the goddess speaks to those who listen at her sacred places. But we must listen very carefully, with all our quiet and peace within us to hear."

"But the Lake speaks to us. Won't it speak to him too?"

"He..." she began and thought a moment, as she often did when she wanted to explain something to me that I might not yet grasp because of my age. "Sometimes, it is the small voice of the goddess that can't be heard among a kingdom like ours, if one needs to hear it. Just as it's easier to hear a mouse in the storehouse when it is quiet, so it is when we listen for the goddess to speak to us, individually, that we must go to a quiet place where we can truly listen to her."

"At his house—" I began.

"You went into his home?" she asked with consternation in her voice.

"I didn't think he would mind," I said. "I thought he might..." I tried to come up with a good lie to cover up. "I thought he might need help."

"You must not do this again, Mordred," Viviane said, and for the first time in my experience, she seemed stern and unyielding. "You cannot just run roughshod over strangers and their lives."

"I'm sorry."

"What did you see there?"

"I saw his sword," I said. "It was gold at the handle and silver along its edge."

"Would you like a sword, Mordred, my love?" she asked. I wanted to ask more of the hermit and the strange home, but swords caught my attention, and my young mind easily skipped to a subject dear to my heart. Later in my youth I'd learn that she had changed courses so that she would not have to tell more of that man I had not yet seen.

I nodded. "I want to fight dragons."

"Oh, but dragons are our protectors."

"Then, I want to fight the boars of Moccus."

"I suppose you're at the age when boys wish to do such things," she said, and then she promised me she would ask Lukat's father to teach me the art of the sword. "If you will not learn it from me."

"You know the sword?" I asked.

She laughed. "All the Crones know the uses of the sword. I trained many young men—and, yes, maidens in my day to wield a half-sword. But I put aside the sword when the wars of my younger days had passed. It is not good to draw a sword for no reason at all, but it is good to know its uses in this world."

6

Many nights I lay awake and in my mind returned to that small house at the fountain, against the forest fence and the desolate territories. I wondered about the man who lived there, this wild hermit who could speak to no one but the gods themselves. I wondered if he were pretty and if he ever donned that armor and raised that sword.

I dreamed sometimes of what he must look like, and in the dreams he took my hand and we walked into the thatched-roof house.

Chapter Five

1

My friend Lukat took me to his father to learn how to carry a dagger and a sword and how best to use a shield, though our only shields were made of wood and our swords were birch branches that had fallen in a storm. His father was a large, thickset man, but when he wielded a sword he was as agile as a dancer. He taught us how best to avoid situations with swords but, when cornered, how to use a dirk as well as sword to fend off attackers. My mother taught us both how to make meatless stews that tasted as if they were filled with venison instead of barley, herbs, and wild grasses. She also took time out to teach us the use of the double sword we called the Broad-Tooth, and the Saxon long knife that we simply called the Seax. Danil taught us the use of the bow and arrow, as well as the way to guide the horses at chariot.

All the children of the isle would rise early in the day for training in the arts of the hunt and of war; the Eponi families would bring out their young horses that we should learn to ride fast through the forest, and how to bring a horse to near silence when hunting. Though we were not at war with any kingdom, still our elders knew the past wars that had swept Broceliande and felt that even their youngest should be prepared.

Lukat challenged me to races, and we ran for what seemed like many leagues across the meadows and deep into the fern beds until I was out of breath. We stole herbs from the Viviane's gardens and in chewing them had visions that made us laugh at nearly everything we encountered. When my great-aunt found out what we'd done, she scolded us for the thievery and made us work from morning until nightfall building stone walls around her gardens just to protect them from robbers like us.

It was Lukat who inadvertently taught me to swim in water, for I had no such training. We had gone out on a flat boat that was used to transport those from the far side of the Lake to the isle, and thought we would try to catch the bright orange fish that seemed to live only at the center of the Lake. We had spent an entire afternoon making a net from horse-hair and spun wool, and when Lukat passed it to me in the boat, he said, "When you dip it in the water, I'll paddle to the left. Just lean over so that the net stays beneath the surface."

Then, as I did this, I heard him laugh and then felt his foot press against my backside as I went sprawling, losing what little balance I had, and fell into the Lake itself. Beneath the water I tried to climb up to the boat but could not seem to get anywhere as I flailed my arms and legs. The water was dark but clear because of the intense sunlight from far above, and it was so warm that I could not tell where my body ended and the water began. I held my breath, hoping to draw myself up from below, yet I continued to sink down like a stone.

All I saw was the sunlight above me and a shadow where the flat boat floated. And then, a hand grabbed me by the wrist and tugged me along, drawing me upward. It was Lukat, who had dived overboard to get me. When I broke the water's surface I coughed up water and grabbed for his neck to keep from falling again. He pulled my arms from his throat and instead pushed me toward the boat. "Grab the edge, Mordred. Grab it," he said, more patient with me than I would have been had the situation been reversed. I went to his neck again, to cling to him as if he were himself a boat. But again, he pushed me away. "The boat. You can do this, Mordred. Go to the boat." And so, I at last moved my hands in a slapping kind of way, just beneath the water's surface, and made it to the flat edge of the wood-and-bark boat and grabbed hold of it.

"Kick your legs beneath the water," he said. "Kick them. Come on. Not like that! Kick them as if you're trying to be a fish. Like you're swimming with a school of yellow fish."

And so he guided me slowly through the process of remaining afloat in the water. As the summer days passed, he taught me how to glide near the surface of the water so that I would not sink, and how to measure my breaths so that before autumn came I could swim from one end of the Lake to the other and back. We often swam out to the rock ledges and outcroppings of the cavern walls, and saw the strange man who was whiter than all others, named Maponus. He squatted upon his perch, thick fur blankets beside him and offerings of food from the isle. His droppings, which were numerous, added a sulfurous stink to that alcove within the cavern walls. He seemed nearly blind, for his eyes had no color in them, yet he seemed to hear any new ripple upon the water's surface that approached his place.

"They say he never leaves," Lukat whispered to me, swimming close as we both looked at the old man.

"What's down there?" I whispered in return. "Why does it need protection?"

"We'll know when our midsummer rites come," he said.

"We have to wait so long."

"And you will drown if you do not keep swimming," he said, kicking out at me.

Lukat swam off toward the far shore, but I remained for a few moments, treading water, looking at the pale white man with his white eyes and long mane of white hair and beard. He sniffed the air, sensing my presence, several feet from him in the water. He reached behind his back and drew out a thick stone blade, pointing it across the water. "Come no closer, boy," he said. "I will cut your throat if it is not your time."

When I made it to shore, Lukat lay back on the cavern floor, panting with exhaustion. I drew up beside him and told him of what Maponus had said. Lukat looked up at me sternly. "He killed a boy before. I heard. Stay away from him. Stay away from that place."

"Would he really kill me if I tried to get in there?" I asked.

"If he could not kill you, you would have to kill him," Lukat said. "My grandmother told me that the boy who stole Excalibur from the Lady had to murder the man who guarded that way into the labyrinth."

I lay back on the stone floor, staring up at the cave paintings over us. I could not tell him that the boy who had stolen the sword was my father.

Father, I thought. He was fifteen years old when he went toward the doorway to Annwn to steal the sword that claimed many kingdoms. He killed the man who guarded that entry before Maponus had come to atone for his own crimes and keep that way shut. My father had gone to a forbidden place, right at the door to the Otherworld, for Excalibur. *A sword of power*, I thought, as I lay there beside my friend, both of us breathing too heavily from the long swim. *A sword like no other, which sings to the man who will wield it. A sacred, magickal sword. It brings war, and it promises peace. My father holds it and rules the kingdoms of the Britons on the great island of our people to the west, and keeps the Saxons at bay as if they were hounds on the hunt. He must be a great man to do this. He broke the law of the Lake to get Excalibur, but it has brought him greatness. He had to kill the guard of the labyrinth to get it. He was fifteen, not much older than I am. He was not yet a man, yet he became a king and great warrior.*

I hated my father with a passion though I did not yet know him. And yet I also wanted desperately to know what kind of man he was

and what would he think of me, his son that he had never before laid eyes upon. I glanced over at Lukat, envying him his father, though he had lost his mother to the arms of death at his birth.

I wanted to tell him that my father was alive, not dead at all as he'd been told by the elders. I wanted to tell him that my father was King Arthur himself, my mother's half brother, and that the blood of the king ran in my veins. Yet, it was the one promise I could not break to Merlin or to my mother. It would change how Lukat saw me, how he would treat me, and he might even hate me for this. I could not lose him as a friend. Even thinking of such a thing brought sorrow into my heart.

On the cave ceiling above us was a depiction of Arawn himself, with the ram's head crown upon his scalp, his mouth opened it the voice that brought death to those who heard it, with the skulls of slain warriors at his feet—his hounds all around him, and the old woman known as the washer at the ford, who cleaned the souls of fallen heroes on the battlefield. Not far from him were his sacred black swans and several hares and stags.

"Do you think it's beautiful?" I asked.

"Annwn?"

"Do you think it's as they say? Beautiful and wonderful, full of fruit trees and stags and horns that give every kind of drink to those who wish it? That there are jewels in the roads into the Otherworld and greater kingdoms than have ever existed in this world?"

"Some souls choose not to be reborn from it," Lukat said. "People stay there for thousands of years before returning here. It must be wonderful. My mother's there. The Druids told me she has not wished to be reborn, and they speak with the dead. She would not remain there if it did not bring her happiness. When I die, I'll see her there."

"It makes me scared," I said finally, as if it were a secret I'd kept too long. "King Arawn looks like a monster."

"I think all kings look like monsters," Lukat said, and again I thought of my father. *Was my father a monster, as my mother had told me? Was he a good man as Merlin had said?*

Lukat reached over and scruffed up my damp hair. "We don't have to think about Arawn for a long time to come. My father told me that when his chariot comes and you feel the heat of his horses and the howls of his hounds approaching, you seek him out. But you, when *you* hear his hounds, Mordred, you just run as fast as you can and maybe he won't catch you."

2

All the swimming and running and swordplay had its effect on my body. One day I looked into the mirror bowl and did not see the chubby face with its odd little nose but instead a more sculpted face of a boy who showed the man within himself through muscle and cheekbone, and I barely recognized this new youth in that reflection. I had lost much of my weight and had begun to take pride in the contests and competitions. We had yearly races and archery contests on horseback. We hunted, after the blessings of the deer and the boar and the fish. Lukat and I often slept in woven blankets out beneath the trees as we tracked a stag for many days and nights. I had begun to understand what the work of men was, and I enjoyed being among the horse herds and the charioteers, who showed us their skills and their labors. The shepherds, the root and seed gatherers, and the watchers, who protected our home from the tallest branches of the trees, also took us on their journeys that we might understand the ways of the forest.

3

Lukat and I had many adventures together as boys, and sometimes, when we escaped the daily work, we'd climb the tallest oak we could find to look out over the haze of the forest after a rainfall, and just sit there, looking out over our domain. All we could see was forest and hill, and the balding areas of the desolate lands. Sometimes, the wild horses ran across the heath in the distance, or we'd see the Lake's hunters out stalking boar and deer. I remember the first time we spotted the standing stones of the grove—they had always been there, yet we had never noticed them. These gray stones that were nearly as tall as a man. "They were hunters who met with Lord Arawn's wrath," Lukat's father told us. "Many hundreds of years ago, these were men who boasted of their prowess at the hunt. And when one of Arawn's stags escaped from the Otherworld, these hundred men of the forest set out after the stag for many days, for a stag of Annwn would never die, no matter how many times it was slain for meat. It would rise up again the next night and might be slain again. It was greatly prized, as you may imagine. But when they had quarried the stag, here in the grove, Cernunnos himself

came to the protection of the sacred animal. And these hunters, in seeing him, turned to stone, for we are not meant to look upon the face
of the gods directly. And though their features have washed away over
the years of rain and snow, these were once men. And buried beneath
them, in the mounds," he added, "are fallen Romans who came to burn
the forest and murder the Druids themselves."

"Were they killed by the goddess?"

"Or the Druids?" Lukat asked.

"No," he said, his voice lowering in thrilled excitement as if he
meant to gleefully terrify us with this tale, "the earth itself swallowed
them whole, and the roots of the oaks strangled them after they had
spilled the blood of many Druid priests."

I loved Lukat's father's tales, and my time with Lukat during the day
always seemed too short.

We laughed with the jokes that little boys make, and for which we
were scolded by our elders, for they often involved belching or farting or
playing pranks on the gullible. Lukat had a penchant for filling sheep's
bladders, stolen from the butcher's table, with water and then tossing
them from the trees onto our friends who passed by. His punishment for
this was cleaning up the butcher's ice-cold chamber after the salting of
the meat. Together, from the age of ten onward, we often stole horses
from the paddocks above and rode them out into the desolate lands,
playing as if we were knights with swords, or even the gods Cernunnos
and Arawn, fighting over the Lady of the Lake.

Once, when Lukat and I rode out along a sunlit road between the
thick alders and yews, with me behind him amd he before me, and a
colored blanket as our saddle, I leaned forward and kissed him lightly,
just below the ear, at the place where he had a curl of dark hair that I
could not resist touching.

I did not then even understand why I did this, and my heart beat too
fast in my chest as I drew back from him again. He glanced back and
gave me a look that could only be one of scrutiny rather than delight
and said, "No."

We rode on in silence, and that night I lay on my bed, furious with myself for what I had done before only in dreams. I had not even understood my own nature in wishing to kiss him, or how I was affected by seeing that place at the back of his neck and that curl of hair and the way his ear looked to me, as if it wanted a kiss. The way the sun had felt upon my skin and the smell of the wildflowers on the soft air while the stag thistle's seeds were carried on the gentle breeze around us. It had seemed like a moment stolen from time, like a dream that had come into being, and I had broken that spell with my actions.

I felt I had taken a terrible risk and had, in the process, lost my one true friend.

4

Though many believe that the heathens are full of those like me, I could not find other boys who shared my desires. Now, when I look back at those days, I think it was good, for being unable to fulfill desire, thought about it much and considered what my life would be as I got older.

My mother, though she told me she had long understood my nature and that "the gods bless those such as you with great insight and understanding," did not herself seem to carry much understanding for me. She had begun withdrawing from others, including me, as I reached that point just before manhood, as if I had gone over to the enemy camp. She had sought out the goddess of the waning moon as her patroness and in so doing had spoken much of my father and of the wounds inside her that had festered during the years since she last saw her beloved homeland. Now and then, she would offer up a tenderness to me or ask me how my studies had been, for I had learned both the old language and the new, and also could read some of the ancient Greek writings that Merlin had brought to me.

"You are special to me," my mother would say, "but you are reaching those years when we will not agree on anything. Sometimes, I think boys should be stopped at sixteen."

"Killed?" I asked, surprised at the thought.

"No, just drawn away, for they are old enough to father children, and they are still good and kind, but as their blood boils, they bring war and worse upon the world. What a pleasant place it would be if youth were the last of men, and afterward they would go off to sea or away until old age."

I laughed later about this with Viviane as I worked in her many gardens. I squatted down to cut and then plant new growth while she sat watching and guiding me from a curved rock.

"Your mother has wicked ideas," she said. "But do not let her words bother you. She loves you and would not have you vanish after your sixteenth year."

"I am full of confusions," I said. "And Merlin will not speak to me of what I feel. Nor will my mother, though she did once when I was a boy. Well, I suppose I don't feel comfortable speaking with her about it anymore."

"But you do with me?"

"Yes," I said. "You are...well, you're a Crone."

"And what does Crone mean to you?"

"It means that...well, that you're wiser than many of my elders. It means that you have seen much. That you listen to the goddess with finer ears than I do."

"Sometimes it means that I'm simply old," she smiled. "But if you want to talk about your feelings."

"About *things*," I said.

"Ah, it is of your dual nature."

"Dual?"

"The sun and the moon together," she said. "It is like an eclipse when they meet, and people are scared as the darkness covers the sun. But even when this happens, the light is more intense than if the sun and moon had not come together. You have the strong muscles of one who will be a man among men and the mind of one who will be a scholar. You bring the philosophy you learn from your studies as if you were a philosopher in Rome. But you have that other side to you. It is that part of you that desires men, for love. It is that simple, Mordred. There are those, even here, who do not understand it, although they forget that Arawn and Cernunnos have shared a single bed—the forest and the Otherworld together. It is what brings you the spark of life that others do not readily have. You will have an understanding of men and of women that those who are attracted to their opposite sex will never possess. In some ways, you are more fearless because of it. In other ways, more withdrawn."

I felt my face burn as she spoke, for I had not mentioned my inner anguish to her. Yet, I should have guessed that she would know the malady from which I suffered. "Is there a cure for this?" I asked.

"A cure?" She looked at me strangely. "Why would you cure what is from your very nature?"

"My friends, the other boys, do not feel as I do."

"Some of them do, but they hide it. When I was a girl, few hid it, but as with all things, in times of trouble, fear grows. Most don't hide it, and there are men here you may meet who are like you and have taken their love. They live above, usually, among the forest paths, in the turf houses; or else they go to the villas, for they find the towns of more interest than the woods. You have known of the priestess who has hand-fasted with the Eponi herder?"

I nodded. "But it is accepted for the women."

"No more than for the men. But when you are not yet a man, many have difficulty understanding it. It is worse in the world beyond this forest, so look to the blessings of your life. There are those of your age who are turned out of their homes merely for love, or the lack of it, among their kinsfolk."

"I have lost a friend," I said.

"Ah, your friend Lukat. Have you indeed lost him? Or have you simply frightened each other with the power of your feelings?" She smiled as she asked me this, and when the gardening was done and I carried her on my back toward home as the evening sun dappled the darkening leaves above us, she said, "I suspect he loves you as you love him, but he has not the same nature as you. This may be difficult for him, for the youths who only feel drawn to maidens are frightened of what they do not understand. But this is not your fault, Mordred. You must follow your heart in all things. In the life I have led, that is the only truth that has never proven wrong. I once knew a boy like you, many years ago. He felt confusion in his nature, and he followed paths that were not his."

"Did he like other boys too?"

"Yes, he did," she said. "And he was beloved of the Lady of the Lake, as you are. He would swim her waters many days, and when we spoke of his yearning for a boy like him, I tried to help him understand that he would one day find that boy—that man—but that life did not hand us these wonderful loves too early lest we take them for granted."

"And did he?" I asked. "Did he find someone to love?"

"Perhaps," she said. "He left us. He left us because he could not accept his nature, nor could he accept the waiting for the gods to send him love. But patience is all the gods ask of us, Mordred. I hope you will have a little patience."

"I will, Aunt Vivy," I whispered. "I promise."

5

I would tell more here of the tribal councils that were held; of the many messengers that arrived with news from Cornwall and Wales and from the Dragon's Mount at the coast, those who came for charms and potions and salves of healing and in exchange brought news and wine and honey, of the study of the grove and its trees and beasts, but these were not the direction of my life. Outside of athletics and the reading of the scrolls, I was concerned with friendship, and love, and what my place in the world should be.

In those days, I did not think of myself as the son of a king and a queen, for my parentage was kept secret from those around me for the shame my mother felt it brought with her. Instead, I was seen as one of the many youths of our home, with no greater rank than the lowliest of goat herds, and if I did not hunt for boar or deer with the others, if I did not work the summer gardens until I was exhausted come the late sundown, I did not gain a good word from anyone, even Viviane herself, who believed that work for self and work for the tribes were interconnected. "You work a full day as all do, as to your abilities, and if you choose not to, why should we suffer for your lack of dedication to your own welfare? Do not expect alms here, as did your cousin Gawain when he lazily spent his summer protected by Morgause, who ruined that boy with her coddling. I do not care for knights or kings, and princes are worse than the most pampered of princesses in all the world. You are servant to yourself, and as you serve yourself, so you serve others." She had said this on a particularly rough day for me, when I had let the sorrow of my lost friendship allow me to moan and grumble and stay in my bedchamber half the day.

Neither was the life on the Isle of Glass one of devil-may-care, for if we sought idle pleasures when the harvest of the forest needed tending, the herdsman lost no time in bundling birch strips and swatting us as we passed until we went out into the orange-gold of the season to gather up the grains and bring them to the earthen storehouses. My cousin Gawain had never liked it there, and when he had returned before he took up a position with his father and with mine as a servant-soldier, he mocked our country ways and called me his "little rabbit," because I was always "hopping about, doing the bidding of these old women."

During the changing of seasons to winter, Lukat was out at the edge of the Lake, for we bathed often in winter in its warm, healing waters. He called to me as I passed by, carrying the wood for the bread ovens, and I set my burden down and went over to him. Farther out in the water was a maiden I knew by the name of Melisse. "I think she is the one I will hand-fast this coming Beltane," he said.

"But that's before our midsummer rites. We won't be brought into the Mysteries for a while yet." It was the only thing I could think of to say to him, because it shocked me that he had fallen in love. It made me feel lonely to even know it. Lonely to imagine the hand-fasting ritual between my friend and a maiden, where the ceremonial rope would be bound to both their wrists before all of the Isle of Glass, for the Lady herself to see their love for each other and how they had bound their souls together.

"Rituals of manhood?" he grinned. "The Mysteries are ceremonial. Why wait for them? You've seen youths hand-fast before the rites. Those Druid rituals are meant as signs, Mordred. They don't change you into a man. You become a man when you understand love. And the debt of love."

"The debt of love?"

"Yes. I know it with Melisse. My debt is to love itself, that I will nurture and protect and grow with her. That's how I know I'm a man," he said, his eyes shining with this sense he had acquired.

"That's wonderful," I told him and glanced out at the girl who was my rival. She was pretty and fair-haired, and I could not think anything unkind of her. Or of him. *I am petty and low*, I thought. *Mean and small and stupid. I am living in a dream to think he could be my closest friend all of our lives.*

"Join us," he said, and I could tell by his gentle smile that he had forgiven me that small token of love I'd pressed behind his ear. Soon enough, we were splashing each other in the waters, and Melisse swam up to us and reminded me that I had told her that she looked like a frog when we were both no more than five years old.

I loved those years, and I cannot say much bad of them. I learned the way that I imagine children the world over learn of things, and I longed for things beyond my reach and dreamed of them, as many others do and have and will.

I could not know the terror that awaited me, so soon along the road of life, for I had been kept innocent of the greater matters of the world and had not yet been touched by madness or by death.

But before the winter was through, the terrible times would begin, and I would learn too much of death and of the beginnings of grief, nearly as well as I knew my friend Lukat and my mother, and yet I would also learn of that love that haunted my dreams.

As the seasons wore on, my mother's spirit failed a bit. I awoke some nights to find her standing over my bed and whispering to me, "Arthur. Arthur. What have you done? What have you done?"

I recall a night when I heard her whimpering, and I lit the candle by my bed. She was huddled in a corner, staring at me and speaking in languages that I could not understand, but it terrified me, for she did not seem to know me at all in that trancelike state.

Far too often, she called me "Arthur," as she stared at me with cold eyes that held neither fear nor anger, and this frightened me more than anything else in the world.

Part Two

The Stag

Chapter Six

1

As my mother began to lose something of herself in the nightmares she had, I went to others to seek remedies for her. Viviane and the priestesses reassured me that Morgan would find health in the goddess, "for her mind has been torn at by wolves, but she will heal as all things mend." Some nights, my mother slept through until dawn, so I had begun to believe that the elders were right.

All in all, we lived a sheltered life on the Isle of Glass, for when the storms came, we could retreat to our warm cavern paradise and believe that the nameless goddess walked among us.

In the summers, Morgause often arrived in her great pale-green garments, and with a great cloak of pure white that shone in the sun and sparkled at twilight as if it were made of faerie dust, for she loved finery and refused to wear the more modest and humble white-brown robes of the wise women. She returned without any of her sons, complaining of them constantly, and took part in the priestess activities though she had become ambivalent about the rituals. Merlin came and went during the warmer seasons of summer and spring, bringing with him more manuscripts and scrolls, so news of the outside world came to us through them and others who were wanderers between the worlds.

We learned of the great peace that had lasted since the time of my birth among the southern kingdoms of Britain. Yet we also learned of the ravages of the wars to the north and the many deaths of Britons in defense of the kingdoms.

Morgause told my mother, so that I might hear, that her sons were being drawn into service for Arthur, and though she fought her husband bitterly over this, my cousins had already begun training for battle with hopes of knighthood.

"I should have stayed here with them when they were still young. I should have told Lot that they died at sea, so that they might never grow too fond of those robber kings." She wept bitter tears against my mother's bosom, and my mother comforted her with memories of their childhood, of the moments they had stolen of happiness and tenderness and joy.

"I should never have agreed to marry King Lot," Morgause said more than once. "I thought it would bring peace and safety to all of us. I thought Orkney would not join with Arthur in his wars. I did not see this in my visions of the future. I did not see any of it, and I do not know why the goddess blinded me so."

"What *did* you see?" Morgan asked. "For I saw much of it when I was too young to understand, and I warned you of it, though we could not know the form these dark days would take." My mother had lost much of her ability to scry after my birth. It was thought that her anger of the past, or the violence of Arthur's act against her, had blocked the future from her. She was intensely interested in anyone who saw what was to come.

Morgause looked up at her and closed her eyes before saying "I saw the kingdoms of Arthur burning. I saw the isle of Avalon as if I were a raven, flying over frozen sea, rapidly, toward the towers that seemed like torches. I saw...Arthur's battered, wounded body and...your face, but it did not seem like you...holding him."

I held my breath as she spoke, for these visions the elders had terrified and fascinated me too.

"Then," my mother said, comforting her with a hollow voice, "all will be made well."

When Morgause saw me spying on them, she drew me aside long

after supper and took me into my bedchamber. She drew back the door, and in the darkness of my room, sat me down upon a chair and squatted in front of me, holding my hands. "You are to take care of her now, as she and I have cared for you. You are old enough, Mordred, to watch out for her. I trust you will have the Druids send messages to me should anything happen."

"What will happen?"

"I don't know," she said, her soft voice growing colder than I had ever heard it. "But I have seen enough of this life to know that there are those poisons that take many years to work upon the soul. And I am afraid for your mother. Once, she...she tried to hurt herself. I was able to stop her then, but I am afraid if she were to do that again, I could not. All I ask is that you watch out for her and protect her from any danger, for her spirit is waning in these times and I cannot be here for her much of the year."

"I promise," I said, and when I spoke the words, I meant them, although I did not find myself able to truly protect my mother from her own dreams and furies.

2

My daylight hours, when not shepherding, or working in the fields that needed seeding and tending, or chasing the bulls that wandered the desolate lands that we gathered up as cattle for one month a year, I spent with Merlin, who came to Beltane each year and left before Samhain had arrived at the beginning of winter. My studies were harsh, and often I stayed up late into the night, reading by the glow of the watchfires in the clearing above our caves. It took me six years of my life to learn the damnable Latin tongue, even though Greek seemed simple to me and I loved reading the old parchments, stolen from that library of Alexandria by Merlin himself in a previous lifetime. He brought me scrolls about our tribes, and the Etruscans of Italy and their temples, and of the Great Alexander who had conquered Egypt and the East, and the kings of Troy before its fall. Persian mathematics also gave me headaches and strained my eyes, and I found the most difficult of the studies to be about that Ogham language of the Druids, though I was not quite wise enough to master its intricacies of meaning, which only that priesthood knew. I had been learning the magick of numbers and their uses, and found that cities could be built from the calculations of a scroll. I was made to read the gospels of Christianity that I might understand the wisdom of their beliefs, and I read what Merlin brought me of the law of the Hebrew people and of the moon gods of ancient Babylon. "Truth is not owned by one tribe, you whelp bastard!" he shouted at me when I told him that I didn't want to be corrupted by these other religions. "These are the many lights of the gods, and you cannot choose to claim that you seek truth if you douse those lights as others might! You talk like those who wish to see the gods of our tribe wiped out just as they burn our histories and our lives! You Cornish son of a jackal bitch from the prick of a gob-arse robber king, sit down and read until your eyes bleed, until that mind of yours opens to what these scrolls tell you! This white-raven shit upon your brain will addle you—I should never have let you grow up here. I wanted to take you to Rome, to those labyrinthine halls beneath the fallen city, deep where the Etruscan Mysteries are still practiced, that you might avoid this... distraction here. The world is a wider place than Broceliande, and there are greater seas than the Lake of Glass."

His curses often went on and on. I was barely affected by them anymore. I had heard worse from him when our lessons had begun when I was a little boy. Sometimes, I even laughed and called him a son-of-a-bitch-goddess, which got him laughing as well. He taught me phrases that my mother forbade me from using in the daylight hours, and I learned all the insults that could be made of the body parts and of mating from him, some of them in the Roman tongue, some in Greek, but most in the language of the Britons. My favorite of his was when he said of someone with whom he disagreed, "He talks like a plague-carrying prick-discharge of a Saxon mouth-whore!" It took me more than a few nights to even understand it, and when I did, I awoke laughing in the middle of the night imagining the disgusting image of it. He once called my great-aunt Viviane "a hag without a hagdom!" when they fought, which was often and as if they had been married for several lifetimes; though she gave as good as she got by calling him "a great old wrinkled ball sack without a ball in sight!"

But when it came to my lessons, Merlin, for all his rages, taught me well.

I was not particularly talented toward learning, but I found in it an interest that seemed to bring me out of any loneliness I felt in the Lake Kingdom. I read from the stories of heroes and gods that had come from those ancient places, and my mother and her friends delighted in them and told me more of their own lore learned from their childhood teachers; and of the Lady of the Lake and her stolen sword, and of the cauldron of Rebirth, which had been tricked by an ancient hero from the god Arawn; and brought from the Otherworld, which had caused Arawn to loose the boars of Moccus upon the world of men. But the nameless Lady, our Lady of the Lake, hid the cauldron that Arawn should never find it, and she brought it forth in the times of great need of its healing magick. Merlin told me he'd seen the cauldron once, and only once, in all his lifetimes. "It is gilt-edged and covered with rubies along its lip, but the bowl itself is dark black and shiny as glass. It can be carried by one man, but is too heavy for all but the one who is destined to hold it."

"I am surprised my father did not steal it when he took the sacred sword," I said.

"Ah." He considered this and shook his head. "Your father tricked me, as I am too often tricked by those the gods favor."

"He tricked you? But you are Merlin," I said in wonder.

"Yes," he said. "And he was a boy of fifteen, and often those are the greatest of tricksters. But I had merely told him of the sword's existence. He had a friend—more than a friend, I think; like a brother to him. Like your friend Lukat is to you. And the friend guided him to the sword, though I do not understand this friend, for he did not stop Arthur from it." Merlin's mind seemed to wander away from him as he spoke of my father, so I quizzed him, since few would talk at length of the high-king.

Merlin glanced up to the cavern walls, as if they would remind him of my father and his friend stealing the sword Excalibur from its burial mound within a hidden cave. "Well, Arthur has much good in him, though your mother and her sister will never believe me. He was like you, not in most ways, but of a curious mind. He learned the Art, as well, though he was not as good as you at it, and much of it was clouded from him after he took the sword, for the Art does not always respond to a boy who uses it for his own gain. But he has had a different path. Each of us has a different path to take. Sometimes, whelpling, there is no sense to it, and I have taken many paths in my lifetime."

"But if it was bad to take the sword, why wouldn't he put it back?"

"It was destined for him, I suppose, though the Lady of the Lake has not yet forgiven me, nor has your mother or her sister. And in particular that great old harpy Viviane. She still growls in my presence. The she-bitch. But she knew what Arthur would do. She saw it in her scrying bowl, and *she* did nothing to stop it, so she is no less guilty than I, and I could not see what would come of it."

"If my father knows the Lake of Glass, why does he not come here?" I asked him. "He must know that Morgan lives here. He must know that his son also is here."

"Mordred, your father is one who is afraid of this place. He understands the Art, though its practice was taken from him. He has seen things here, in taking Excalibur from us, put doubt in his mind that he could ever return here. He is brave. He has goodness in him, but like all men, he has shadow. I had to unravel his memory of finding it, and to plant doubt and fear of the place in him. It has kept you safe here. It has protected Morgause and her sons when they come, for few who set foot within Arthur's court may find this place so long as it is under the protection of the Lady."

And then, I asked him the one question I did not understand, though it plagued me in those early mornings when I lay upon my bed and looked up at the red and yellow rock of my bedroom ceiling. "Why does my father wish to kill me? I would not harm him, though he has hurt my mother and taken from her and my aunt their kingdoms. Would he not understand that I have no wish to take his kingdom?"

When I asked this, Merlin grew dark and pressed his face into his hands as if washing it in despair. Then, he looked at me again and said, "He understands too well the prophecies. But do not be concerned so much with him. He lives across the sea that separates this small Britannia from the larger one. He has Saxons to fight for years to come and has quests whose calls must be answered. Concern yourself with your life here, with your studies, and the Art itself. Are you happy here, Mordred?"

"Yes. I love the Lake and I feel the Lady here with me at all times."

"Does she comfort you?"

"Yes, my lord, she does. I felt her when I was little and had dreams of terrible places, and she held my hand as a mother would."

"And do you love your mother?"

I nodded.

"And Viviane?"

I nodded.

"And me?"

"More than any father I could wish for," I said.

"Then do not think of that distant kingdom of Arthur and his knights and warlords. What's done cannot be undone. Arthur may have sons and daughters by women other than your mother, so this prophecy of doom may not speak of you but of another. He has not yet taken his bride from the provinces to the east of us. You may not be the destroyer of his kingdoms. You may live this entire lifetime here and perhaps even your next."

"That is all I want," I said, and then we returned to our lessons.

3

Without Merlin, I doubt I would have been able to dream of the world beyond the Isle of Glass; his teaching brought me visions of the vast expanse of kingdoms and wilderness, and though I was privileged to learn of it, I shared as much as I could with my few friends so that they too could dream of other places and times.

One midsummer's night, Merlin sat me down in a boat upon the Lake and said, "You know of the raveling."

I nodded.

"Your mother stole it from me, against my will."

"Yes," I said. "She told me of it when she brought the memories of her past into me."

"I long ago forgave her. But I must ask, did she pass you the Art of it?"

I wanted to lie and say she had not, but I could not, not to Merlin. I was at my utmost serious with Merlin, for I could not take his disdain or anger and had long ago trained myself to be the obedient pupil to him, my master in all things.

I nodded. "But I do not know it well. She took me into it once so that I might understand the days before my birth."

"And did you? Understand?"

I shook my head. "But as I grow older, I begin to see why we had to leave my grandmother's kingdom. But I am confused by much of it."

"And were you sick after? When the raveling and its unraveling came to pass, did you have nights of pain?"

I remembered these all too well. "Yes. I had a terrible fever for weeks, and Viviane brought me into the healing circle that I might not slip away. I had aches in my bones as if they wished to break free of my flesh, and my thirst could not be quenched for many nights no matter how much water I drank."

"I do not teach this Art lightly," he said. "And I would not teach you, had your mother not already brought it into your body. Once in the body, it will not leave." Then, a newborn fury rose up in him, and he began cursing with all the languages known to him, of rutting and of the male and female parts, and words in many tongues that all meant those things that the body expelled or was diseased by. Finally, he muttered, "By the gods, if she has taught her sister this Art, I will—"

"My mother raveled to no one but me," I said, hoping to calm him. "She regretted what she had done, and Viviane herself and the Druidess they call Manann both made her swear upon her own life that she would never partake of this Art again, for it brought suffering with it."

He grunted his assent to this. "Viviane is a wise old wench. She will be raveled at her death, that her wisdom will not die with the passage of her spirit. She understands the uses of the Art. What do you really know of it?"

"It is for you alone," I said. "For it is used in the moments before death that the memory of the great and small may not be lost from our people."

"Memory?" He shook his head, sighing. "You do not understand its power. The raveling itself may bring death to the one who is already near the doorway of the dead. The fever and pains you experienced, Mordred—your mother should never have inflicted those upon you. It was selfish of her. It has killed people, this Art, and it does not simply drink from memory. It may drink the soul itself if not done precisely. When I perform this sacred act, I take upon myself the spirit debt, and I too grow sick from this that the soul might go free into Annwn."

"My mother told me she wished she hadn't stolen it," I said. "She told me that it was an accursed Art to practice."

"Yes, she swore this to me but too late for you," he said. "By raveling into you, she passed this into your body, and the body does not forget such things. If I could, I would remove this from your blood knowledge, but it is impossible. Once the fevers of the raveling have entered the blood, they remain there, sleeping, waiting to return. So, you must learn this Art, though I wish you never to practice it on pain of death."

"Yes, my lord," I said.

"When someone ravels, whelp," as he had called me from my earliest days, although when I had behaved wrongly, he had called me "worthless whelp," which made me laugh, "they also unravel. It is a strong art, not for someone of this lifetime. Do you understand?"

I nodded. "Will we learn this now?"

"There is another Art you must master first, and once you have done this, we will begin the raveling. This Art is called the Vessel of Mercury."

"Is it a healing art?"

"No. It is of the voice of the mind. Have you ever spoken into a vessel?"

"A vessel? Like a bowl?"

"Yes," he said. "Just like a bowl. Or a cup."

I shook my head. "No, my lord."

"Here," Merlin said. He reached into the folds of his snow-white garment and drew out a wooden trencher. He passed it to me.

I looked down at it in my hands. Then, I looked at him. "What shall I do?"

"Speak into it."

Feeling silly, I lifted the bowl to my face and said "Like this?" into it.

"Did you hear anything?"

"No, my lord."

"Not a sound? Try again."

Again I spoke into it: "What am I meant to hear?"

He remained silent. A few seconds passed. He said, "Again."

"I am speaking into a bowl," I said, slowly and softly.

And then I heard it. The slight echo of my voice, a whisper returning to me.

"It's the curves of the vessel that bring back a tincture of voice," he said. Then, he added, "You may put the bowl down."

I passed it back to him. "Is this about an art of speaking in bowls?"

His eyes flashed with that distant lightning that I knew might end up with a slap to my face, as Merlin did not refrain from hitting and slapping or boxing ears when I was slow to understand him. "The bowl is an example," he said, keeping his temper. "Now, look at the air between us."

Again, I felt foolish, but I looked at his face and then tried to imagine the air between us.

"It is curved, like a bowl. But not just the air. We are actually touching now, boy. I am sitting here and you there, but the aura around each of us touches and mingles together, as when one pours water and wine into a vessel and it becomes one thing. Somewhere between where I sit and where you sit, our essence has been poured into a vessel." As was the custom for Merlin's teachings, when not accompanied by a Greek or Latin or Ogham text, he grew frustrated with my inability to grasp his meanings, and I became slightly amused and annoyed that he spoke in such riddles half the time, the way the Druids often did. His face seemed to brighten with an idea. "Watch." He reached into that large leather pouch of his that rarely left his side and drew out a piece of parchment.

Using a bit of red chalk-rock, he scratched out an oval.

"This is your head." Then he drew another oval. "This is mine." He drew a series of swirls around his oval and then around mine, and somewhere between them, these swirls intersected and his swirls reached as far as mine. "When I speak to you, my voice carries to your ears. But when I vessel..." Here he closed his mouth and began speaking even without the movement of his lips: *I pour my thoughts into you, using these paths that are invisible to us. You hear the echoes of my thoughts, like so.*

I sat there stunned. I understood that Merlin had great power and the raveling itself was a sign of it, but this vesseling seemed even more remarkable to me, for it did not involve the absorbing of a vision from one to another but of a voice, as if he had spoken clearly. As if others might heard him if they had sat near us.

You see? I am speaking but without my tongue. I am using this aura field between us to move the sound of my voice into your brain without my mouth and without your ears. I could not do this if we did not have sympathy for each other, boy.

"Sympathy?"

If you and I weren't as...understanding of each other.

I tried to speak to him. *Can you hear me?*

He did not respond.

"I tried, just now, to speak to you. Did you hear it?"

"No," he said. "It is not a trick of some traveling wizard, whelp. It takes years for it to work. Your training in the vessel has just begun. And it is not to be used for sport. In the ancient days, when men had not yet been given the gift of language by the birds, they spoke through their vessels. You hear the echo of my vessel, for it is into it that I speak."

"How do I do this?" I asked, excited by the prospect of a new trick. I had learned the secret calendar that predicted the rains and the stars and the moons for years to come. I had spent three summers with Merlin learning of the many numbers and their mystical uses; I could cipher as well as any Druid. But this speaking into the mind of another seemed like a wonderful new magick, and I loved the very idea of magick, let alone its uses. "Please. Is there something I can do now? I want to."

"It's not a game!" he shouted. "You arse-end of a woodcock. It will take you years to master it."

"Do you know what I'm thinking? Is that what it's like?"

"I don't go into your mind," he said, snorting as if I were an idiot. "As much of a whelp as you are, I have too much respect for you. Mordred, this is important. Get your hands out of your mealy trousers and wake up your mind. I want you to focus on this. I may go away for a while, perhaps a long time. But I want you to be able to call to me, wherever I am."

"You're leaving?"

"I might leave," he said. "Whether I leave or stay is not the point."

Then he began cursing, using the words for rutting and the various male and female anatomy that he liked to cry out when he was angry. The words "prick" and "ball-sack" flew from his mouth like summer green-flies from a dead man's mouth. "Whelp, you will need this Art. And you are reaching a point where you might lose the ability to learn it at all."

"Lose? But there are many arts, my lord, that I do not yet know."

"When you become a man—when all youth has turned to man-hood—much is lost. Those arts and wisdoms not yet imparted are often waylaid." He chuckled as he said this, as if something about the word "waylaid" had been a particularly clever turn of phrase for him.

"Why? Why would it change? What will happen when I become a man that has not already come to pass?"

"I've told you before about the energies?"

I nodded. "The points of the body that hold the expression of the soul."

"Six points along the body. Six points of energy and of expression. The mind, the heart, the solar plexus, the snake of devouring, the organs of the seed in men and of the womb in women, and the funda-ment. But manhood stops the energies of the upper body from reaching the lower, unless as a boy and youth the man has kept this open."

"But my mother learned the raveling when she was older."

"Women do not lose the ability to learn the Art. Only men."

"And not boys?"

"I will speak plainly, Mordred," he said, squinting at me as he looked me over. "You have not yet known a woman. Or a man?"

I felt my face burn a bit on the inside. "I have not."

"Virginity among males is a state in which learning of the hidden arts may occur. It is not well-thought-of, this state of existence, but anyone who practices the Art understands. It is not so with females, who may learn the arts into their hundredth year. You must remain in this state for as long as you can, for it will allow me to pass you this knowledge and this Art. Once you are a doorway for the magick itself, you may cross the rites of manhood and continue to gain a few of the other secret wisdoms. There are other arts of manhood that will come later for you, but to learn these particular ones, the raveling and its twin, the unraveling, you must approach them with energy untarnished by the unsheathing of the sword. Do you understand?"

"I've heard that some virgins see the faeries."

He wrinkled his face up, from chin to forehead, as if he had just smelled a fart. "Those blasted elfin faerie revels of the superstitious mind. Those pretty little people? No better than gas and hallucinations, Mordred. Have you not drunk mead and seen spirits dancing? The elementals exist, though they do not have the wings of butterflies nor do they rein and saddle rabbits for their steeds. They invade the mind through scent and the invisible boundaries that exist in the world though men do not see them. They are energies of the forest that play with our minds when we come near these areas. Many are weak when near them, but the strong will resist this manipulation, which is but the forces of the rock and water and air and flame."

"Are these elementals as powerful as the gods?"

He thought a moment, calming from his tirade. "The gods are masks of an eternal truth, Mordred. The elementals are very different. In that ancient city where Jason left on his ship, the Argos, the priests of the stars wrote of great energies, called the *magnes*, documented there many centuries ago. These are the elementals of which we speak, and of the cause of the magick of the faerie realm. Rocks and water, and gas produced from them as well, combine with this to create feelings in us, ignite senses, and cause these visions. You must never let this sort of thing overpower you."

I was not sure if I had angered him or not, but I pressed further. "May I learn the raveling? If I remain untouched?"

He ignored this question, which was as good as him yelling at me for asking it. Instead, he said, "I want your word that you will keep your studies sacred. That you will not break the vow I ask of you. You will remain chaste, though all other youths you know follow their lusts. Will you do this? For I have much to teach you and not as much time left to do it, as the nature of man takes you from me."

"Yes, my lord," I said.

He spoke within my mind: *I will give you the greatest gift I know, Mordred, and I will bring ancient secrets that only a handful of mages have learned. These are mysteries of the Otherworld from which most men are forbidden. We will, one day, speak together, and vessel within each other from great distances. And if you keep true to this promise, you will become greater than even your father. You will one day speak with the gods themselves.*

We spent many long days sitting across from one another, whether in the world above, on the flat altar stones in the groves, or upon the boat in the Lake, or, on the warmer nights, under the stars, upon the cliffs overlooking the distant hills, turned blue-gray in the misty darkness.

After many months, he said to me, *Yes. I can hear you now, whelpling prince. You are pouring yourself into my vessel. You have broken through the wall that has separated my mind from yours. Welcome to this, my boy, for it will protect you in dark times and in places of shadow, and will prove its use to you in ways you do not now know or anticipate. When I see you next, if you keep your vow to me, I will train you in the raveling, for you are ready for its thorny path.*

4

Merlin spent six weeks with me in isolation, out in the desolate lands where there was little food and less water. I lost weight on a diet of roots and berries, with but a few sips of water every few hours. I was asked to chew on the stag thistle when my hunger became overwhelming, and he spent one boiling hot day of summer spreading over my body a salve made of a mixture of belladonna and foxglove, and while I felt myself floating as if to the sky from this, he began to press himself to me. It was in a way that was nothing like my dreams of mating but even more intimate, for I felt him move through me, as if he were in my blood and I were in his, and our eyes were so close together I could not even blink, and our skin pressed tight for more than an hour as I felt that salve on my body heat both of us until I thought we would burst into a funeral pyre.

And then, the raveling began, and I unraveled into him and he into me. I knew then what real power was, for the union of two minds in the raveling—not simply the one practicing the Art but the two at once raveling into each other—it was as if I had become a god.

I went with Merlin through his past and saw my father as a boy; the great towers of the world; Morgan, but three years old, in my grandmother Ygrain's arms; and Viviane at fourteen riding a great black horse along the Cornish coast. I began to fly within his memory and see even the edges of things and nearly touch what was before me.

Through his direction, I was even able to move back before his birth at this incarnation, and for a moment that seemed as if I'd gone underwater, I saw the world through the eyes of a previous Merlin, as the great Roman armies lit the forests of Britain with cages of prisoners of our people, burning.

I reached the point of exhaustion with the raveling, but it was like a delicious drug, and I wanted more, I wanted to suck at his memories, through his thousand lives, that I might see the making and unmaking of the world itself. I awoke one night lying on a blanket while he sat beside me. Blood had poured from my mouth and nose, and he had begun calling to the gods for healing that I might not pass into Annwn before my time.

In that time, I had traveled to the realms of the gods, though these were merely dreams and hallucinations, a side effect of the raveling and of the poisons rubbed upon my body to heighten my senses during this time. I saw the hounds of Annwn hunting the souls of knights and chieftains along a battlefield blanketed with the torn bodies of the dead; behind them a wine-dark sunset and a man upon a low hill, a spear raised, a large round shield glinting in that unnatural light. He wore the blood-stained armor of a prince of distant lands, and upon his head, a helmet as none I had ever seen, with the antlers of Cernunnos upon it and a crown upon the helmet, encircling the antlers. He faced another warrior who held up a sword that seemed to be on fire. Upon his head, a helmet that was also encircled with a crown. Surrounding these two, a yellow wind of spirits, like locusts whirling about them, even as the two men seemed frozen in their battle.

The sky itself darkened, and, as if from the clouds, the black swans of Arawn's flock descended from the sky, and as they touched down upon the battle-scarred earth, they transformed into beautiful maidens, with the black-feathered wings of angels.

My visions turned to darkness, and I fell ill for days. I found myself on my hands and knees throwing up those berries I'd ingested before the raveling had begun. My fever broke.

Merlin squatted beside me. "You have learned it, I think." He rubbed my back, and that night we slept at the edge of a river so that I might bathe and rest. He told me that it had to be used sparingly. "The raveling takes much out of us. It may damage the mind and pain the soul, for it is not a game. The soul has a substance, Mordred. You must understand that the raveling also unravels the one who practices its Art. But you have withstood it, twice, and while you were within its realm, I brought you the strength you would need for its use that you might not die from it."

He did not have to worry about me using it ever again, I thought at that moment, for I felt sick to my stomach for weeks and fought a fever that left me no good for anything but the simplest of chores for the remainder of that summer.

5

My lessons with Merlin only now and then took my mind off the problems with my mother.

I loved her dearly, but she had begun hurting herself—and me—in small and large ways since I'd been a child. I had grown less patient with her drinking too much of the barley ale during the winter festivals, and bringing home men that I did not know, though I did not begrudge her lust, for at times I, too, felt lust for men. But living with her, in those seasons when Merlin or Morgause and her sons did not visit, I felt unprotected in some way when it was just she and I in our rock chambers along the cavern cliffs. She had her happy times as well, and she did not drag me through her many miseries, I will give her that. And worse, I understood her unending fury. I had heard her cry out in the night during a dream that my father still came for her, that terrible night when I was conceived. I covered my ears that I would not hear the whimpers and cries she made as her dream carried her back into that nightmarish event. I knew of how her brothers and father had been killed to make way for Uther pen-Dragon to take Ygrain and to bring Arthur into being. I knew the tale, told me by Viviane, of how Arthur had tricked Merlin into helping him retrieve the sword of the ancient kings, called Excalibur, stolen from the rock outcroppings of the Lady of the Lake, meant to remain buried in that watery stone for centuries, an amulet of our tribes, not to be held by any human hand without bringing power and glory and destruction to all. "The Lady tried to drown Arthur as he left in his boat clutching the sword as if it were his birthright. Her waters boiled that day, and the fish within it died, and was poisoned for five years until we had appeased her with our atonement."

"And does the sword hold so much sway in the world of men?"

"It is a sword of terror and retribution, and though it brings peace to one land, it brings suffering to another," she said. "For there is no peace without many wars in the world of men, and while a war may save a kingdom and exalt its king and his knights, it will leave many dead in their fields and blood will run in rivers beneath the highest of castle walls."

The lake had suffered greatly from my father's action as a boy, as had Merlin, as had my mother, and when I think on it much, my life also had been a suffering from his actions though I did not wish my own undoing in order to make it right.

I simply wished for a better world and for peace to come into my mother's heart and for her to recognize my love for her, because I put her above all other women. I held her as the finest of our tribe, and I saw her as the Queen of the Lake, as did many. Without saying a word about it, she had been silently abdicating her throne there, beginning to lose her grasp on daily living, forgetting to meet with the wise women at council, leaving the stews on the fire too long while muttering words that sounded like spells to me, though I could not understand them, and avoiding her responsibility for the groves during the festivals. My heart broke often when she spoke harshly to me over minor offenses, and I felt renewed hope each season that she seemed to regain her spirits.

My mother's mind had always been both strong and fragile. When I was younger, I did not think unusual those periods of winter when, like a bear in its cave, she went to her bedchamber for days at a time, drawing the woolen blankets across her body and covering her head with her pillows—one of the few luxuries she'd brought with her from Cornwall—as if she didn't want to even hear a human voice. I was used to her sudden anger at me if I misplaced the bowls, or if I did not draw enough water for the stew. When Gawain was there, in my first few years of memory, he complained loudly of her constant punishments of the two of us for the minor crimes of childhood (bringing frogs into our chamber and leaving them among the hay, or lighting a fire when we weren't supposed to have stolen kindling from the communal fire pit). "Your mother is mean," he wailed to me once, his face the usual mix of handsome looks from his mother's tribe and those wolfish attributes from King Lot's family. "I don't know if I can stand to be here another summer." He regaled me with tales of the castle at Orkney. "It is a long hall, full of dogs and knights, and the smell of honey-beer all around us, and the kitchen is always warm and full of freshly baked bread. Someday, Mordred, you should come back with me." He told me that his mother was sweeter than mine and that she did as her husband told her to do. "All women are meant for that," he said.

"Not the women here," I protested.

"The women here are strange," he said. "In my father's castle, the women do the bidding of the men. Here, the men seem to obey the women."

"Aunt Morgause isn't like the women where you live," I said. "She does no one's bidding but the goddess."

"She is different here than at home," he said. "My father says she deceives much."

I didn't like Gawain as a boy, but sometimes I longed for my cousin's home though I could only dream of it, for it sounded wonderful and so different from the Lake.

My aunt Morgause was warmer than my mother. As the seasons passed, and she and my cousins came less and less often, I missed her embrace as she whispered to me that I was a "prince of all lands."

My mother often watched me, on her sadder days, when the rains came, when the winds were too strong to go much into the world above the caves. And as she watched me, I had the unhappy feeling that she saw my father in my face and in the color of my hair and skin, though my eyes matched hers. I tried to be a comfort to her when I was a boy, but she often seemed to have retreated to another place.

Then, even Viviane spoke to me about her. "You will enter manhood soon enough, Mordred. Even now, I feel we have kept you too much a boy, but it has only been from love and our longing to protect you. But you will learn much of the world in the years to come. Merlin returns before spring, but it may be for the last time, for the Lady of the Lake calls to him, as she calls to Merlin in each lifetime. So, your life will change. Your mother has been in pain these many years. No herb or spell or prayer has helped her much, and I have watched the long spiderlegs of shadow cross her face and her soul. Do you know where she goes in the dark of the moon?"

I shook my head but said, "She has her duties as a priestess. I am forbidden, as are all men, to know of this."

"It is not that," my great-aunt said and offered me a few puffs on her pipe, something I had begun enjoying. "It is to those Roman outcasts called Strega by those who have met them. The ones who sell their potions and poisons to the villas and the soldiers. I do not know them, nor do I wish to meet them, ever. I am glad that they are far from us, a good day's journey on horseback, for I could not bear the stink of them. I understand they make cheap love philters and create elaborate curses to be brought down on those who will not pay their price. They are dream merchants as well, for they sell the ability to invade sleepers and give them restless thoughts. They are the dark side of a foreign goddess. She is from Greece and Italy, and has been calling those who despair to her. Some believe they worship Hecate, the owl goddess of the Greeks."

"The goddess, in all her forms, is good," I said, having learned this in the teachings of the Druids.

"No, that is not correct," Viviane said. "The goddess in all her forms is blessed. A blessing to one may be a curse to another. But there is a dark side to the gods. The boars of Moccus are not good, though they serve Arawn. The flying pestilence, though an incarnation of the Lady Nimue, is not good, for it brings disease and eats our crops and kills our cattle and sheep and goats. We suffer from the goddess, but this does not mean she does not bless us. And so this Hecate, stolen from a foreign land, brings her own pestilence to our forest. Your mother has shared blood with those Roman sisters." She said this as if she'd forgotten that I sat beside her. "She has taken vows with them."

I drew in a smoky cough from her pipe and passed it back to her. "She has much to be angry about. I wish it were not so. I wish all those who hurt her would…"

"Do not forget: The greatest law we know," Viviane said, "is the law of three. And this law tells us?"

"That what we bring into the world will return to us threefold."

"And nine times nine comes the dark," she finished. "Your mother is bringing something here. In her night worship. She is bringing something terrible to us, I fear. I do not trust Romans or their sorceries."

"I will speak to her," I said.

"Is that enough?" Viviane asked. Tears came into her eyes, and she reached over to embrace me. The smoke around us was like a mist, connecting the two of us, Crone and Youth. "You were blessed, as was she. She seeks vengeance in her life. But vengeance is not for us, but for the gods."

I determined as I held Viviane, as she wept against my neck, that I would find out about these Strega and my mother's nightly excursions.

I would see for myself where she went and what she did there.

Chapter Seven

1

I followed my mother many nights, carefully riding my horse toward the forest paths rather than the main roads she took so that she would not see me.

Once close enough, I dismounted, hiding behind rocks and bushes and lying flat among the ferns as she made her way to that poisoned well where the Strega, those three Roman sisters, dwelt, but by the time I reached the place, I could not find them. They met at the dark of the moon, and I heard the growls of wild cats and the call of owls around me as I tried to search for them in the pitch-black. I did not enjoy spying on her, and I began to sense that she knew I had begun watching her too closely.

"You are curious about my meetings?" she asked one day as we both carried the water pots to the Lake.

"Your meetings?" I lied with the question.

"I have given myself to a goddess older than our own," she said. "And she brings me comfort. She calms my dreams, which have been horrible tempests for many years. But now they are beautiful and show me serenity where I had none within my heart."

"That is good," I said. "But I have heard they are terrible hags and this frightens me."

She laughed. "I suppose, to men, they do look terrible, and you are nearly a man. How can I expect you to understand differently? What makes Viviane a Crone and the women I visit hags?"

"Viviane does not like them."

"She does not have to like them. She has never met them and never will, for she is against the foreign manifestations of the goddess."

"But they are *hags*," I said. "Night hags. I heard they steal dreams and in their places leave nightmares and terrible visions."

"And you heard this from?"

Although both Viviane and Merlin had told me this, I decided to mention only my teacher. "Merlin told me they work a rough sort of magick."

"You believe the word of a man who sleeps with the Pictish whores and bathes but once a century? He does not know much of women, Mordred, though he may have been a woman for a few lifetimes. And you do not know them. To me, they are wise women, though their aspect is frightening. Yet it is so that men may fear them and tremble at their power," she grinned, and I could not tell if this was a joke or not. As if reading my mind, she said, "And no, you are not going to meet them, Mordred. I'd be afraid that they might take too much to you and wish to keep you. Youths such as yourself are attractive to such *hags*."

"I thought you said they were Crones."

"Neither Crones or Strega! All of it, simply words," my mother said. "Words. Men created language simply to insult women and enslave people. There's more to existence than the barbs that fall from the tongue. I am tired of words and curses and vows. Tired of it all." Then she went silent, and any good humor in her was gone. I watched a shadow cross her face as if she meant to tell me more about the Strega, but it was as if to do so would require the breaking of a vow.

2

In the autumn of my fifteenth year, I learned too much of the struggle of life that had been hidden from me and only existed in scrolls and parchment or in the tales told by Viviane and the Druids during the grove worship. I had been dreaming too much of boys my age and those a few years older. I thought of their faces, their bodies, the way their legs moved when they ran or when they clutched each other as they wrestled in games. I thought too much of them and how I wanted to hold them. But when I awoke, I remembered Merlin's warning to me of the sacredness of the arts I still needed to learn before manhood took me over. I did not understand why I couldn't seek out others like me and fulfill these dreams of mine, but I longed for power as I'm certain my father before me had also longed for it, though he had grabbed it while I waited patiently for those magickal arts that Merlin might pass to me.

We had warnings of the Moccus boars, that someone had entreated Arawn in the Otherworld for favor and this brought these dangerous beasts roaming into the woods. Lukat and I went to our treetops to watch for them but only saw stags and their mates out along the desolate lands beyond the trees. All the youths and maidens and those of ancient years were told to keep to the thicket at the cavern and venture no further than the paddocks and streams that led from the Lake of Glass, until the watchers and herdsmen gave word that the Moccus boars had passed on to other hunting grounds. At the far rim of our forest, the Druids put out scraps and roots and baskets of berries in offering to Moccus and Arawn that the boars should feed and leave us untouched.

Soon after the Samhain Festival, the harvest in, and the first frost upon the ground, the time of the boars had passed, and the sun gleaming bright though the air was like ice. Lukat and Melisse invited me out with them for an afternoon horseback ride. The two of them rode together, and I felt a twinge of jealousy, not just that Melisse had captured the heart of my closest friend, but that they had each other. They had love and seemed as one when together. I longed for that love—the touch and the closeness of another, what Viviane called the "twin soul."

I rode alone, thinking of my promise to Merlin to remain chaste, though it seemed against my very nature to do so. In my head, I argued with him, though he ignored my vesseling calls. *Does not the Lord of the Forest call all creatures to mate when it is their season? Does not the goddess bless the act of love and creation?*

Youths my age had often hand-fasted and begun raising families, though many waited until their twentieth year, for in our tribe we had rites of maidenhood and rites of manhood that would not be crossed until maturity of both mind and body had been reached. Still, I didn't think Lukat and Melisse would wait that long for the ritual of hand-fasting—anyone could see their love on their faces, like the spirit of life itself waiting to bring new life from them both.

And yet, I had no love, nor had I found any youth like me in the cliff homes of the cavern. But riding close behind my friends, I was happy for their future and for what they had found, despite my envy of their having it. We raced our horses through the winter meadows, though the chilly wind whipped my cap off and nearly tore the cloak from my back. Among the alder and ash, we dismounted and walked our mares to the crooked emerald stream where it was said the faeries bathed. Like the waters that fed the caverns, it was a warm heat that came up from the stream in a very light mist and warmed us greatly as we drew off our shoes and dipped our feet into it.

Melisse spoke of their plans for the next Beltane fires, when they would hand-fast, and Lukat made jokes about how they would have to carve up a new home in the caves if they were to bring children into the world.

"I won't have children yet," Melisse said, with a scolding laugh. "I am going to be a Druid."

"A Druidess?" I asked. "Have you begun the training?"

"For six years," she said. "And for seven more."

"Seven years with no children? Shall I wear a chastity belt?" Lukat asked, almost surprised. "A year from midsummer, do Mordred and I not become men? Will we not ride the bull and wear the sacred antlers and learn the secrets of men that we may no longer be called boys? So many years without knowing the pleasure of you?" Then, he laughed. "I guess I will have to find another bride."

"And I will have to find a bride too," she said. "If you expect me to be a wife as the kind that the horse herds marry. I want that kind of wife who will be a slave to a foolish husband. I will not carry water from the Lake, nor will I wash your filthy undergarments. And if one of us has to cook, you might want to start learning, because I would rather eat raw barley than spend my days over the hearth-fire."

"She has bewitched me," Lukat said, and reached over to grab her hand and squeeze it. "Do not ever fall in love, Mordred. You will become its slave, as I have."

"But it is a lovely sort of slavery," she said, and grinned. "Mordred, someday, you will meet a man, and then you'll be arguing over who does the washing too."

"Yes, and may he be a better man than most, for I know how you stink at dawn when you first wake," Lukat added.

"It's you who stinks," I said, laughing as I splashed water up at both of them.

We sat on a long, flat rock, and Lukat brought out the lunch he'd packed into his serving pouch. It was a long flatbread cake, with dried mutton with swamp apple sliced across it and long-stem mushrooms that were called "little amulets," all slathered in rosemary butter. To drink, we had skins full of heavily diluted unfermented wine from the wild grapes. We divided up the food, passing bits to each other that tasted especially good. Lukat kept claiming that the wine made him drunk, although it could not have, for there was so little of it and it had not even fermented. Melisse talked a bit about her brothers who had left our forest sanctuary, knowing they could never speak of the Lake of Glass, to go join King Hoel's army at the northern coast, which fought against the provincial governors who paid allegiance to no people, as well as the Saxons who had come to those shores, all in service to the great court of King Arthur and his knights of the round table and for the glory of that sword Excalibur. As she spoke, I felt more isolated from the world around me, feeling I could not speak of the reasons for my mother's well-known furies and silences, and her inability to leave our home in the winter, even for the feasts of the nameless days at solstice time.

Lukat turned to me as the afternoon dwindled and put his arm over my shoulder. "You are more brother than any brother to me. I hope when Melisse and I have children, you will be their guardian and uncle."

"Yes!" I shouted and could not help myself—I kissed him on the cheek, feeling that welling-up of friendship and affection.

He blushed, and grinned, and Melisse said, "No stealing my husband-to-be, Mordred. With your looks and talents, you will have many handsome men to choose from, You don't need this horse herd from the caves." We laughed and then Melisse stood, offering her hand to me. "Do you know how to dance, Mordred?"

"I have watching dancing but never done it."

"Come on, then," she said. "Take my hand." She had that kind of girlish smile that seems like the sun coming out from behind a cloud: there was no guile there, no hidden meaning to her. I loved Melisse in that moment, as I hadn't completely loved her before. She had accepted me for who I was, and she wanted my friendship and she offered hers in return. I took her hand, which was slightly cold. She drew me up, and Lukat reached into his shirt for the pipes he played when we guided the sheep along the dusty trails.

He began to play a lively tune that reminded me of the wild Beltane dances. Melisse guided my hands to her waist and then began moving her feet in a lively fashion as we twirled around on the cold ground. "Faster!" she cried as Lukat's tune picked up. "Lose yourself in it, Mordred. Yes! Like this!" She held my hands and spun away from me, and I did the same, still touching her fingers. Then, we came back together, and Lukat's music seemed to linger in the air in that green paradise, and I have frozen it in my memory above many others, for it was the last of its kind for me in this life.

This is my memory that I ravel into you: the beautiful red-wine–haired girl of sixteen, her fingertips touching mine, her skirt and cape swirling in a blur of dance, the mist of the stream and the green of the fern at its edge, while the white frost speckled among the mosses like faerie dust, and the boy of sixteen on the flat rock, playing the five-fluted pipes, looking like beautiful Pan serenading children just before they entered the world of men and women.

How I would return to that moment, the tincture of time, if I could, that moment before my left foot returned to earth and while my right leg had just landed on the dead leaves below them.

For the hour to come would be one I could never wipe from my thoughts as long as I lived. That brief moment of the dance held my hopes before the darkness swooped down like a crow upon us.

3

We were back on our horses too soon, but we went slowly along the path, catching the last of sunlight between the oaks. "I want to begin farming the Lake itself," Lukat said. "No one has tried it yet."

"They've tried," Melisse said. "But no one has the ideas you have, my love."

"Cress and eel-spice can grow in the water easily," Lukat said, looking across to me. "I think we can use the far shore to plant, and I've already grown swamp apples there. If we grow them far enough away, near the luminous pools, the branches won't get in the way of the boats."

"You've done this all in secret?" I asked.

He nodded.

"He wanted to make sure it worked before he said anything," Melisse said, leaning forward to whisper something to the mare, for the Eponi could whisper to their horses in order to train them and guide them.

"If we are to have many children," Lukat said, "I need to make sure we bring more food to our people."

"Two children," Melisse said. "A boy and a girl."

"Two boys, two girls," he said, laughing.

"Seven years from now, we can fight about it like old people," she said gaily. "Once I'm a Druid."

"Mordred, my brother, I'm going to be a Druid's bitch," Lukat smirked.

"And you'll love every minute of it," she said.

"And after I come back from my service," he added. "For all I know, that will be seven years as well."

"Service?" I asked.

"To our kings," he said.

"But you can't leave the Lake."

Melisse leaned forward to rest her head upon the horse's mane. She looked over at me, offering up a wan smile.

"Our cousins and families are in danger on the coast," Lukat said. "I won't leave until next summer."

"And the coast may be safe by then," she added.

"But...but you belong here. We are not people of those kingdoms."

"Mordred? Of course we are. Haven't you noticed others who have gone? Besides Melisse's brothers and my uncles, many of the boys younger than you and I have already left."

"But the wars are for Christendom. They are for the nobles of Britain. Not for those in service to Our Lady."

"Our Lady of the Lake is for all who call themselves Briton and who keep her sanctuary safe. Those Saxons may come and burn these woods some day. Or the Romans may return in another few years, for their new kings to the east grow restless and hungry for power. In Paris, there is a king who seeks favor with Constantinople. You've heard the messengers' reports at each council meeting. I can't ignore this," he said, his mood darkening. "I knew I should not have told you yet."

"The wars may be over by Beltane," Melisse said, keeping her gazed fixed upon me. "Do not fear. We will ask the goddess for peace. She will surely bring it."

"The source of our strength is our lake," I said, as I felt my heart beating too fast, thinking of Lukat leaving for war. I had ignored the men who left our forest to go to follow the call of duty, for exiles came and went from the Isle of Glass, off to serve with their fellow Britons to protect the southern kingdoms. But I had never thought Lukat, whose family was Eponi, would ever join them.

"All the lakes of the world and all its forests will not stop the attacks on our people," Lukat said.

"This is the first I've heard such talk from you," I said, with a bitter taste in my throat as the evening grew colder and our horses seemed to stop to graze too much on our lazy way home. "You won't do it. I know you. By spring you'll hand-fast, and by summer you'll have your water garden and be tending the sheep in the summer meadow."

Lukat turned away from me, looking up the road ahead. I could tell he was angry. Melisse watched me, sadness on her face. "I tell you," she said. "The wars will end soon. There is peace in Cornwall and North-galis, and only in London do the Saxons rob the old Roman towns. Do not fear."

"The king of all Britons, the high-king who rules the warlords of the lands, Arthur, is the greatest of all emperors and frees our people as his great knights lead the armies to victory in east, west, north, and south. And I intend to serve him," Lukat said.

I was dumbstruck. My closest friend in the whole world could not know the evil that high-king had brought to my mother and to me. Could not know how he had torn at my mother's family, murdering many and seeking my death as well as my mother's.

The man he thought of as the great liberator of the Britons in the islands to the west and the Hebrides, and Orkney and the White Coast of Lyonesse, and the Dragon's Mount and its coastline was, to me, the one human being I wished dead in the world.

And yet, within that hatred, I had a longing to see him. He was my father, despite the monstrous things he'd done to my mother before my birth. He was a man who commanded the armies of other kings who served him as if they were his vassals. He had been predicted in the ancient scrolls, the high-king of the tribes, and his legend, it was said, had spread across the world and even the Romans respected and feared him.

But I was certain that I would never see my father as long as I lived. And I would never leave the Lake of Glass and its secrets until my father had breathed his final breath.

I rode a little ahead of them, prodding my mount with my heels. I had to resist the urge to argue with my friends, for fear that I might reveal the secret of my birth and thereby risk even Lukat's life should he ever be called before the King's Guard—known torturers and thieves—to testify to his knowledge of the existence of the king's bastard son.

I knew that I would have to let my friend go where he would in life. We had reached that crossroads, and my world might never be his again as he sought his future and his life. He would marry, go to war, and even if he returned in another harvest season, our friendship would change. I did not like the way life went, and I began to wonder if the Lake were sanctuary or prison for me.

They caught up to me, and Melisse challenged us both to race our mares along the twilight path. "We take the longer path home and race until we reach the shepherd's stones before the grove itself. Whoever crosses the last stone first, wins."

"And what do we win?" I asked.

"A kiss. From either of us," she smiled.

"If I win?" Lukat asked.

"Well, I hope you'll want a kiss from me," she said.

"I want more than a kiss," he grinned wickedly. He glanced over to me. "My horse is called Wind-mare, for she is like the wind in a storm."

"I've heard her wind," I said, laughing again, letting the trouble of my mind melt a bit. "And it truly is a mighty wind. Mine is named," and I had to make up a name quickly, for I didn't know the true name of the horse I rode, "Boadicea, for she has the spirit of the great Iceni warrior queen who vanquishes all!"

"But can she run?" he asked and then he clicked his tongue and pressed his feet against his horse and took off, Melisse crying out, surprised by the suddenness of it.

"Cheater!" I cried out and soon had my mare racing to catch up to his. The path to the shepherd stones took a few turns and twists along the heath before returning to the woods, and then as we raced, I saw ahead of us both—for we were nearly neck and neck along that wide well-trodden path—the opening from the Groves onto the meadow where the stones stood. It had grown so cold that I could see the steam coming from my mount's nostrils, and when I briefly glanced over at the two of them, Lukat had wrapped his arms around Melisse and they bounced together up and down on the poor mare's back while Melisse giggled and cried out with delight. As we had just cleared the trees and the expanse of meadow lay before us with its dips and rises, I thought I saw movement among the brambles by the wayside. I didn't imagine it was anything to be concerned about, and it had become a blur to me as I faced forward again, seeing the stones ahead of us, hoping to outrace Lukat and Melisse so that I might kiss him again, though I knew he would never be mine.

My mare seemed to gain great energy as we passed the brambles, and I felt a surge of movement as she seemed to gallop so fast it was as if she had wings, and the thunder of her hoofbeats were in my head.

And then I heard a terrible noise behind me, and Melisse cried out. I drew back on the reins, but my horse didn't want to slow down at all, so I kept trying to turn her to stop her galloping. When I finally glanced back, bringing my mare around, I heard a noise as if some growling bear had bounded up behind us.

When I turned in my mount, I saw Lukat's horse on the ground, being torn at by a beast the like of which I could not make out. My blood rushed fast within me, and I turned my horse around and went riding back to them.

Melisse lay beneath the fallen horse, and for the first time in my life I saw one of the boars of Moccus, crouching there, tearing at the dying horse.

Lukat had been thrown clear of it and lay upon brambles and grass, his eyes closed.

I had nothing but a dirk in the scabbard at my shoulder, but I drew it from beneath my cloak and ran swiftly to face the beast.

Chapter Eight

1

The great creature was nearly half my height, and I was considered tall for our people, though not as tall as many of the Druids. It was wide and thick and reminded me more of a bear than of a boar. I held my small blade up, hoping that it would at least be wary of one who was taller than it might be. I tried not to think of Viviane's encounter with the Moccus, which I had somehow doubted, for her tale had seemed too far-fetched. And yet, it was as she had described the animal to me: its spines were thick and like small daggers themselves, and it had two long crescent tusks to the left of its snout, cutting through the skin of its muzzle, and three to the right. Its coloring provided even more wonder and terror, for it was pure white; its eyes were blood-red; its muzzle spattered with the blood of the now-dead mare.

Steam came from its mouth and nostrils, and it dug at the turf beneath its feet with its hooves, as if it would charge me.

I could not take it on, for my small dirk might at best penetrate an eye or, with luck, its tough hide, but I would be dead before I was able to stab it more than once.

Merlin, help me, I tried vesseling to my master.

Merlin, come to me now. Bring me magick that I might stop this hell-beast.

Time itself seemed to freeze as I stood there, hearing Lukat moaning with pain. The boar, also listening for this, twitched his head and looked in the direction of him.

I took a tentative step forward, holding the dirk before me with a trembling hand.

Lady of the Lake, be with me now, and at the moment of my passing into the Otherworld, I prayed. *You are blessed of all the forest and the waters within it, and you may entreat Arawn of the Otherworld to call back his creatures that we might gain safe passage. But if we cannot, be with me at that passage into darkness, for it is from darkness to darkness we go.*

I heard Merlin in my mind, although it was not his vesseling of me at some great distance. It was my own memory, bringing up his words as one draws water from a deep well. *You have the blood of the great kings within you, Mordred, and the queens of power and right. You have learned the Art of the vessel. It is the auras that come together that all living creatures possess. Use the magick that you have, for it is good to do so.*

In less time than it takes for a soul to pass from the body, I spoke to the boar's mind in a way that I hoped it would understand. Not with words that would be foreign to it, but with visions of its own slaughter at my hands. My anger and fury rose to such a degree that in the vision that I wished to vessel into it, I tore it open and skinned it while alive, drenched in the blood of that beast.

The boar of Moccus seemed to calm, as it looked from me to Lukat; to Melisse, who lay silent under the dead horse's weight.

The watcher along the trees and hilltops had seen this from a distance, and soon I heard hoofbeats behind me as horsemen and -women rode along the path, and it was perhaps their coming that scared off the boar and not my imagined vesseling of a vision into the beast.

But as it ran off into the ferny shadows, I thanked the Lady for her blessings and asked her to bring life into my friends.

Then, I ran first to Melisse and, with two other men who had just leapt down from their mounts, drew the horse from her body. One of the men, named Marlet, wept as he lifted her. I knew without him saying it that her spirit had passed to Arawn's arms in Annwn, where the souls went soon after death. I glanced over at those men who had gone to Lukat and was heartened to see him open his eyes and cry out, though it was in despair as he called Melisse's name into the darkening air and heard no reply.

2

I stayed at Lukat's bedside for three days, barely sleeping and hardly eating. His father remained in chambers as well, cooking stews and accepting fresh bread and herbal remedies from others who came to offer their blessings and prayers. When alone with Lukat, I wept and crawled beside him that he might feel warmth. He remained unconscious for those days and nights, though his eyes fluttered open during moments and he took water by a damp cool cloth that I pressed to his lips. The back of his scalp had been torn at by the brambles, and their thorns had been driven into his neck and back also by the force of his fall. These wounds needed daily washings, so my mother came with her salves and balms. She was slowly withdrawing from me in many ways, but she had not abandoned her knowledge of the goddess's healing. She taught me how to rub the salve along his back and shoulders, and how to massage it into his scalp so that he would heal better. His father brought a large round tub into the chamber and poured heated water from the hearth-fire into it. We undressed my friend and lifted him up, bringing him into the bath to clean him in the health of the Lady of the Lake's lifeblood, which was that crystal-clear water full of minerals of the earth that brought health and vitality to her people.

Finally, at the end of the third day, as nightfall blessed us, he stirred in his sleep and turned, reaching for me. His eyes opened, and he whispered, "Mordred."

"Yes," I said.

"I dreamed she had died. Melisse." His voice was scratchy from the dryness of his throat, and before he spoke again, I had him sit up, his arms ringed around my shoulders. I dipped my hand into the water font by the bed, and he drank from my hand as if he'd never tasted water before.

"Where is she?"

"Gone."

"To Arawn," he said. "To Annwn."

I could not answer but began sobbing, clutching him that I might never let him go again.

"To Arawn," he repeated as I clung to him.

3

Before dawn, my arms wrapped around my friend, I felt the terrible fever that had come upon him, leaving his back slick with sweat. "Mordred?"

"Hmm," I murmured.

"When we die, do we go right into a new life?" His voice had a moan within it, as if each breath took some life from him.

"I don't know. I suppose. Sometimes."

"Could Melisse be born right now?"

"If Arawn wills it."

"Perhaps even here, in the caves?"

"Shh," I said. "The sun hasn't risen yet. Sleep."

"Do you love me?" he asked.

I didn't answer for a moment. Then: "Yes. You're my brother that I never had."

"And you're mine. But you love me like I loved her."

I sighed. "Yes."

"I wish I could love you back. Like that."

"I do too."

"I wish I didn't hurt so much. On the inside. Thinking of her."

"If I could, Lukat, I'd change places so I'd feel that pain. You would not suffer so much."

"It is a suffering I want. I see her face the more it hurts. I feel her with me. With us here. Right here."

We lay there silently. I began to understand something of love that I had never before known. It was greater than the love I had felt for him when I had felt my heart pound next to him before. I felt the pain of love, which was sacrifice. There was no way around it. I knew then a wisdom that no priestess or Merlin had yet taught me. And it was that love is a sacrifice, but not to the gods or goddesses. It is a sacrifice to the soul, and the chambers within the soul enlarge because of it, and we find within those chambers more doorways into other rooms and corridors. Each love—each genuine love—we carry expands the vessel of the soul. And if the vessel should crack and break, and not be mended, it is none the worse for being broken.

The vessel of the soul is meant to break, to expand, to be larger and more full at the end of our lives than at their beginning.

I kissed the back of his neck with tenderness, without lust, without want, without need. I inhaled the aroma of him: the sweat and the flower of it, and the fresh-grass odor he carried as well as the herbs of the bath that remained on his skin. If I had been able to ravel then, I would have raveled into him and he into me so that neither of us would feel that terrible loneliness that one feels when the ache for love grows too great to bear.

I felt as if he and I were one, there, in that feather-stuffed woolen mat, covered with the layered blankets of the weavers. I whispered to him about our games of childhood and how we were punished many times by our stern elders. I reminded him of the day he taught me to swim by trying to drown me and of our races along the desolate lands, and of chasing down a stag in the hunt one November day when we had both begun to understand our differences.

After a while, he turned to me and whispered, "I wish I could love you as you want to be loved, Mordred. For other than Melisse, there is no one in this world I care about as I do you. If I could, I would handfast with you. I would be with you forever."

"It wouldn't be you, Lukat. It's not your nature, though I wish it."

"But I would." His eyes filled with the gleam of tears as the light came up beyond the chamber; and I embraced him, and he, me, as he turned. He pressed his eyelids to my lips, and I tasted the saltiness of his tears.

He kissed me just below my lips and drew his head back. "I'm going to leave the Lake forever," he said.

"I know," I whispered, afraid of this, and knowing in my heart it was what he must do.

"One day, I will find Melisse again. The Druids say that the young child will remember, sometimes, the life lived before. I can wait many years. I can wait for her soul to return and to grow up into a great lady again."

"They say it is not good to remember the pain of past lives," I said.

"Because it brings fear to those who must face this life," he replied, as we had been taught in our childhood lessons with the wise women.

"But you will find her," I said.

He nodded. "Will you love many men or one man?"

"I hope one," I said.

"I thought I would have many women when I became a man," he said. "But Melisse was all I ever wanted. I knew her soul as she looked into mine too. I knew her in ways that I know no one else but you." His voice became almost a bleating, as of a lamb. It tore at my heart to hear him. "*Mordred. Mordred.* I don't want to ever have to hurt like this again. Please tell me I won't rip in two. I feel like I may. I feel it."

"Shh," I whispered, hoping he would rest.

We rested a bit, a delicate calm upon us.

Then, he spoke again. "When I go, I promise I'll come back. Someday."

"If you leave, we will never see each other again."

"No," he said. "Don't ever believe that, Mordred. I will always find you. I will always come home to you. If we could see our past life, I bet you were my father. Or my lover. Or my sister. Or I was your daughter.

We too are somehow bound. Do you not feel it?"

"I imagined it," I said. "But did not know if it was true."

"What we imagine may be true," he said. "I thought I imagined love, but it *is* true. I know it. Do you know love? Really know it?"

I could say nothing in response, though I felt love in my heart for Lukat himself and love for Melisse, whom I had just begun getting to know through his love for her.

"If you ever find it, Mordred—love—the love that comes from the gods," he whispered, clinging to me as if I were Melisse and he spoke to her through me, "if you ever find it, it is worth going to the Otherworld to bring it back. Be afraid of nothing. Be afraid of no one. If you have the love that is the two souls in one, you have nothing to fear in all of your lives." He must have known that I was sobbing against him. All the loneliness of my childhood had come up from a deep well, all those moments when my mother had looked at me as if she had recognized my father in my face; or when I could not play with friends for fear that I would reach over and kiss Lukat and embarrass him and me, or not talk to someone about my feelings and thoughts, lest they be mocked or, worse, taken gravely seriously by even Merlin as an indication of an unsteady and wavering mind when I was too young to even know my way.

Lukat closed his eyes. "I need to rest. I will see Melisse in my dreams. I will ask her into what new life she goes that I may find her."

And so, I held him as he slept. He was my child and my brother and the best friend I had ever known. While he slept, I hummed the soft song of summer winds that was taught to us by Viviane. It was the song of the Lady Nimue, who had sacrificed herself to the Lady of the Lake many centuries before so that she could travel to the underworld kingdom of Arawn and beg for mercy for the tribes, for the Romans then slaughtered one and all, and the spirits did not come back to the flesh for new life, as many women had gone barren. And the Lady of the Lake, seeing her great sacrifice, rescued Lady Nimue's spirit from Arawn, who had fallen in love with the priestess. The nameless Lady released Nimue's spirit as wind on water, that Nimue might guide the boats of the tribe to safety when their enemies came for them, or bring storms down upon the invaders.

Later that night, when all was quiet, I rose from our bed and went out to climb up the steps to sit in the moonlight. The fires of the Eponi were lit, and I went to sit with some of the men and women who would remain up all night, praying for young Melisse's safe passage between worlds.

In my head, I began writing a song to her, stealing much of it from the Nimue tune, but enough was new that it was wholly mine. It was for Melisse and Lukat and I do not remember much of it, but it began what would be a lifelong love of writing and poetry. It would be days before I'd find a parchment and begin to write upon it, my own words, my own thoughts, but that night, by the fire of the Eponi, watching the flames and thinking of Lukat and his beloved, I sang a song in my head for them, for it was my own prayer. It was to their love and to my friendship with them, and even the white boar of Moccus, who had brought death and sorrow to us.

4

The funerary rites for Melisse were held in those days after the priestesses and the Druids had purified the body and spirit of the departed. Far from a solemn occasion, it was an awakening.

The minstrels, who came from among the artisans, played the old songs of the gods and of the early heroes of Troy and of Rome and of the southern mountains and of North-galis and the Wastelands. Maidens of Melisse's age or younger danced in the stylized slow movements that reminded me of the Greek mystery dances of which I'd read so much. The Eponi, who were Melisse's tribe, raced their horses in the darkening fields lit by torches, and Melisse's own horse was honored with garlands of wildflowers and scented evergreen branches. Along the Lake, all who had known Melisse told stories of her, and then one by one, we youths stripped off our clothes and dove into the Lake, swimming toward its center. When we reached that point, we were to dive down deep to see if one could touch the cauldron of Rebirth, which was the Womb of the Lady and covered the entrance to the Otherworld. If one could touch it, he would rise up and be praised and covered with flowers and given the best portion of the roasted pigs, for he had sent the prayer to both Arawn and the Lady for Melisse's swift return into a new life with her tribe, there at the Isle of Glass, before her soul might move away.

I swam with the other boys, having told Lukat that I swam for him since he could not. All the years of swimming the Lake and the rivers above had made me strong and ready for this. Other youths, older and younger, did not travel so far into the Lake, or so fast as I did. And when I reached the center point, marked in the rock ceiling above by the beginning of the chasm doorway to the sky, I took a deep breath, and dove down, kicking my legs like a frog behind me that I might push further into the depths of the water. The heat was greatest at the Lake's center, and was nearly too hot as I went farther down, but I bore it, thinking of Lukat and Melisse.

I had to come up, for I did not find the lip of the cauldron. I glanced about: two other boys, one a year older and one three years younger had joined me, though others still swam from the shore toward us. They, too, dove down as I caught my breath. And I went again, below the surface, and as I did, pushing myself deeper and deeper into that silent darkness, I saw an eerie yellow-green light, as if the Lady's Lamp, that glowing residue of the hot springs, was smudged beneath me. I followed the light down, and nearly had reached it when I felt my hand burning hot as I pressed it forward. And there, at the edge of the light, I saw the gold and bronze of the rim of a large bowl or cup.

I reached forward, though my fingers blistered in the blast of heat around it. I touched the edge of the cauldron of Rebirth.

My skin felt as if it were on fire, and I swiftly drew my hand back and allowed my body to float upward, kicking as much as I could, hoping to break the surface at any moment, but as I went, I was sure that I would drown, for my face did not emerge above the water.

I took water into my lungs but finally broke through that surface, and spat the water from me, coughing. The other youths around me took me up upon their shoulders and backs, swimming with me toward the shore's celebrations. When I had recovered my strength within the hour my hand had turned red and blistered from the heat from where I had touched the Cauldron of Rebirth so that Melisse could return to the Eponi in her next life.

That night, a great dance was held, and her father and mother got drunk on honey ale, and even I drank too much wine, which dulled the throbbing pain of my hand. As I was the one who had brought the cauldron's blessing to the departing soul, I had to dance with every maiden who would come to me, and every youth, for it was known now of my nature, and though the youths danced as close to me as the maidens, none interested me, and I did not detect one among them who had a love for men as I did. Lukat danced with me twice, though he grew dizzy and had to rest, for he had not yet fully recovered from his own fall nor from the shock of Melisse's death.

The revels went on into the early dawn. We made quite a din, and the songs to Arawn and to the Lady and to Cernunnos and to all the gods known and unknown continued until the sun began to rise over the caverns.

I raised my cup to Melisse before the Druids took her body for their sacred rite in the grove at sunrise, from which the rest of us were barred.

After the Druids had passed her body to the arms of the goddess, Lukat collapsed again and took his bed just at the first snowfall.

5

A month went by, and the worst of winter came upon us, so I did not leave the warmth of the Lake or the bedside of my friend. He grew stronger, and I grew sadder, knowing he would leave when he had regained all his health. I brought Viviane to him that she might bless him and speak on his behalf to Cernunnos and Arawn, as well as to Sulis and Diana, and the gods of the four corners, and the elemental spirits of the rock and wood.

Then, I went down to the Lake and shed my winter clothing and stepped into the steamy waters that felt so loving to me in the midst of that season of frost.

6

I swam the length of the Lake, and each time I grew tired and the muscles in my shoulders and stomach seemed to want to rest and even drown, I asked the Lady for strength and was able to continue onward. I looked down into the luminous darkness of its bottom and saw the yellow and red spires of that underwater kingdom, thinking of its depths that went well below the level of our cavern, and of the legend that this was from the baths of Arawn himself, broken open by the Lady so as to escape the Lord of the Dead, who had held her prisoner. When I reached the round pools that came off the Lake, out where the ancient paintings were upon the cave wall, I rose up. Naked, I shook off that last of the water and sat shivering, looking at the Art upon the rough-hewn rock.

The Art of our tribe was magickal, and it showed the hunting of the Carnac bulls, each of which granted a blessing and a power to our ancestors. I saw the sacrifices of the elders, which occurred only once in our long history, when those who had lived long voluntarily gave up their lives for their children and grandchildren that they might have long life in a winter of extreme hardship. When those people had sacrificed their elders, they turned next to their children, the grandchildren of those who had died, and were nearly going to kill themselves that their blood might sustain their children through the dark nights. And it was then that the white ravens came from the thickets in such great numbers, and the wild pigs were found at the lip of the caverns that our ancestors might eat and find shelter.

There, on that painting, was an image of the Lady of the Lake. I had seen it many times as a child, but had not come to this place in several years.

She wore a blue-green robe, though it might have been the Lake itself surrounding her in a rippling halo. Her nakedness was not covered beyond the robe that flowed down her shoulders and back. Her hair, a burnt-red, nearly black, like that of my mother and aunt and many of our women, curled and undulated like a crooked stream.

Her breasts were not overly large, but a crescent moon had been painted upon one where a nipple would be, and a star or small sun was at the other. Her legs were long, and she stood upon two large fish, as if they were twin horses for her ride.

Her left hand was placed across her belly, which was small and rounded. There, held by her hand and across her belly down to her pubis, was the great cauldron of Rebirth, represented simply by a circle and the face of Arawn himself within it.

I looked at my left hand, still healing from the blisters brought from the touch of the cauldron.

I thought: *I have touched her womb, the place of rebirth. This is the sign that I have been blessed by the Lady.*

In the painting, her right arm raised up to her shoulder, her hand drawn as if inviting the viewer of this Art into her domain. Above her, the sacred white ravens and the gray doves that were her heralds.

"Our Lady," I whispered, "do not forsake my friend."

I closed my eyes, for though we had paintings and statues of our goddesses and our gods, we were not meant to worship stone or chalk. "The picture is so that you will not be frightened of her," Viviane once told me. "For the countenance of the goddess to the uninitiated may be full of terror or awe. She wishes for us to see her as we see ourselves. But when we pray or ask for blessings, we must go into ourselves to find her. For that is where she hears us. You must not ask for yourself, but for others, that they may prosper and might also ask the goddess for blessings upon you."

Lady, whose name is unknown to us but who has loved our people and saved us from our enemies, please be with my friend Lukat. Bring him comfort in this time of grief. Bring him the joy of your gardens and of your healing waters. Forgive me for my desires for him, for they were the desires of a child. I will become a man. You have opened my eyes to what life is, through the love I have for him. I will seek that love in one who will return it, but I would like to ask that if I need to be cursed in this life, so long as it makes Lukat, my friend, and Morgan, my mother, heal and forget their pain, I will happily be cursed. Let me take on their torments and their sorrow, for I can bear them on their behalf, but I cannot bear to watch Lukat suffer more, or my mother reach to the darkness to ease her pain.

You are the beautiful and the merciful. You heal and you bring life. I pray that you will speak to Arawn that he might trade my life for Melisse, so that she might return into the flesh and be known to my friend that he will find joy again and peace. You brought the cauldron of Rebirth up from the Otherworld and hold it within your womb. I beg of you to bring Melisse into its holy circle and raise her again to life.

I opened my eyes, half hoping that I would have a vision or a sight of the Lady, as some claimed to have during the solstices. But all I saw was that drawing, with the faceless and nameless goddess upon her fish mounts, her hand beckoning to me, the eternal circle of the cauldron upon her form.

I wanted more than this, more than the Lake. I wanted to be able to find love as Lukat had, with a mate, with someone with whom I could bind and hand-fast.

I wanted Lukat, and if not him, then someone who was everything a man could be. I did not want to settle for the men of the Lake anymore.

There were others in the world, others who would understand me.

Men who would love me as I could love them, and I only wanted one. I only wanted a mate as anyone on earth would want.

I sat there and prayed that Lukat might one day love me, for I could not imagine that I would find a friend like him again. Someone to whom I could offer body and spirit, even if it meant asking nothing in return.

I had worshipped the goddess too long, I thought, as I sat there.

The Lord of the Forest, Cernunnos, called Cerne by some, with his great antlers, riding the white stag—he was the one to whom men prayed.

He brought lust and love to men, and as I saw that soft Lady with her beauty and gifts, I knew that I would need to turn to the god of men to find a man who was like a god. I was done with the boyhood dreams of one who did not demand of the world what he wanted. Done with waiting and praying and hoping and watching, as if I were a flower in a field waiting to be picked or trod upon.

I hungered for that burning of the flesh that I had denied within myself.

For that moment, of looking at the ancient paintings on the walls, was the last true time of innocence for me, the last second of childhood, gone, as if it had never existed. I loved Lukat, I could not deny it. I was hurt for him too, and felt pain, but I did not wish Melisse back. I did not wish for Lukat's happiness. I wished for my own, and my pain was for my own grief at knowing that however close I got to him, he would always abandon me to a maiden, whether Melisse or some other that he might meet. I had given him all my love, and though he professed to give me his, he would not take that step toward me, that animal step that I desired. I hated myself as I sat there and then I exalted myself, for I did not truly believe that Lukat did not want me. I did not, in the deepest well of my soul, believe that he loved *any* more than he loved me.

I had lost that innocence as I contemplated the Lady and the Lord. And in its place was something dark and wild, something that had not been tamed by any goddess.

I was nearly a man, and I would do all things that men do.

I wanted love for myself. I wanted a man who loved me and wanted me and would come to me naked and willing and happy and with excitement in both his gaze and his flesh.

I wanted to be a hunter of men.

I turned to the painting of Cernunnos, his great antlers rising like a forest and his great organ erect, and around him the stag and the rabbit and the bird of prey.

Lord of the Forest. Lord of men. Lord of the rutting and the mating. Lord of the hunter and of the hunted. Hear my prayer that I might now become a man.

I dreamed that night of the deep emerald forest and of a great bow studded with dark red jewels in my hand. I was naked but for a cloth wrapped around my waist that hung down and tied between my legs as the hunters of old wore them, and there in a clearing I saw the great stag of Cernunnos. Five times the size of any deer, the stag was magnificent and mottled of color. His antlers were as tall as the trees themselves.

I brought an arrow to my bow and aimed for the stag's throat. When it sensed me, rather than running from me, the stag nodded its head as if acknowledging my presence and began to take steps toward me.

I lowered my bow and dropped the arrow to the fern-covered earth. And when the stag had come close to me, I saw it more clearly. It was a man wearing the skin of a stag upon him, the headdress of antlers worn in those ceremonies of the Lord of the Forest and of the Hunt.

He looked at me with eyes that were like the game stones of the Druids, polished and shiny-black.

And in that dream, I wrestled with the stag until we both lay upon the earth—the fresh, damp earth—and as I lay atop him, the dream faded into dawn.

I awoke to hear the sounding of the horn at the arrival of a messenger from the kingdoms of Britain.

7

That night, the council of elders called a meeting around the great fire in the clearing above the caverns. The messenger spoke to all of us, elders and the tribes that gathered to hear the news from the west. The news was of King Hoel on the coast of Armorica, and the sea-nation king, Tristan, of Lyonesse, whose fleets had defeated the Saxon invader along the islands for the glory of Arthur.

Then, Viviane, sitting closest to the fire, for she was the eldest of all elders, told what the messenger himself would not reveal. "King Arthur of the Britons has set his sights on the Roman provinces to the east, and he will bring his wars to Broceliande soon enough. He accepted a betrothal to a princess of the province to the south of Gaul, along the Mediterranean Sea. Gold is her dowry, and armies as well. She is the youngest daughter of that Roman family who once ruled all of Armorica and much of Cornwall before the wars of our fathers. Her name, as far as I can tell, is Guinevere. And in tribute, Arthur pays to her father..." Viviane could not continue, and she glanced down at her hands as if she could read some future there.

My mother, fire in her eyes and venom in her throat, stood up at the meeting and finished telling the news as if she were a warrior calling us all to arms: "Arthur has given this Roman family the forest and all that are in it in exchange for this half-Roman whore princess! She is of the same bloodline that stole Cornwall and Lyonesse in our great-grandmother's lifetimes! She is the Roman wolf coming back to the den, and Arthur opens his hand to her that she may feed upon our people. We will not just have the Saxons howling at our caves, but the Romans will return as well, this time, we do not fight them. No, we bend over for them!"

"It is but a betrothal, Morgan," Viviane said to calm her. "He has promised to wed before but has not. Three girls of the provinces have tempted him, but each one has broken a promise of the dowry. This is all politics, and politics change with every breath of the gods. He may break this before the girl is even seventeen. Though her father is Roman, her mother is Briton, and from the kingdom of North-galis, from which many of us are descended, my niece. She is still a child, and many things may happen before a child grows to become a maiden. A few years will pass before this may happen. The world changes in a few years. Even the world of the Romans. We must trust in Our Lady, for she guides our fortune in all things. Even that dark goddess to whom you pray cannot know if this will come to pass or pass away."

But my mother, whose anxiety and moods had taken her over, and whose vigils with those poisoner witches had begun to frighten me when she came home at dawn bedraggled and talking of blood and power, did not believe it.

"He will marry the Roman whore, and they will have sons who will bring Rome back to our lands. He is passing the kingdoms in one generation back to those who would see all of us dead and our children tortured and sold into that vile slavery that they practice. Do you not remember the torques? The chains? Viviane? You still have the scars from childhood. Do not tell me that this is simply a betrothal. Arthur is our enemy!" She raised her fists up to the night sky and cried out, "You stars in the heavens! You gods! You are indifferent to us! You stole my kingdom and murdered my brothers! You watch while he raped me! And the sacred Lady laughed while he forced himself upon me! Why should we live in exile? Why?"

I stood up, wanting to go to her, for the pain was upon her face. The others all remained silent, allowing her this outburst, but I could not stand to see her suffer like this. Nor did I like to hear of these things, for they made me think that she might have had a sweet life without me.

"He has Excalibur," my mother said. "The Lady did not stop him. Why are we so kind to that traitor knight who brought him? Why are we so welcoming of that traitor priest Merlin? Why do we not raise an army, as none the world has seen? My son! My son!" She pointed at me as if about to curse me with some terrible spell. But seeing me, her eyes filled with tears. The pain of seeing her was too much for me, and I felt that tightening of my insides as if my heart would break. "My son, does he not deserve that kingdom? Can any of you sitting here, you wise women, you Druids, you men who once fought for Briton until you were turned out like dirt beneath his shoes? Do you not think my son—my only child—should not be king one day, oor that I should ever rule the kingdoms of my mother? Merlin sat by while Uther raped my mother and murdered my brothers and father. And he taught Arthur the Art that keeps us from him, yet he betrays the goddess with his new religion of Rome. Merlin stood by while the traitor took Arthur into the Lady's treasure! And now he is going to marry a Roman whore who will pass our homeland back to the very monsters whom we had chased out within the memory of many of you here? What have we done? What have I done? What terrible thing did I do that I should be torn from my home? Where was our goddess? Where was she?" She broke down sobbing, and three of the elders went to her. "Don't touch me!" she shouted, brushing them away, her hair covering her face. "I should..." she began to calm but swayed to the left and then the right as if slightly drunk. "I should..." She drew her hair back, and in the firelight, she looked like she had gone completely mad. Her face was shone with sweat and tears, and her eyes seemed red, her mouth open in a grimace.

It was as if she were hypnotized by the great fire around which the council of elders sat. She took a step forward. Viviane called out to her to return to her self and take her seat. Danil, the charioteer, came over to my mother, stepping into the circle. He grabbed her around the waist to draw her away from the flames lest her robe catch fire. As he lifted her up, she fought against him and cursed us and cursed the stars and cursed the Lady of the Lake for all that had been done to her.

Chapter Nine

1

With the coming of the rains of spring, Lukat left the Isle of Glass. Though we embraced at his parting, I could not weep, for I felt hollow within myself. Hollow as the caverns themselves, for the emptiness of the world had begun to crawl into me and to find a home there. I had accepted sorrow and grief, and had taken on the bitter and weary aspect of my mother's face. I spent the next year studying more seriously with Merlin, and I obeyed his law that I might not yet discover those pleasures of mating that my friends and others all had been enjoying. I decided this would be easy, for my love for my friend Lukat kept me from wanting to find love in other youths. I saw myself as celibate for his friendship's sake, and I would someday take a vow to that, though I could not do it then.

"The creative spirit in a boy is important, and to develop it further, so that the Art becomes funneled by the goddess herself, it is imperative to refrain from these desires, whelpling," Merlin would say. "It won't be forever, and once you have crossed that border into rutting, you will not be good for much other than mating, desiring to mate, trying to mate, or warring that you might mate again—until your old age. That is often the problem of men, and I will not have it happen to you until you have learned more of the Art."

"But at night, when I am alone, I—" I began.

He hushed me up with a slap to the back of my scalp. "Don't be a

Saxon helmet-rat! The virginity is of the flesh and spirit commingling with another. It breaks the ability to vessel in men, if the Art is not strong. What you do in the dark of your room or at the edge of your bath in private is your own matter. And I don't need to hear about any winking going on, so don't regale me with stories."

The truth of it was, I had taken to strolling, when free from work and studies, out into the forest in summer, bathing in the streams and dreaming of men and how I would love them, and how they would love me.

It was on such an afternoon that I came upon a rust-colored pool bedecked with lilies and water ferns, and I saw a man of such intense beauty, a stallion of a man, with long dark hair, bathing and speaking to the sky as if a god were there to reply to him. I could but watch him from a distance, and I gave myself "free rein," as Lukat had called it when the hand went to the trousers, but I trusted that I was unseen. I could not resist, for his body alone overwhelmed me with the strength of it, the sinewy muscles and long limbs and even that part that is called by some the worst part of a man and by others the best. When next I came to that pool, waiting for hours, he was not there again. Before dark, I slipped into that same pool and closed my eyes, imagining him with me, his breath upon mine, his weight pressing down on me, and my imagination became so focused on this that when I opened my eyes after, I was surprised to find myself alone.

In another summer, I searched for this man. Finally, I saw him swimming down in the Lake called Lugdun and decided that I had to meet him and know who he was. I shed my clothing, and stepped into the chilly water, so different from my own lake. I swam out toward where he was, and when he saw me he moved to the shallows, away from me. As he stood, I saw him smile, and he raised his arm up in greeting. I felt my heart beat fast in my chest and remembered Merlin's words about my studies in the Art. And yet my body did not seem to recall the specific warning Merlin had given me. I splashed toward him, and as I did he turned his back on me and walked to the shore. I saw the tattoos along his shoulder and the smaller one just above the cheeks of his buttocks as he stepped onto the mossy rocks of the bank. He did not turn to wait for me, but instead moved toward the birch trees that were in clutches just beyond the Lake clearing.

I stood there in the water, furious for his leaving.

Furious for my wanting to touch him.

Furious for believing I could find a kindred soul in this forest at all.

2

I had no love for anyone, nor did I believe I had hope, though it is always the smallest of flames in dark times yet does not ever go out.

At Beltane, when my Aunt Morgause came, brought from the coast by charioteers, I met her at the rock stairway, and she crossed her arms over her chest when she looked at me. "I've been away too long, I see," she said. "You have lost all that baby fat, Mordred, and soon you'll be too handsome to have time for your aunt."

3

I need to shine more of a light upon Morgause herself. She had come early that year for several reasons. First, she had grown to dislike her husband to such an extent that she did not even like living within what she called his "mean little country." He had whores, she said, which made her happy, as she did not want him in her bed ever again. She was far too frank with me about her intimate life, but it was what I loved about her. "There is a truth in life, Mordred, which you will need to know, since it seems you foolishly will love men rather than the more wonderful female sex. The larger the broadsword that a man carries, the smaller the dagger sheathed in his trousers. The longer he talks of his love to you, the shorter the time he spends between your legs. I bore him three sons, but during those brief bouts of his rutting lust I prayed to the goddess for a tincture of pleasure or at least a good laugh. And if not a laugh, something of a prick that might tickle me in some fashion."

Her bawdiness never ceased to make me smile, and how I wished at times my mother would be more like her.

Since my birth, she had lived among the three worlds of Orkney with its severe kingdom governed more by bishops, she said, than by her husband, the king; Camelot, where she went in the winter for her duty as Queen of Orkney; and, finally, the Isle of Glass, from which she could not be forbidden as she was a priestess of the Lady of the Lake, and even the bishops and clerics of Christendom did not yet have power among the kingdoms to stop the worship of the goddess and her consorts.

Whenever she came to the Lake, she brought the filthy jokes she'd heard at court and told of the affairs of the noble ladies who one minute were at Mass praising themselves for their piety and within the next minute mounting the hounds keepers, or the ladies-in-waiting, or even the bishop himself. "These ladies of the court who stink of spiced oranges and thick perfumes from Rome at least have a time of it. I find none of the men of those castles in the least appealing. So few wash well enough to make me want to find out what is under their armor and tunic. So, instead, I try to imagine the charioteers here, with their oiled bodies in summer and the muscles on their arms as round as the ones on their backsides. I hope I am not embarrassing you," she said.

I shook my head, grinning, as I sat with her over a cauldron of mint tea.

"Have you yet taken a man?" she asked. Before I could answer, she said, "Try not to let the lechers find you, Mordred. You have that masculine beauty that old men of my age desire, but they shouldn't ever have it in their bed,m for they lost their chance in their own youths and now chase phantoms of their mortality when they chase young men like you. Are you in love?"

"No. Not as you mean it," I said. "Merlin forbade me from it."

"Oh," she said, nodding. "The problem of your sex. The goddess brings the Art, but she prizes virginity in youths. In maidens, she prizes their minds and spirits. But to her, the only gift a boy may give her is his chastity in exchange for her secrets. It is strange how that happens."

"Very strange," I said, sipping the hot tea.

"But you have loved a boy?"

"In the way that friends may love," I said.

"Good. Love is a wonderful part of life, Mordred. I myself have never had it, though I felt it briefly for each of my sons. But I, too, prized their virginities, and once they, one by one, went off with their whoring father, they became dull and stupid. Gawain talks only of Arthur, and if not talking, he is eating, and if not eating, he is whoring. I wish he'd been more like you," she said, reaching over and stroking my hair, which had grown long in the past winter without tending. She had told me often enough that she could read the mind of someone simply by touching their hair, and she did this now. "You have a man, somewhere. You are hiding something from me, dear nephew."

"I have seen one man. One man I think of."

"Ah," she grinned wickedly. "The kind you dream of?"

I nodded. "I've watched him bathe."

"Naughty boy," she said, laughing. "And was he well worth the view?"

I chuckled but was too embarrassed to say more, afraid she had already read my thoughts about him. "I am so happy you've come," I said. "You bring joy here."

"And you bring me great joy as well. Morgan is blessed. She doesn't know how blessed she is. Look at you. My sons wear armor and make enemies of any they see in order to call battle. My husband...well, I should not speak so much of him, for if I do I might end up liking him for his thousand flaws." Then, her voice calmed a bit, and she whispered, "Are there many like you here at the Lake?"

"I don't think so."

"Oh, I don't know," she said, knowingly. "I saw a charioteer washing the back of one of the Eponi herdsmen out along the Albi River. Years ago, we had many lovers who were men. Perhaps there still are some among the Eponi. I think if you open your eyes a little and don't look so downcast, you might notice these things."

"I would like to meet someone."

"What would this someone be like?"

"He would be..." I thought of the dark-haired man I had seen at the Lake and at his pool bath. "Older. But not too much. Perhaps ten years. And experienced."

"A knowledgeable lover," she smiled, nodding. "Yes. You are smart to wish for that. Nothing is worse than a clumsy man."

"With long hair, very dark, and eyes like the summer sky."

"You dream of this lover well, Mordred."

"I have seen him," I said and then regretted it.

"Ah. The one whose name you will not tell me."

"I've watched him bathe."

"I give him my highest blessings, then," Morgause said. "My husband hasn't bathed since the wedding feast. If you find a man who bathes regularly, Mordred, do not let him go. Tell me about this man you've seen. Is he a shepherd or does he tend the horses? A hunter? A messenger? A guard?"

"I'm not certain," I said. "He lives apart from us. There is a little house I've seen. Very rude and dirty. Covered with sod and thatched on the roof. Viviane told me that he is a hermit who has taken vows to the gods."

"Oh." The peaches and cream of her face seemed to turn ashen as a realization came to her. "*Him.*"

"You know him?" I asked, eagerly.

"I knew him very little. Many years ago, it seems."

"Is he that old?"

"Not so terribly old. He was very young then. Terribly young," she said, and I could tell by the look in her eyes that she had gone into a memory. I wished I could ravel her memory at that moment that I might peer into her past to see this man I had begun watching from afar, dreaming about. Then, she looked at me again, bringing her face close to mine and rubbing her nose against my nose as she had when

I'd been a little boy. When she drew back from me, she finished her tea and said, "I think you should find your love within the Lake, Mordred. Leave that man alone, because he...well, he will not be good for you. I can see by your look that you want to know more about him, but accept my word that he has brought suffering to many people and he does not live among us because of a past wrong for which he must atone."

"Just as Maponus guards the labyrinth below?"

She nodded. "Yes. A crime against the goddess herself. But do not ask more of me about this hermit, Mordred. Leave him to his burdens and his atonement."

"As you will it, so I shall," I said, repeating the phrase I'd been taught to say to the elders of my family.

"Promise me," she said, leaning forward and taking my hands in hers. Her hands were warm, but her eyes seemed harsh and distant as she watched my face as if detecting any deception. "Promise me you will not think of him. Banish him from your thoughts as the goddess herself has banished him from her sight."

I nodded, but my mouth had gone dry, and I felt my heart thudding against my chest as if I were a deer facing a hunter whose arrow was aimed and nearly shot from its bow.

She tightened her fingers around mine. "You will meet other men. I think you will have lovers before you meet the one you will love forever," she whispered, brightening slightly as she let my fingers slip from her hand. "I am so glad we may speak freely, Mordred. My sister and I can't seem to talk of these things between us."

"She won't talk with me about this either. Not anymore. When I was younger, she sometimes let me know that..."

"It was your nature?"

"Yes."

Morgause took a deep breath and then exhaled. "You understand about your mother." Her eyes shone with tears that remained there like drops of dew upon clover. "She has had the worst of the burdens of this world."

"I know what my father did to her."

She turned away briefly and then said, "I have learned, my dear, not to dwell in the places from which I've come." She set her cup down, brought her knees up under her chin, and wrapped her arms around them, allowing her long garments to spill onto the floor, hiding her bare feet. Morgause reminded me, at times, of a cat with her crouching and her stretching—there was something very free about her in those days. "But your mother lives in the past, still. I do not think she left Tintagel, in her mind, though her body has been here so many years. Your entire life, and yet she does not seem to be here at the Lake at all."

We were quiet for a bit, and I finally said what I had wished to say earlier. "She has turned away from the Lady, away even from Cernunnos and Sulis."

"Ah," Morgause said. "Do not worry about the goddess from whom she seeks blessings, Mordred. All are the masks of the one goddess, though some of the masks are more fearsome than others."

"And this Greek goddess of darkness, called Hecate? Worshipped here only by those Roman poisoners at the ancient well?"

"You say it like a challenge," she said. "These are masks, and beneath them, the true goddess. She wears the masks for us, so that we might understand her better. So that we might go to her with everything we feel and know, for the mask reflects our desires and not her true face."

"The Lady of the Lake wears no mask."

"Even that is its own mask," my aunt said.

4

While the dances and the bonfires went on in the world above, and the season of lambing had begun, and while the Druids began their sacred duties of augury and of tending the grove and its oaks and birches, I remained in the cavernous chambers I shared with my mother and aunt. Morgause, never one to miss the dancing and all-night festival of Beltane, slept for days once the fires were out. I found her abed with a young man of twenty, and when she saw me staring at the two of them—sleeping, for it was nearly noon and she rarely rose before the midday meal—she stuck out her tongue at me. She later told me not to be jealous because she found lovers among the horse herds and the young priests. "I am a foolish woman to sleep with men young enough to be my children," she said.

"He wasn't that young. I know him. He reached his midsummer rites two years ago."

"I might've given birth to him when I was fifteen," she said, laughing. "Some maidens marry at that age."

"But not a daughter of Ygrain," I said.

"True. I waited until I was eighteen, and even that was far too young," she laughed. "But I am foolish, Mordred. I married out of fear and now simply am married *to* fear. Morgan has always been the wiser of the two of us." As she said this, her still-half-asleep eyes lit up wide as she glanced around. "Where *is* your mother?"

"She has taken to sleeping above. Once I found her near the bogs, curled up in ferns."

"Ah. The bogs hold the spirits of past sacrifice. The call of shadows," she said. "It is the way of that dark moon tribe. Or whatever they call themselves."

"Witches," I said.

"Do not say it like a fearful cleric from Ravenna," she said, laughing. "They say it with a bit of spite and bile for good measure. But the Art itself is called witchcraft by those folk of the church and the villas. Your father thought she was a witch. He calls her the Witch-Queen whenever her name is brought up." As soon as she said it, she clapped her hand over her mouth. "By the gods, the white ravens should swoop down and tear out my tongue by its roots lest I tell all the secrets of the grove."

"No, my mother told me. He called her a Witch-Queen once, when he caught her at her scrying bowl. She told me it was an honor to be called it."

"Your father mistook wit—and witch—for wisdom. Arthur could

steal Excalibur from Our Lady, learn the sacred arts that the goddess allows boys to learn, and then turn on all his teachings, suddenly wearing a cross and claiming that Excalibur is not the sword of pagan conquerors, but blessed by the Nazarene, who, as I recall, was not one to suggest taking up swords in the first place."

"He was a good man," I said. "The Nazarene. Merlin has taught me much of his life."

"Yes," she said, "he believed many of the things that our path teaches, though those bishops don't seem to want to acknowledge the Old Ways. We are witches, after all."

"But there is that dark side of witchcraft and the Art itself," I said. "They say that even the Lord of the Dead shuns it."

"Sometimes, Mordred, you sound like your father," she said rather sharply. She pointed her finger at me. "You need to understand your mother. Always seek to understand before passing judgment. She loves you very much and has given you this world that, I will tell you, is better than the court at Camelot."

I loved when she talked of court. "Is it full of handsome knights and beautiful ladies who wear jewels stolen from the Saxon treasuries?"

She gave me a look as if I were the most naive dolt in the world. "Every castle looks the same after a few visits. And Arthur does not welcome me much."

"Does he...does he ask about my mother?"

She bit her lower lip and nodded. "He believes her dead. We have allowed that belief to be known."

"But someone will tell him. Someday," I said.

"No. Who? Who besides me? Will Merlin?"

"My cousins. Gawain hates me. He will tell."

"They are too frightened for their own skins," she said, fanning the air as if to dismiss her sons. "They are greedy little knights, Mordred. If it were known that they had come here. That they knew of this place and how to call to the ravens that the horsemen might come...well, they are afraid they will lose their lives in the bargain. They speak of nothing of their summers here, and Arthur will never ask them of it."

"So we are dead to him. To my father."

"That makes you sad?" She put her finger to my chin and lifted my face up toward hers. "I do not care for your father, Mordred. I have lived to regret—in too many ways to count—the mistakes I made in my young years. I married not for love but for escape and to ensure the position of our bloodline within the kingdoms. I brought children into the world because it was my duty as a wife to a king. I have watched your father create a wonderful court and bring much peace to the southern king-doms, though wars continue in the farthest reaches of the lands. But I would rather be dead to him, to that world, and live here, until my bones are dust in the crevice of rock, than have to return to that life, that bargain I made, in order to survive. You have so much here. And your mother, for all her moods and disturbances, is ten times the person that your father could ever hope to be. She is a Witch-Queen, and I say that as the Iceni once said it of their greatest warriors. She is gifted of the goddess, and whether she brings thunder or gentle showers upon this land, she is one of the finest women I have ever been fortunate enough to know."

5

Morgause had been right; my mother was gifted of the goddess, and it was said by the wise women that the one who is most gifted by the goddess is also thrice cursed by the gods.

So when an entire day and night passed, and my mother had not come back to our home, I went to the paddocks for a horse and told Morgause to send out the message among the people that Morgan le Fay was missing.

6

I rode for one full night, until I had exhausted myself and had to find a warm, soft place for sleeping. I slept but a few hours and had eaten only the sweet bread I'd packed into my cloak.

I raced my horse to the point of his exhaustion as well, traveling along the desolate lands and the heath, hunting the very edges of the forest and out along the cliffs, through the grove itself, among the old stone temples and the earth-hovels and deep into the fern-spattered woods. I called out to my mother and to the goddess for guidance. Nearing twilight, I brought the horse to water not far from that well of poisoners and, with a dollop of fear and a bit of false courage, went to find those three Roman sisters who might have kidnapped my mother into their service.

The well itself was older than even our tribes and had been there since the early times of the land, when the gods walked the Groves and the mistletoe grew as tall trees. The elders said that children had been cast into that well by the Romans and that to drink of it was to become invaded by their spirits. But these Roman sisters have poisoned it so that none would drink without the taste of death upon their lips.

Behind the well, one of the old Roman grottoes could be just barely seen through the overgrowth of twisting vine, rimmed by stone blocks that had been carved up with the symbols of the Latins. The vines here had once been a grape arbor that had gone wild, and the grapes were milky-white and as poisonous as anything that grew in this cursed place. The stories of the elders were that the Romans of centuries previous had made blood sacrifices of the Celtic youth and maidens, spilling their blood into the grotto that they might divine future events. Debaucheries and lascivious orgies had taken place here, usually with the slaves of our tribe being badly abused. They said that for each stone at the edge of the mossy grotto, there had been a child buried beneath it, some of them still breathing when they were placed in the large urns that were sealed as their tombs.

The Druids shunned the place, and I had been told my whole life not to go near it, but I feared for my mother's safety, and I also feared for her mind—that it had taken her to this place of nightmares.

As I stood at the edge of the grotto, I glanced through those snaky vines and branches that overhung the rounded cave entrance where the shiny black water flowed. There, in the water, was a statue to that goddess of the howling night, Hecate. Her three faces were of the bird of prey, and the feral cat, and the jackal. Both female and male was she in this statue, though I had never heard before that this Greek goddess was a hermaphrodite, which was a blessing and a sign of wholeness of self. Her breasts were large, and the chest beneath them was muscular as a warrior. In her left hand, she carried a dagger that was the poisoned blade. In her right hand, she carried a rounded globe that I suppose was meant to be the moon itself.

Through the doorway, I saw the flickering of lights and heard the muffled sound of women's voices.

No man was meant to ever cross this sanctuary, so I waited at the edge of the water and knelt there.

I looked at the statue and closed my eyes and prayed to the goddess who watched all and wore the masks of eternity that she might help me with the Strega.

And then I opened my eyes and called out, "Strega! I have come for Morgan le Fay! Strega! Witches! Poisoners! I call to you! Come out of your pit!"

7

After several minutes of such calls and shouts, I heard a strange howling from within the grotto's mouth. The flickering of lights grew in intensity from that watery doorway; and a woman as naked as the goddess herself but covered in mud—with slender vines wrapped into her long hair, which was the color of sand—came out. She was older than my mother, perhaps as old as Viviane, but her face had been painted with blues and greens such that it gave her a vital appearance, though I suspected she had not slept in days.

"Do you bring an offering?" she asked, still crawling toward the water, her breasts hanging down, her thickly painted lips drawn back over gleaming white teeth, each of which seemed to have been sharpened into points. As she got to the very edge of the water, across from me, she slipped into it, just as a lizard might, and continued to crawl toward me.

Behind her, there was a noise like a scuttling crab along rock, and the first I saw of her were fingers extending at the roof edge of the doorway into the grotto cave. Then, a face appeared, upside down, with long oiled black hair shining. This Strega clung to the ceiling of her lair and crawled out from it onto the ledge that was just above the entryway. She righted herself and crouched there on her haunches, looking down at me. "Do you bring us pain or pleasure?" this one asked.

In the water, the one that now slithered toward me drew herself up to the statue of the goddess and clung to the stone, watching me with eyes that seemed like the dead eyes of the adder, causing one to freeze upon seeing the creature. "You are a pretty youth to come to us," both sisters said in unison, and to their two voices, I heard a third. The Strega upon the ledge sniffed at the air. "You have not yet used the power between your legs," she said and grinned a terrible crescent-moon smile. "Hecate blesses you for this."

"She drinks the blood of youths who have not yet unsheathed their blades," the Strega at the statue said.

Then, an inky shadow moved out from the doorway as the flickering lights brightened, and following this shadow, came the third of the Roman sisters, who was carrying a torch that seemed to burn along its entire length though it did not burn her hand. This woman was of a less horrifying aspect as her sisters, for she was a crone of some beauty, with her hair golden and plaited, though she too was naked and covered in mud. "We have been sleeping," she said, but as she said it, the other three also repeated her words, like an echo. "You have come from the Lady's island." Again, as she spoke, her sisters repeated, watching me with their snakelike eyes.

I was about to say something, but this third Strega smiled and stepped into the water, and set her torch down upon the surface. The fire from her torch burned upon the water, and a ring of flame raced to encircle the grotto.

"No man may enter our sanctuary," the beautiful crone said. "But you may ask of us what you wish. If you bring us meat, we will give you roots and berries which may heal or kill."

"Heal or kill," her sisters echoed.

"Do not be afraid, virgin youth," the crone said. "My sisters' aspect frightens some, but they are blessed with our mother goddess. But you, yourself, have an understanding nature."

Watching her through the fire, I nodded.

"You search for your mother," she said, and the others echoed her. "We know that fair lady, Morgan of the Faerie, who is Queen of Three Realms, which have been stolen from her by men. You are the one who was brought into her by the goddess, to bless her when men had taken too much to bear."

"Too much to bear," the sisters repeated.

"I am Anthea, and my sisters are also myself."

"I hear you share one soul," I said.

"One soul," they said. "Three bodies. We cannot share more with you."

"You are Strega, and of the Roman mysteries."

"Older than Rome are our mysteries. We are Anthea," the three said in a mumbling unison. "We are not Strega, as your tribe has called us, who are of the ancient Etruscan dynasty. Our goddess is not that Greek, Hecate, but her mother, who was blessed among the Canaanites, called Namtareth, who brings light into the deepest well and darkest night."

The one who had curled herself around the statue pointed to the blade in the statue's hand. "She is a surgeon for those who are sick."

Over the ledge, the sister said, "She brings death when misery is too great to bear."

At the statue, the sister reached up to the goddess's right hand and the globe within it. "This is the soul, which she carries over the waters of night to him whom you call Arawn but we know as Plutonis and Hades in his Otherworld kingdom, for the soul is like a ball of light and it seeks light, which Namtareth brings with her presence."

"Her holy presence," said the Anthea who stood in the water, clutching the torch.

"Many die," they said in unison. "And many come to know the light of Namtareth, who lifts them up from the deep and returns them to the clay of the flesh."

"Your mother is not yet dead," she said, "but only sleeping. She lies among the brambles and the sedge."

"Her soul has not yet traveled," said the ledge Anthea.

"Her blood has spoken to the earth, and we hear its call," said the Anthea upon the statue.

"Do not fear us, gentle Mordred, son of Morgan," said the torch-bearing Anthea, "for though men fear the Crone and the women who live in the wilderness and the dark, it is these women who bring peace and safe passage into those other realms. There will come a day, Mordred—"

"I can see it," said the statue-clinging Anthea.

"In the chambers of my soul, I see that day," said the sister who crouched upon the ledge above the entrance.

And then, all three said, "A day when souls shall twin within one body, and you shall grow dark with the maddening fury."

"If your mother should die," said one.

"If she should breathe her last," said another.

And then, a confusion of tongues began, and in many languages, though I could only understand the Roman and my own language. It was as if many small birds flew through the air around me, or a plague of bees buzzed at my ears, their words crisscrossed and came at me so quickly from all three of them.

"Then it shall come to pass, and the world will be unmade."

"Unmade, until that sword."

"That evil sword."

"The sword of tyrants."

"Tyrants who once were great kings."

"That sword called Caliburn."

"Excalibur."

"That sword stolen from the nameless Lady."

"Lady."

"Of the Lake."

"Of the cauldron."

"Of Rebirth."

"Until that sword is returned to her from whom."

"Stolen, it was."

"Stolen and sullied."

"Taken from its rightful owner."

"But meant for kings."

"Meant by its sorcery to bring peace and war in equal measure."

"Meant for none but the Lady herself."

"That sacred Lady."

"Namtareth is blessed by her."

"Namtareth, our mother-father."

"Mother-father."

"Namtareth, whom Hecate serves."

"Namtareth, the Lady of Necramours, who lights the way with the dark lamp of the soul."

"The Lady of Necramours who brings us the tongues of the dead."

"Of those sacrificed in the dark bogs, dwelling with Arawn for hundreds of years, she brings us their eyes and their ears that we might know their secrets."

"The Lady of Necramours, Namtareth the Terrible and the Beautiful, who blesses us with sleep-spirits and the voices of the dead."

"Who teaches us to fly through the dreams of men that we might love them."

"That we might bring forth children of nightmares."

"Blessed art thou Namtareth, who brings terror in the night!"

The echoes of their words seemed endless, and as I stood there in twilight, the gloaming of mist around us and the brightness of the ring of fire along the black water, I felt as if I had entered a place holier than any before and yet it was the most fearsome of places.

When silence returned, I opened my mouth to ask a question, but the three Anthea sisters all opened their mouths and with my voice—my own voice—they asked the question: "If my mother is in danger, where might I find her? I have looked in all places."

They closed their mouths, and the one upon the ledge leapt like a lion, splashing down at the edge of the ring of fire and then leaping again toward me, knocking me down onto my back.

Her weight was heavy as she pressed her slimy hands against my shoulders. Her breasts hung down and nearly touched my throat. She brought her face close to mine and looked me in the eyes. Spittle dripped from her lips onto me, and she whispered, "You must let her die, Mordred. She lies at the bottom of a chasm, offering herself to Arawn's embrace. If she lives, she will never know peace. It is not ours to choose life or death."

"I will not let her die," I spat back.

"Her life will be your unmaking," the one at the statue said.

"I do not care," I said.

"Her death will bring her to you again," said the Anthea pressing down on me.

"I do not believe that. Where is she? There are a thousand chasms and quarries and cliffs in Broceliande. Where is my mother?" I cried out, trying to push her away.

"You may pay us for this."

"If you tell me, I will pay anything," I said.

"The cauldron, then," the one atop me muttered.

"The cauldron," the others repeated.

"The cauldron of Rebirth."

"The sacred grail."

Then, they all three began speaking in echoes and across each other's words until it was like the buzzing of flies over a dead body.

"It is held by the Lady."

"She stole it."

"From Arawn."

"We do not want it for long."

"A short time only," said the one at the statue.

"I won't steal it," I said. "I don't know where it is."

"We can show you."

"Yes, we know."

"We have always known."

"Oh!" they cried out at once, and all three pointed at me as if accusing. "You lie! You bastard prince of many lands! You lie! You have touched it! We see the burns upon your hand!"

More quietly, they whispered, "You have been blessed with your vision of it, Mordred. You could not touch it were it not meant for you to take. The Lady of the Lake adores you, and Arawn thrice blesses you. Our goddess of Necramours blesses you and will bring you the tongues of the dead if you but bring her that cauldron."

"Our goddess Namtareth, the Queen of Necramours, who calls the dead to her service that they might not be reborn."

"Nine times nine she kisses you."

"Your mother lies dying."

"Six times six, she touches your heart."

"Morgan is bleeding into the earth, and her blood sings."

"A beautiful song, like the hymns of the owl."

"Like the sweet chirps of the ruby-throated frog."

"Three times three, she whispers in your dreams."

"It is a crime to steal from the Lady of the Lake," I protested. "And I might never find it again. It was upon the soul-passing of an innocent!"

"Souls always pass," they said. Then, they laughed. "Unless the Lady of Necramours calls them to service as her lamp in darkness."

"She might call your mother to service if she passes now, and she has but hours to live in that place where she lies bleeding."

"It is not stealing but borrowing," the statue clinger said. "The cauldron will not go missing."

"All law is meant to be broken," said the torchbearer.

"And yet the sword was stolen and built a great kingdom," said the one who held me down, low growls coming from her throat like she was a lion.

"She will understand."

"She blesses Mordred, son of Morgan."

"She blesses the Prince of the Wastelands and of North-galis and of Cornwall."

"She thrice blesses Mordred with the love of men that he may see the truth of life buried beneath the lies of the kingdoms."

And then, the Anthea crawled off from me, nearly slithering like a snake back toward the fiery water.

I sat up and looked into the burning flames and saw the cauldron of Rebirth, which was covered with the muck of the Lake, and small fish that flashed silver and gold swam among the eel-grass surrounding it.

"It is at the deepest pit of the Lake of Glass."

"We know you have touched it, Mordred. We are in dreams and see."

"On a ledge, beneath where the healing waters bring rain into Arawn's kingdom."

"We cannot leave our grotto."

"For we will die and never return."

"For we have lived our thousand lives."

"We share but one last soul between us."

"Given to us by Namtareth the Beautiful."

"The Lady of Necramours, the Terrible."

"A soul shared by three, but the last of it is soon gone."

"But the cauldron will bring us the youth and beauty stolen from us."

"Tortured from us by our own countrymen as they denied the old ways."

"Denied and tortured."

"Flayed our skin."

"Buried us alive."

"That we had to crawl up from the earth to breathe again."

"In this, our final life."

"Morgan le Fay lies dying."

"The rightful Queen of Cornwall and North-galis and the Wastelands, the mother of the future King of All, Mordred. The Faerie Queen Morgan, whose death will bless us."

"She must die."

"She must die."

"Unless you pay the price."

"The cauldron."

"It is but a bowl."

"A chalice, nothing more."

"Made of stone."

"We may leave if we bathe in its waters."

"Called 'grail' by Romans and 'cauldron' by your tribes, it cannot bring harm to steal it."

In my mind, I agreed to the bargain, for in those fires of the grotto I saw my mother's face and its pain.

And the sisters heard me.

The fire died down into the water.

"By midsummer's night, our payment is due."

"You must swear to speak to no one of this."

"Swear upon all the gods known and yet to be known."

"Speak of this price you pay us, and you will be cursed above all men."

"But you do not have to pay us, virgin youth."

"No payment is needed if you stay pure."

"Remain chaste and you do not need the cauldron."

"Keep your sword in its sheath."

"Your cod in its piece."

"Your flesh unyielded to another."

"You are a man and have waited so long, surely you can wait longer, for you have outlasted your companions."

"There are those who remain chaste their whole lives."

"Men devoted to the goddess."

"Like Attis, they castrate themselves for purity."

"But you do not need to do this, youth, for you have mastery of the flesh."

"A man among men."

"If you remain so, you need not steal this bowl on our behalf."

"We will forgive this debt as long as you are untouched by man or woman."

"Untouched in that place where men hide their fury and seed."

"Untouched and pure and virgin, then the debt is forgiven and the cauldron forgotten."

"But should you give that virginity."

"In all ways that virginity may be offered, for it is a praise and a blessing to achieve manhood in that way."

"And womanhood."

"If you offer up your sword to another and yield your body."

"Then, payment is due."

"We will keep the cauldron but a single night."

"From sun to moon to sun."

"And then you may take it back to the Lady that will not have noticed that it was taken."

"She will not mind this."

"No, for she is blessed, and blessing."

"Thrice blessed."

"Nine times nine blessed," they said.

"We send you this dream that you might find Queen Morgan," a single voice said, though I did not know which sister had said it.

I saw in my mind where my mother lay as if I were dreaming with my eyes open.

Morgan le Fay lay against rocks and stream, to the western cliffs of the Valley of No Return, near where Viviane had been driven over the edge by the boars of Moccus.

Chapter Ten

1

I did not hesitate, nor thank these daughters of Namtareth, whom they called the Lady of Necramours. I returned to my steed, mounted it swiftly, pressed my heels to its flanks, and whispered to it in the tongue of the Druids to fly as if with raven's wings to the valley.

2

As if guided by those sisters, I found my mother by the time of the first stars in the sky. She lay as if dead, but I felt her breath against my hand, and her heart beat softly. I drew her up and cradled her in front of me, with her head resting upon my chest as if she were my child.

When we returned to our cavern home, the wise women and the Druids gathered around her and began the medicines and healings. Viviane drew me aside to say "She may live, Mordred. You must not fear. But if she does, she may desire the peace of death again. Long has she been troubled, and long has her soul, in its suffering, wished to leave her body. Once a soul has decided to leave this life, it is nearly impossible to stop it."

"I cannot believe that!" I shouted at her as if she were deaf. "She will live. I will bring her back. I will do what is necessary to cure her of this spirit ache. All of us will, Viviane, and you also must."

"I have seen many souls pass to the Otherworld, Mordred," she said.

"You cannot stop a soul's journey, though you may bring an army to try and hold it back."

"Crone, you may believe that, for you have lived long enough to know the breadth of life. But my mother is still young and has not yet given up this fight to live, though she may have had a misguided thought along those cliffs. Or she may have fallen without intention," I said.

"I do not mean to bring you pain," Viviane said and called for an initiate to come carry her to the healing circle. "I only mean to speak to you of the concerns of the soul and the comfort you must find in it."

3

Out on the Lake that night, I saw the entreaties to the Lady, for many boats were on the water, with torchlight upon them to light up the ancient paintings along the cavern roof and to the floor of the Lake, far below. The reds and gold and blues and greens of the Art of our ancestors seemed alive within the luminescence. As was the tradition during a great healing, the boatmen and women wore cloaks and the gold and silver masks of Cernunnos as well as of the Lady, whose face was unknown. The songs of old were sung by little children whose voices had the purity of their passage from the previous life.

I sat upon the mat at the doorway to my home, watching it all from that height, and prayed that my mother would live, though her bones were broken and her spirit seemed to have nearly departed her flesh. The smoke from many fires moved like a storm cloud up through the caverns to the chasmic opening in the earth above, and in it I saw the faces, I thought, of those daughters of Namtareth to whom I had promised to pay a terrible price if my mother lived.

In the night, when others slept and the boats still rocked gently upon the waters off the shore of the isle, Morgause came to me, wrapping her arms around me. "Thank you for finding her," she said, kissing my forehead. "I could not live if she were to die."

"She wanted to kill herself," I said.

"But she did not," Morgause said harshly, as if I had spoken a lie or had somehow wished my mother's death. Then she softened again, and begged my forgiveness for her mood. "I was worried we would lose her, and I could not live without her beside me. It is a miracle that you found her before it was too late."

"More than a miracle," I said.

Morgause raised an eyebrow. "How did you find her, Mordred? Was it merely by chance? Did the goddess show you the way?"

"I am sworn not to tell."

"What secret is this?"

"It is about the Well of Poison."

"Those Romans," she said, her nose wrinkling. "I should have known they'd have a hand in it."

"I promised something terrible."

"Promised?"

"They call themselves as one name, Anthea, and their goddess is called Namtareth."

"Namtareth," Morgause nodded. "An ancient name. She is a stealer of spirits, and it is said she lights her path with their darkening souls." She looked at me, a crease in her brow as she tried to read my face. "Even dark places bring light for those who must live in shadow, Mordred."

"I promised..." I began but then remembered that I must tell no one of this price I had agreed to pay. "Have you ever promised something because you had no choice?"

"There is always a choice."

"If the choice were the life of someone you did not want to lose?"

"Ah. And you cannot tell me of this choice or of the price you must pay, for you are afraid it would hurt this someone?"

I nodded, and she wrapped her arms around me, kissing my forehead and my cheek. She drew her lips near to my ears and whispered, "For my sister, no price is too great. Life demands a great price for every breath we take, so do not fear this. If you or I suffer from this price that is paid, then I for one welcome the suffering."

"As do I," I said, but was still unsure of it.

She drew back again from me, keeping her hands on my shoulders, peering into my face as if able to read my thoughts.

"Those well poisoners are tricksters," she said. "They do not think well of men and will lure youths to destruction if given the chance. Did they hurt you?"

"No."

"Then you're blessed."

"They guided me to my mother in a dream. But they asked something of me that I am not sure I can give."

"Pay whatever it is," she said. "And then be done with them, for it is not good to be in debt to those grotto creatures. Though they serve the goddess, I do not trust them and believe they had a hand in my sister's misery."

4

Although my mother did not speak for many days, she began to heal. The Druids had set her bones so that they might grow together like the oak sprig that is cut in spring and tied to the trunk of another oak so that the two grow into one. I went to her daily and, as I had with Lukat, washed and fed her, and brought her news of the Lake and of the approaching summer.

Morgan was kept within the grove for healing, wrapped in a bed of herbs and asleep upon the willow bark that brought such peace to the sick, and upon her the ancient ram's fleece that had come from distant lands and had old magick still within it. Morgause took a lover from among the charioteers, so I did not see her for many nights. I remained alone in my chambers, and night brought dreams of the Anthea and of that statue of Namtareth with her beast faces and the black water of the grotto afire. They were dream-hags, using the spirits of the dead to invade the dreams of men and women, and so they brought me back to their well and their water and that fearsome strange statue of the Lady of Necramours, Namtareth. I saw their snake eyes and their long hair and the gleam to their sharpened teeth. Several nights I woke crying out, for the dreams seemed real as they chanted to me of the price I must pay for my mother's life.

But as the nights passed, I began to dream of more soothing things and to forget the Anthea. Instead, I dreamed of great seas and distant castles. I dreamed of that man I had watched bathe and swim, and beauty of his body, like a god's. I dreamed of Lukat and of the nights we held each other in warmth and comfort and love. I dreamed of the charioteer Danil, who had been my mother's lover for some years, and his thick-corded neck and the devilish mischief in his eyes as he went to my mother, though in the dream, he came to me. I dreamed of other men too, faceless and beautiful, whose bodies covered mine like a cloak, drawing me to a blistering heat.

From these dreams, I often awoke feeling as if I were on fire and needed to bathe so that I could cool myself from that burning sensation.

I had begun to feel that I wanted to sleep with a man, nearly any man, and hated that feeling because it plagued my mind, for I could not break my word to Merlin nor pay the debt to the Anthea that they required.

And so I burned from these dreams, and I became obsessed with thoughts of the sparkling eyes of men and the want of their touch.

5

Merlin had not returned this year, and the news from the watchers and messengers was that the war battles along the coast had been severe. I worried about Merlin, and Lukat, and my cousins, though Morgause thought poorly of them. I went to Viviane to ask her to scry the fates of those I cared for, but she told me that the scrying bowl was not a game. We shared a pipe together, and she said, "Your soul is darkening, Mordred. Will you bring light into it that I might see your troubles?"

"I cannot," I said. "But it is my mother and her health that concern me."

"As I am concerned for her too," she said, and then, as was her way, she diverted my mind with a tale of old. She recited the tale of the legends of the ravens of Brana and how they had come to lose their beautiful shiny black feathers when they flew too close to the sun on midsummer's night. "They became the sacred white ravens of the goddess and were thrice blessed for disobeying their mistress and flying into the heavens." When I asked her why she told me this tale now, she smiled. "Sometimes these legends of our woods mean more today than they meant in the long ago."

"I am tired of stories," I said. "I want to do things. I want to...I want to leave, sometimes. Go out where other men go."

"How old are you now?" she asked.

It was a strange question, for I had stopped counting the years of my life. The Isle of Glass had taken time away, and I measured life by its seasons and harvests, not by my age.

When I told her my age, I realized I had reached that age of being a man. Youths my age had already begun their lives with their mates, had already apprenticed to the field or the hunt or the herding or the farming and gathering or the priesthood, or had gone off to the border wars. She sensed this as well. "We have kept you a boy too long, Mordred. Out of protection for you. Out of love," she said. "We did this—all of us here—because of what came before your life: the suffering of your mother and those exiled. Sometimes, it is worse to protect the nest than to set the birds free. Sometimes we think the birds will die if they fly to the sun, but we may be wrong. Sometimes, the gods bless them for their freedom and bravery."

"As the ravens were blessed when burned by the sun," I said. "As they became sacred by it."

I realized that I could not wait for Merlin to bring me into the rites of manhood through his Art. I had become a man, and I had to find what manhood was before all of life passed. I felt that urgency of youth that may be looked back upon with gentle humor in later years: that sense that everything was *now* and nothing could wait.

I needed to forge my destiny as all men and women must, and leave behind the childhood that had held me in its thrall for too long. But I was also determined to retain my chastity, now at any cost, though male chastity was not prized and certainly not at my age when many of the youths had already hand-fasted and had their first children.

But if I could avoid the lures of the pleasures of mating and the erotic joy of flesh, I might never have to rob the Lady of the Lake of her cauldron and pass it to those sisters at the well and grotto.

My mother would remain alive and perhaps find the happiness that had eluded her for many years.

6

But the bargain struck with those Roman sisters was not meant to be delayed. I should have understood this, for Merlin had taught me the ways of the trickster-gods who brought men to debts that could not be paid without great tragedy.

But I was not yet a man, though I was by age and development. In many respects I was still too much a youth, and I had underestimated the powers of those three women. I had not understood the true price that would be paid to the daughters of Namtareth.

And yet, my midsummer rites were approaching, as all the youths of the Lake would pass the guardian Maponus and venture into the deep labyrinth where the Druid priests would bring us forth as men at the very doorway to the Otherworld.

Chapter Eleven

1

The Anthea, whose goddess Namtareth granted me vision that I might see where my mother had fallen, had tricked me well with the notion that the debt would be forgiven if I did not lay with man or woman.

For just having planted that seed in my mind, they had ensured that I should think of nothing else but of rutting and flesh and of the over-powering urges of the loins. I tried to stop up the dreams they had sent me by what my friends called "skinning the adder," which involved a warming salve applied beneath the tunic, with the palm, and a stroking motion outward. I became obsessed with this activity for a while and even bored with it. No matter how it seemed to satisfy my midnight lusts, I wanted someone with me, not simply my hand. I did not seek the pleasure of release but of a physical man to be with me, to wrap myself around, to awaken the energies of my body with the ride that only two people could take together.

In the dreams that haunted me, I saw that dark-haired stranger, that hermit whose body had turned my thoughts toward rutting and plea-sure. I began to wander toward that turf house of his, though I never went beyond watching it from a distance—and dreaming. Sometimes I caught a glimpse of him at a distance, having just caught two rabbits for his supper, walking back to his home alone. I tried to throw myself into swimming and into shepherding and horse herding and my studies, but my mind wandered to these daydreams, and I began to think I would go mad if this quickening of the flesh wasn't satisfied.

I may look back on these events and wish I could have forced that youth whom I was to not allow the dreams sent to him to take him over in such a way. Those demon sisters had surely brought me this craving that had only been a mild one previous, and I went to the Lady for her blessing of chastity, but even while I did, I thought of that image of Cernunnos, of his great antlers and large ball sack with its extended prick, and I felt as if I had turned into some kind of soldier's whore, in heat like a wolf-bitch. At the bridge into manhood, I had begun drinking mead and honey ale with the other young men my age after a day of work. They would talk of the maidens they'd coupled with and how it felt to be inside them. The whole time they spoke, I wanted to tear at their shirts and trousers and show them other feelings they hadn't yet had with the maidens. I was disturbed, and the mead never helped this, for it disordered my senses and sometimes I would stay late with the other men, hoping one would take me by the hand and lead me into some fern bed. Sometimes, I fell asleep out in the meadow, having drunk too much and dreamed that I had been taken by two of the more muscular horse herds and laid across a wolf's fur rug while I glanced over and saw the horrible sisters of Namtareth laughing as my men's mouths covered mine, one after another. Waking up, I had the hammering headache of drink and dryness in my mouth, made me run to the stream and dunk my head under the surface just to feel alive.

I may have reached manhood by my age, but I had certainly not yet made it there through balls or bravery.

But Midsummer's Eve would change all that.

2

To try and take my mind off my urges, I spent more time with my mother, who still lay recovering from her fall. She had not been able to speak, and so I tried vesseling into her. Though I told her much in this fashion, I did not hear anything in reply from her. She would look at me, now and then, as if she barely recognized me. All around her, garlands and small carved statues of the goddess had been laid. I sat there with her, holding her hand and trying to speak into her mind, but it was as if I pressed against a wall of darkness.

3

Before the first light of day on Midsummer's Eve, the Druids gathered upon the site of the seven stones that surrounded the gaping mouth of the cavern: there, a sacred thanks was given to the sun and to the coming of the harvest in the months ahead, and such rituals as Druids keep to their orders were performed. I was awakened by a Druid priest in a dark blue robe, which was not the usual garb. He pressed his hand to my mouth to keep me silent and leaned over to whisper in my ear, "I have come to take you to the edge of Annwn so that you will become a man today."

4

I went beneath his robe to leave my home, as did other boys of my age, some slightly younger, some older, for the blue robes the Druids wore were large and meant to hide us like a great tent that we might not yet be seen by the rising sun. On flat boats, perhaps a dozen of us, along with six Druids, went out across the Lake to the ledge where Maponus stood, blade in hand.

When I stepped off the boat, the blind old man held his blade to my throat and muttered, "As you pass here, you shall die to the old ways. All that you see below must remain secret even until you pass into the arms of Arawn."

We were each blindfolded at that place, and as I walked farther along, my head was held down to avoid bumping the low cavern ceiling. Then I felt steps beneath my feet, and I took these rough-hewn stairs slowly. I felt as if we had walked for hours, although I had lost track of time in that darkness of the mind. But my bones ached, and I had grown thirsty.

At the bottom of the stairs, I was led to a place, with my back nearly touching the rock wall behind me. Heat rose from this place, a dry but not uncomfortable heat, and I smelled the herbs and incense of Druid ceremony as the sweat began to pour from my skin. It felt like a cleansing, and we were instructed to remove what clothes we wore. After I did so, I felt the sharp sting of small whips along my back and shoulders, but soon realized that these were the thorny branches of the stag thistle, a poisonous plant if eaten, but if pressed against the skin would draw blood to the surface.

Then, someone came up and slipped a cloak of some kind over my shoulders and whispered in my ear, "You are the son of Arawn, the light of Cernunnos, consort of the great Lady." I heard many whispers of this, so I imagined the other youths each heard this from one of the various priests who had brought us. Then we were told that we each would be taken into individual chambers of the labyrinth that we might experience the great god Arawn for ourselves.

Fingers pried my lips open and that sacred stag thistle berry was squeezed upon my tongue. It tasted bitter but also carried with it a sweet tartness of the wild strawberries often found in the meadow in early spring.

"The stag thistle was brought from Annwn in the paws of the hounds, and its seed fell in our grove, where they chased the stag of life. It may kill a man if too much is given," a Druid told us. "But in these sacred rites, it will bring your spirit forth from your body that you may be instructed in the ways of midsummer, of the men of the tribes, of the old ways of our people. We perform this in secret now, by the sacred doorway, because we are hunted by Romans and Saxons and even Britons who have abandoned the Groves. But in our past lives, we performed this ritual in the full light of day, by the sunlit waters of the goddess. You may never speak of what you do here, for to speak of it will press a thorn deep into your heart and kill you instantly."

As he spoke, the stag thistle had its effect upon me, and judging from the moans I heard from those around me, I knew I was not alone.

My body became soaked in sweat, my lungs filled with that rich perfumed air, and a smoke as of something sweet also rose up, which made me cough. I felt light-headed, and it reminded me too much of the salve that Merlin had once rubbed upon me. I seemed to be floating beyond my body and yet, blindfolded, saw nothing.

"You will see visions here," the Druid said. His voice echoed in this chamber, and the drug that I'd taken had stretched the echo out in such a way that his words seemed to change into other words, and their meanings evaded me. "You will know who you will become by these sights. Fear what you see, embrace what you find, but all is at your peril. Remove the coverings from your eyes."

This last part I understood, and after what seemed a long silence, someone removed my blindfold.

I had been brought down into a deep circular pit. There were many carved arched doorways leading out of this chamber. The cavern ceiling above seemed many leagues upward, and there was a round hole at its very top, barely more than a pinprick at this distance, as if it were the top of a well far above us. From this hole, the light of the sun brought a thin spear of white to the center of the stone chamber.

Only four other youths stood with me, and a Druid whose face was covered with a silver mask conducted us in the first rite of the day.

From the corner of my eye, I saw faint light down the other arched doorways, and from the murmuring sounds and the mist of incense that came up, I gathered that the other youths were in their own rooms with a mentor or Druid who would guide them through this sacred rite.

For some reason, I stood watching one particular young man, who looked as if he were too drugged to see me; his staring eyes seemed to look right through me. He resembled someone I knew—a friend, perhaps—though I could not recall his name. Now, I knew! As I looked at him, he looked like my cousin Gawain, though, no, his face less canine in some way, and in some respects I felt as if I looked at some lost brother of mine, for in feature he resembled me. His hair, though tamped down by sweat, was much like mine, and his nose and lips seemed borrowed from my mother...I felt a terrible chill, the kind that when experienced in intense heat brings with it greater shivers than if surrounded by ice.

I looked at myself, standing there. I had left my body completely. The stag thistle and its incense and the beating of my shoulders with its stinging nettles had disordered my senses more so than even the raveling might have.

I had stepped outside my body and could watch myself, as if asleep yet wide-eyed, with this Druid speaking to that body while I wandered. I glanced at the others, all of whom were similarly glazed in eye and manner. This self-consciousness began to annoy me, for I could not look too much beyond myself, though I could catch glimpses about my body. It was as if my consciousness were locked upon my own figure.

And then, giving me a feeling of absolute terror, I felt something brush against the back of my neck, yet I could not turn around to see who—or what—this might be. But it gave me the dreadful feeling: *I am not alone.* The others here, they too must have felt that thing brush past them.

We were near the doorway to the Otherworld. It was the feeling of the spirits of the dead moving past us. That is what I had felt. I too was spirit as I watched myself.

And then, the Druid stepped through me and went to my body. He drew my cloak apart and, with a small blade, began carving symbols into my skin. First, along my chest, and then downward. As he did, he drew the cloak back over the skin. I did not feel the pain of any of this and watched with a detached interest, as if I did not care what happened to my body but was fascinated by the Art of the sun and moon and of the stag, drawn with a small sharp blade.

When this was done, two of the elders, whom I had not seen on the flat boats coming here, brought a headdress of a young stag and placed it upon my head. They drew my cloak back and dressed me in a leather tunic as our ancestors might have worn. They brought my hands in front of me and, with a thin leather strip, tied them together.

Then they led me off through one of the doorways. My spirit followed, and we went deeper and lower. At one point, we crossed what seemed to be a stone bridge and beneath was not water at all, but what seemed like burning rock that flowed like a slow-moving stream. Yet I did not feel the heat, though I watched the elders and my body, whose skin seemed reddened from fire.

At last we came to another room with great white walls. It did not need torches for lighting, for at its center was a pool of water almost like a grotto within the rock. The water bubbled and churned and steamed from the heat of that place. On the other side of the pool was a low doorway with many carvings in the Druid tongue at its entrance.

This, then, was the door into the Otherworld.

As I stood watching my body before me, with the antlers of the stag upon my head, with the still-healing art of the Druids upon my skin, the room around me began to fade, just as the chanting began, just as a Druid came up to my body and whispered to me, "You will not die to this world to which you were born, and when you return, you will return a man."

As I stood there, my mind and spirit separate from my body, I began to see other spirits—other souls, like impressions I had had in the steamy mist and smoke of the room—move around my body. This was truly the gateway, and Midsummer's Day, with its long hours of sunlight in the world above, was one of the four days when the veil between worlds was thinnest.

I understood the meaning of the ritual, even as it had not completely begun. To become men, we had to mingle with the spirits of the dead. We had to understand life through knowledge of death. And so, the mysteries of this great Midsummer rite began, though I could not tell of it here, in this life or the next.

5

When we emerged it was nearly dawn of the following day—Midsummer's Day itself.

I slept on the shores of the cave with the other young men, exhausted from a night that had left us with body aches and headaches, and secrets of which we could never speak.

When we returned to the Isle of Glass, the other youths and maidens had already begun making the Summer Cakes of grain milled from the first sprouts of the field, and upon these cakes scored marks upon them of their wishes for love. Then, when someone at the festivities took a cake, he or she had to find the maker of it for a dance, be that person youth or maiden; it did not matter. Within two cakes a small ring had been placed, and the couple who chose those cakes would become the Lord and Lady of the Sun, and would be treated during the dancing and revelry as embodiments of the god and goddess. The Lord wore an antler headdress and a snow-white cloak, and the Lady wore a diadem upon her head that was the crescent moon carved from a boar's tusk, and her cloak was a light blue, like a bird's egg. A tree would be cut down earlier in the day—new growth from the forest, and rich dark earth dug from the muddy banks for the Lake itself. These two would be brought to the Lord and Lady, and all would bring offerings to plant in that mud or hang from the tree. It was a beautiful ritual to begin the great festival of the night of the sun.

The artisans and our old poet, a Welsh Druid named Cian who remembered a thousand tales in his head though he was blind and nearly deaf with age, reenacted the discovery of the Lake by the old ones, and of the forest of Broceliande as a sacred sanctuary of our people. The lyre was played as a beautiful maiden sang of old heroes and the queens of the islands; more was sung of Avalon, those isles out to sea that were so hallowed that only those who were pure and brave could find them, and few ever left them once there.

We were a mix of tribes in the Lake, but all of us had these Celtic ancestors, and the gods and goddesses of each tribe were celebrated that night, for the hours of the day had been extended that we might not forget every blessing.

The dancing began late, and we had our reels and our spins and the old dances of summer and planting, and the ritual bath within the Lake itself of everyone under twenty-five years, symbolizing the new energy of summer. Then the drinking and boasting began, the shows of athletic prowess; the elders went off to their clay pipes and their gathering-fires; there was the stink of love to the shadows above the caverns, as the god and goddess mated within the forms of those who so choose to call the divinity into their bodies. I stumbled along the forest path, having watched friends together, and watched a friend named Basquil press himself between the spreading thighs of a maiden whose face was hidden in shadow. His trousers half fell and I saw the thrusting of his buttocks as he entered her, pressed down into the fern bed. I saw the dark forms of others as they laughed and sang running into the woods, and even thought I saw my Aunt Morgause with a youth, sitting out in the sheep's meadow, their mouths locked together.

The burning chariot of the sun was high and cast shadows that were deep among the woods. I could nearly believe in those elfin tribes who lured the unsuspecting into mischief. I had been warned of what Merlin called "those blasted elfin faerie revels of the superstitious mind... They invade the mind through scent and the invisible boundaries that exist in the world, though men do not see them. They are energies of the forest that play with our minds when we come near these areas. Many are weak when near them, but the strong will resist this manipulation, which is but the forces of the rock and water and air and flame."

And so I had one of those senses—that that elemental energy was near, for the light upon a forest path, edged with luxuriant ferns that grew nearly to my knees, seemed to shimmer as if that waving of air caused by fire. And I saw what I thought must be this elemental energy of which my master and teacher had spoken of—what others called faeries and elves and the goblin-kind.

In that late light that would not turn dark for many hours, I saw my friend Lukat at the edge of the forest.

I rubbed my eyes, and looked again.

He was at some distance, but the bright night sun of that sacred day brought his features and aspect perfectly to me. I called out to him, and wandered away from the music and dancing, a wineskin in my hand. "Lukat! Lukat!" I cried, but as I came to the spot, he had vanished—but not in thin air, for I saw him again, among the fern, mounting a white-and-brown mottled steed, very different from our horses in the paddock. He wore a dirty brown cloak, and now I was not sure this man was my friend. Would I even recognize Lukat, since he'd been gone two long years?

And yet, I believed this was my friend, riding off down a slender path, ignoring my shouts.

6

The wine, the ale, the spinning reels and leaps of the midsummer festivities—or perhaps it had been the dreams I'd been having for many nights previous, where I had men of all kinds, every which way, in every formation imaginable.

But whatever delirium was in me, I kept to the path, following the hoofprints in the sandy earth. I passed the grove, and saw those standing stones that had been hunters of the ancient days, and beneath them, the earth-swallowed Roman army that had come to slaughter our Druids and burn out trees. I felt as if these things were alive on this night, and I heard, at a distant, the hymns of the Druids and their attendant in beyond the grove. The forest burned with its life, and I felt touched by all of it.

Midsummer's Night has always been magick, and so it was that night after I had passed into manhood.

I may have walked many leagues, though the midsummer sun had still not set below the trees but rather gave off that white light that seemed of the Otherworld itself.

I tried in my heart to remember Lukat's face, but the wine had blurred all memory, though it seemed as if I could remember the sweet smell of his skin, and the feeling of him near me—but his face had somehow been wiped from me as a damp cloth wipes a bowl clean.

The path that the horse had taken seemed to come to an end in a bright green fern bed. I looked ahead, through the trees, and the forest began to open up again to a clearing. I continued walking, and as I did so, I took a sip from my wineskin, and then spat it out again for I had too much of it.

At the edge of the forest, I saw a stag, larger than any I had ever before seen, sleek and graceful. Upon his head, a crown of antlers that was like a forest itself. For just a moment, I stood in awe of this creature.

And then, it bounded off across the ferns, deeper into the woods.

As I stepped into the clearing, I began to recognize this place, and saw a familiar stream, though I had not been here in weeks. I took my shoes off and waded in the stream, feeling the cool of water as a blessing. I went along the stream as it broadened, and then a sedge came up, and great tall reeds that nearly came to my shoulders.

I turned my face to the sun above, and its warmth caused me to loosen my shirt. And then, take it off. Then, my pouch, and I drew off my trousers as well, for I decided to bathe there in the sunshine and cool off from the fever of the long day. I sat down in a pool that formed around three trees that had fallen into the stream just as it began to widen further and empty into a larger pool of water just beyond the reeds. The water felt wonderful—chilly and clean—and I lay down on my stomach, dipping my head beneath it to feel the sun on my back, and the water all around my face, and that feeling of quiet beneath the surface.

When I came up, I thought I heard someone muttering, or groaning, I could not tell which. I caught my breath, for I thought these might be the sounds of lust. I climbed up to the bank of the stream, and crouched low, moving among the reeds so as not to be seen, quietly as I could, for the mud beneath my bare feet made a sucking sound as I went.

I parted the reeds, and saw the man.

A stranger, yet not strange to me at all.

7

That hermit I had lusted after before—now spread out here as if waiting for me alone.

His horse was tied to a willow that leaned over the embankment of the widening stream.

He lay across a flat rock, naked also, for I seemed to catch him most at his bath.

His arms were tucked behind his head as a cushion. I had not ever before stared so much at a man's naked form. But his organ was not the only thing that caught my eye, for his feet, which were long and tapered, had a singular beauty, and his calves too, and thighs; and even that way his ears did not seem to have lobes as mine did, but instead curved to his scalp like perfect half shells. He had become brown with the sun, and I felt that familiar arousal that only dreams had brought to me, or those furtive moments upon crawling into my bed to pleasure myself in lieu of losing that virginity, which allowed Merlin to teach me the Arts of the goddess, and more recently kept me from paying a terrible debt to the daughters of Namtareth.

Without meaning to, I had licked my lips, and my arousal had taken a physical form. He seemed to be dreaming, for he groaned and moaned and muttered, but his eyes did not open.

This is a place of that elemental spirit, I thought. The rock and the water had brought up some gas to give me this vision. *That's all it must be*, I thought. It is just what Merlin described when he warned me from the elementals that the priests of stars had described as "magnes"—*the phantom of a man, of an elf prince of great height and thick muscle with that fatal beauty given to just such a vision.*

And yet, I could not resist the pull of the elemental force.

Feeling the shivery fear of the bold and foolish, I found myself moving forward, across the mud, from the reeds. Every few steps I stopped, crouching, hoping he would not open his eyes.

It was as if I were in a trance, but his beauty drew me to him, and soon I stood over him, unaware that I blocked that late sunlight from him.

I looked down at him, longing to touch his skin, just to feel the excitement, and even danger, of the encounter.

When I detected a fluttering of his eyelids, I quickly scurried back into the reeds. I felt ashamed for having intruded upon his private place, this long-limbed stranger with the body of a god. He looked upward toward the sun, shielding his eyes from it. Had he sensed my presence?

Again, he closed his eyes.

I glanced around the woods but saw no one else there with him. I blushed as I watched him, ashamed of my interest yet intensely curious. My mind played tricks on me, for I began wild imaginings of making love with him: rutting against the stone, in the water, even on horseback. He clearly was older, my senior by ten years, perhaps more, and this thought brought more heat to my flesh, for I began to imagine this man my teacher in the sexual arts.

In my heart, even then, I promised that I would find a way to take this man as my own. I did not understand the machinery of love in my youth, but I knew of desire and longing.

The longer I watched him, the more my eyes seemed to leave my skull and travel to his flesh, the more I began to lose any self-consciousness about my own nakedness and about the obvious arousal that I would not be able to hide should I stand upright and step out from the muddy reeds.

He opened his eyes again and sat up, looking about as if he sensed me. Then he lay back and said aloud, "As you have watched me, so I have watched you."

He closed his eyes, and I felt my heart pounding. This was the first any man had invited me to come to him, and in such a way that I knew that there was only one outcome.

It terrified me. It excited me as nothing else might have. I wasn't even sure if I could breathe.

Slowly, I parted the reeds and took a step out in the mud and then another. I stood there, full naked, fully aroused, and terrified of every-thing.

He opened his eyes and gazed up into mine.

He did not seem frightened of seeing me there. It was nearly as if he expected to find me. As if I had moved through the water of the Lady's kingdom into a mirror world, he reached up and took my hand and brought it to his lips, kissing it.

His lips were warm on my hand, and his blue eyes seemed to shine with distant stars. I could not look away from him, and all my skin tingled with a feeling of ice and fire, burning and freezing. I tried to tug my hand away from his, but he drew me down to him while raising up to meet me, to meet my face, my lips, and I felt that burning wetness of our lips, his over mine like a glove over the hand, mingling their waters, our tongues sparring like small blades with small, delicious, thick skin. Moist and sweet was his breath; I felt as if my mouth were engulfed in this man's passion.

I drew back from him, gasping. "I can't do this. I can't."

But he kissed me again and whispered to me of things that I longed to hear: of his loneliness in the forest, of watching me this past spring as I rode the horses or as I swam along the rivers, and how he had wanted me though he did not dare come to me. Of how he had brought messages to the Druids, on behalf of the kingdoms who still honored those priests, and how he had seen me sometimes working shirtless in the field, planting the new crop, or when I brought the geese up from the ponds with my trousers rolled up, my tunic half-torn, my hair in my eyes, and mud all over my arms and legs. He told me of dreaming of me, and I whispered of the dreams I too had of him. He whispered, "There is a god who brings men together, and he has brought us here, like this, for one reason."

"The hunter," I whispered.

"The stag," he murmured.

"You are my stag," I said, our breath mingling, our lips so close.

"You are my hunter," he whispered.

His mouth again covered mine, like a glove slipped too easily on the hand. I was swept into that kiss. I melted against him and felt the rightness of it as his sun-heated body, slick with sweat, pressed to mine. Our chests against each other, his strong arms bringing me closer to his body that I might not know where our flesh had ever been separate. Instinctively, I wrapped my legs across his thighs, and the long-pent-up nature of the gods let loose within me, though we did not enter each other then. It was without thought, without mind, without even my heart, for I felt animal, all animal, all creature of the woods, and I also felt the god within me rising up.

I felt the madness I had seen in the horses as they mounted, in the rabbits, in the sheep in the meadow—I felt that call to the Lord of the Forest of mating and rutting and letting the lower regions of body perform their fire dance while the heart and the mind raced from one paradise to another of memory and dream and vision.

It was madness what I did with this stranger, what I wanted to do with him, what I needed to do.

I felt that rush of blood and of fire within me, in his arms, letting my body move as it would against his. He lifted me into his arms and held me.

We went within each other, sharing our flesh and, I felt, more than that. He lifted me up, laughing, upon his horse, and he leapt on, cradling me in his arms, as we rode across an open meadow. The late sunlight grew dolorous in some way I could not understand, and this melancholy that occurs after the act of love took me over, as we held each other on horseback, naked still, and it was as if I were in the arms of a centaur of those ancient legends, half man, half horse. I turned to face him, and our passions rose again as we went into that fiery place where lovers go when first discovering each other.

Then we returned to that rock where we'd met, and I dismounted from his horse. He followed after, not wanting to let go of me, nor me of him. I had not even asked his name or why he lived in such a humble state, for it was to me as if the god of the sun kept to the shadows of trees and streams his whole life. We lay again, together, the discovery not yet done, the fire on my skin not yet burnt to ash.

The midsummer sun was gone when I next looked up at the sky. Instead, the night was dark with stars and without moon, and we lay on that rock, his hands combimg my hair as he spoke softly to me.

I remembered a dream I had, just as I had this one, and in the dream, there was the rock and the man and the horse and the water and the reeds.

"I dreamed of this," he said, as if reading my thoughts. "Of this beautiful stranger, come to me as a warrior of the old days, when no tunic covered us, when no barrier came between two lovers, whether of cloth or of stone. This young man I had seen before, in dreams and in the forest. I have broken a vow. I promised myself—and the goddess—that I would not ever be with man or woman again."

At his words, my throat grew dry, and the thudding ache of my head returned. I knew.

The Anthea, those daughters of Namtareth. It was the dark of the moon that night.

Midsummer's Night. A night of sacred enchantment, a night of ritual and celebration.

A night when that hammer god of the flesh, Sucellus, the great striker of the earth, might move strangers into each other's arms, into each other's bodies.

I had broken my vow to Merlin, for my studies in the Art of the goddess were not yet complete.

This stranger and I had been loving each other, savoring the flesh and taste of each other, for hours, though it had gone too fast. When I looked at him, he looked well loved, as the men of the caverns would say. He wore a smile of that unearthly sadness of him who has enjoyed and now sorrows for lack of it again.

I wanted to remain with him forever, in that moment, to never let dawn come, never let the world's obligations and duties return. To freeze, as if in winter's ice, that perfect place within the realm of time, where his smile and his eyes were for me, his arms and breath, his every inch, as if this were love itself, love in flesh personified, the stag and hunter together.

But in becoming a man that night—a man not in age (for I had already passed that pathstone) but in that erotic understanding that only arrives with the breaking from the bonds of innocence—new understandings enfolded me. I saw what I had lost, and I saw what I might lose.

The debts of life had just begun, as they always do when innocence itself has passed into experience. I could not now forget that one debt of the Anthea and their goddess, Namtareth, whose predatory faces seemed to be in the night sky above me.

I knew that terrible payment that had to be fulfilled. Or my mother would die.

Part Three

The Twin Souls

Chapter Twelve

1

I tore myself from his arms as if pulling myself out of brambles and ran quickly to grab my clothes.

"No!" he shouted, rising up, still half asleep himself. "Wait! Come back!"

I glanced back at him once, feeling that the greatest distance between us was that short space from where I stood among the reeds, a tincture of a moment as I looked at him and felt that elemental force drawing me back, for I could imagine no home but his arms, no bower but his body curled around me. I had broken from him, and whatever mystery we experienced together, whatever crude animal mating—the rutting that all the other youths boasted of and many maidens whispered about—was finished and could not be brought again.

Although the stranger called to me, I did not heed him and instead felt the terror clutch at my throat. I drew up my trousers, tying them up, and then carried my shirt and shoes and went running back into the dark woods, losing my way, trying to see, but without seeing. I ran through brambles, was swatted at the low-hanging branches of trees, tripping across the slick stones of streams, stepping into a deep pool one minute and nearly tripping over a fallen log in another.

Eventually, the effects of the wine and spent lust took their tolls, and I fell to the earth, my mind turning to darkness.

I dreamed of the statue of Namtareth, with its three heads, of the jackal, of the vulture, and of the cat. Blood had been spattered on these faces and poured down across the white breasts of the goddess. A ring of fire grew around it, and I heard the voices of those three sisters whisper and echo that the great Morgan le Fay, Queen of Many Lands, Faerie-Queen of Broceliande, would die before the sun would set if my promise were broken to Namtareth, on whom I swore a most sacred oath.

And then, worst of all, I dreamed of Arawn, King of the Otherworld, in his most terrible aspect. His cape was long and made of a dark gold and yet seemed more like the wings of a swan than a cape as it trailed behind him. His face was darkened, but the obscene circle of his mouth yawned like a chasm, with the many ridges of small, sharp teeth protruding from the white of his lipless gums. His eyes shone like the last of twilight upon brackish water: red and black with the distant glow of the rising moon. What could be seen of his face was as a mask of ice upon smooth bone. Upon his head, the five-pointed crown of gold, encrusted with the emerald and blue-and-white stones of the deepest caverns of the world, and from this crown, twin ram's horns curled, coming from his scalp just as the antlers rose up from the head of Cernunnos. I had heard from the Crones that Arawn visited those who would die soon, in their dreams, and one could tell if death would be peaceful or terrible by the god's appearance. I grew afraid, looking upon this horrible being. In his right hand was the loin spike, the small, rounded ball of iron with a spike of blade used to cut into a man's lower body to extract the soul. In his right hand, he clutched the thick sword of Death, broken just beyond its hilt, for it came into being, fully, only when thrust into those who died upon the battlefield. Then, when thrust into the body, the sword takes shape as a blade of ice-blue flame, it is said.

Surrounding this King of Annwn were the red-eared, white-skinned hounds that retrieved the souls of the dead as Arawn hunted them down. Their howls filled the air while I watched Arawn's face as the ice began to melt across the bone. When his face finally was revealed, I could not see its features for it was as if I saw this god's face beneath rushing waters. Instead, I looked down as he pointed that loin spike toward his feet, where my mother's body lay, her sweet face turned up toward him as the Lord of the Dead pressed his left foot upon her breast as he bent down, bringing his spike to her flesh.

2

I awoke close to midday, my head pounding, my limbs sore, with the general feeling that I had somehow been beaten and whipped. My face was covered with the pollen of the white thorn flower that had made my bed and scratched me all over my body as I had tossed and turned in the night. I went to the nearby trickle of stream and, leaning over into it, saw my face. I looked as if I had traded my one nineteen-year-old face for one of fifty. My eyes held great sacks beneath them, darkened as if smudged with char-paste. My eyes had grown small and squinty, and my lips, rather than the fullness I had known seemed to be bitten at and parched. My hair was a rat's-nest tangle as well, and I looked at myself a moment only and thought, "Why would a beautiful man—the most handsome I had ever seen—want to have at this bat-faced elf-troll?" And then, I wondered, Was he even handsome? What if it had been the wine? What if my inability to know what to drink had caused me to believe he was beautiful? What if I had...

Mordred, you are a foolish man. Do not blame the wine for your want of him. You watched him before, and he said he watched you as well. This is what you have wanted all these years, what you have dreamed of. He is not Lukat, for Lukat cannot give his love to you the way you wish. He is a gift from the Lord of the Forest, as you are his gift. Do not speak lightly of the mysteries of flesh and the heart, and do not curse them when you have invited them to your arms.

Truthfully, the voice in my head seemed so wise and deep and grave—and angry—that I wondered if Merlin himself weren't vesseling me from some rocky promontory at Lyonesse or in Rome, where he might go to smuggle out more scrolls.

I quickly splashed water upon my face, hoping that all the ugliness upon me would go away, but it did not. And worse, no matter how much water I lapped up from that stream, I spat it out as soon as it was in my mouth for it tasted most foul.

Is this the youth to whom Merlin taught Art and Science? Is this the bastard son of the great King of the Britons? Is this the son of that Witch-Queen Morgan le Fay, nephew of Queen Morgause of the Orkneys? Is this the one who thought that many men would want him in their arms?

Was it a dream? Had last night been a phantasm? For Midsummer's Night was a night of faerie revels as well as those of humans, and though I had still seen no faerie, nor elf, nor actual troll beyond the troll face I wore that day, I could certainly believe that I had merely gotten drunk and wandered into the deep woods, drawn by a phantom of a man I had long dreamed of; and then, under the spell of the magickal night and of lust and of dreams sent by those Roman wolf-bitches and more of wine and honey ale and other concoctions and brews, after a sun-stroked twilight of dancing and singing, that I might have simply fallen asleep among those tiny white thorn flowers and their tiny needles.

My heart gladdened at the thought that I might not have done what I was fairly sure I had. Find a naked beautiful man? In these woods? Lying on a flat rock? His mouth over mine, whispering of secret dreams of Eros that had captured us both?

I had seen magick performed in ritual but none quite so self-serving as this. How could I have gone to him like that? For I had a vow and a bargain that I did not wish to keep. I would surely have avoided a night of passion to keep those hounds of Namtareth at bay!

But as I washed my face again, drawing off dirt and the small thorns that had embedded into my cheek during sleep, I felt that sinking emptiness of the truth that could be called nothing other than truth.

I had been warned all my life of such enchantments. I had been warned that during the great nights—of which Midsummer's Night was one—to stay within the tribal circle, within the hearth-fire's flickering shadow, lest those spirits of unrest and ill will might divert me with their wicked pleasures. I could no longer lay the blame of this on a boy, for a boy might be forgiven. I was too old for those excuses, and I knew it.

I had the ache of body and the sweetness within my flesh that told me that I had made passionate and perhaps violent rut-pleasure with a stranger of whom I knew nothing and had done it despite the wine in me, because I wanted to do it more than I had wanted to do anything in my entire life.

I rose up from that water in a panic. And a hunger.

I wanted fried goose eggs and thick cream across a great dark hunk of bread.

In this hungry state, I rose and wandered back home eventually, far too late in the day for anything but rabbit and barley stew that had been left simmering on the communal hearth.

I fell asleep again, barely making it to the blankets across my bed, so tired from the night and the way it had brought me joy and doubt and terrible confusion.

3

I awoke from a nightmare, though I could not remember a moment later what had so threatened me that I had sat up in bed, my mouth open wide as if to cry out. And then I rose swiftly from my bed, remembering too much, a head full of clattering rocks.

I attended to my mother, but she had left the caverns.

4

I searched about, and when I found Morgause, she told me that my mother had risen of her own strength and had spoken a few words: that she wished to go to the well and the grotto to see those Roman sisters that they might help her regain her strength.

"And you let her go?"

"Mordred?" Morgause asked. "She had health in her. Her face possessed the glow of the goddess. She would not do otherwise. Do you think I *wanted* her to return to them? She could not be stopped." Her eyes seemed cold and harsh. "What do you know of this?"

But remembering my vow to remain silent about my promise and debt to the Anthea, I could tell her nearly nothing of this new sorrow and fear. Instead, I drank great bowls of water to alleviate my intense thirst, and dipped bread in honey that I might satisfy what emptiness I felt in my gut.

Then, I went to the paddock above and asked the herdsman there for the fastest horse he had. As I mounted this steed, I noticed the darkening of the sky—I had slept half the day, and the night was coming too soon.

I rode out to the Well of Poison and prayed that Namtareth herself would allow me time.

5

I arrived at the grotto in the cool of the early evening. The flowering vines that hung down from the ledge above the grotto's doorway had blossomed with magnificent red-orange petals and a yellow-black center. The statue had a sheen to it, as if it had been washed and polished, and the water itself was clear, teeming with eels and small yellow fish.

"Anthea!" I called. "Daughters of Namtareth! Come out and hear me!"

My voice echoed in that place, but I did not hear a sound from within, nor did I see evidence of flickering light.

"Mother!" I shouted. "Mother! Are you here?"

Again, I heard nothing.

I waited for an hour or more and called many times, but the Anthea did not show themselves, nor did I see evidence that my mother had been there that evening.

As the darkness came, I mounted the horse and turned it to go, when I heard a terrible scream from within the grotto entrance. I leapt down and splashed into the pool of water, going up to my knees. The eels swam away, and I waded past them to the doorway of the grotto. Though no man was meant to enter this place, I stepped in through the doorway, and up to the muddy floor. Stones had been piled on either side, and water ran between them. I walked along the stones, crouching down as I moved in through the long tunnel, and as I went I did see a light come up at some distance.

Down that dark tunnel I followed the light, and when I got closer to it, I saw that it flickered like torchlight. I went into a chamber filled with candles, the smoke of which was like bitter incense.

On the floor of the chamber, which was dry and strewn with rushes, my mother's body. Her hands were about a twin-bladed sword that was of the ritual kind of the bloodier religions that still practiced murder, though they might call it sacrifice.

Crouched in a corner, those three harpy women, each snarling at me as I entered their lair. Their confusion of voices was like a plague of locusts flying about my ears.

"You did not pay the price."

"Though you yielded your flesh."

"To a man."

"A beautiful man."

"We know him well, for he came to us for visions once."

"Visions and poison."

"Though he too failed in that quest."

"But for his purity and beauty, we could not harm him."

"But we bring him dreams."

"Dreams of you."

"Your mother has taken her own life."

"She had tried once before, but you saved her."

"Can you save her now?"

"She has taken Arawn for her lover."

"Namtareth blesses her."

"Namtareth curses the name Mordred."

"Thrice cursed is Mordred."

"Nine times nine cursed is Mordred."

"Where is our payment? The sun has gone down."

"You made the bargain."

"You gave us your word."

"Your sacred word."

"Upon your mother's life," they snarled.

"But if you bring us the cauldron, you may yet see your mother."

"For it is the grail of healing."

"Of rebirth."

"It will call your mother back to life."

"From the arms of Arawn."

And then, their echoing snarls and growls silenced for a moment.

I looked down at my mother, the pallor of death on her skin, and could not believe she had taken her own life here. And yet Viviane had been right when she told me *"Once a soul has decided to leave this life, it is nearly impossible to stop it."*

"And if I bring it?" I asked, fury rising up in me. "If I get you your payment?"

The sisters looked at me, their snake eyes narrowing. "If you bring it tonight, there is time, for see? She has a little breath still, and the poison in her is slow as the bite of the river adder."

6

The horse flew like the wind itself, and I came to the cavern by way of its narrow entrance, between the brambles, for I did not wish to call attention to myself to those watchers in the forest that might see my agitation and wonder about my intent. Nor did I wish to see Viviane or Morgause, or any friend or foe who might delay my getting that sacred object from the water.

I had no thought to the Lady of the Lake, for I did not believe she had enough power if she could not stop the evil of Namtareth or stay my mother's hand from desiring death.

I

I swam out to that middling point of the Lake and looked for the markers above as to the center. I took a deep breath and dove down, pushing and kicking and drawing myself as far toward the heat below as I could. And yet I could not find the cauldron, nor did I find that strange green light near it where the burning water came through from far below the earth.

Three times did I rise and dive again and then six and then nine, and yet I could not find it. I had grown exhausted, but my heart beat fast, for I did not want to waste a moment while my mother lay in death's arms.

I dove down again, deciding that if I did not find it on this attempt, I would drown myself trying and perhaps meet my mother at the entry to Arawn's kingdom. Instead, I saw that glimmer of light, and I moved toward it. My hand again blistered with the burning water, but I held to the lip of the bowl and brought my other hand to it as well. I felt as if my wrists and forearms were afire, and then it spread farther as I tugged at the cauldron.

It gave itself up more easily than I had expected, and I wondered if my father, in stealing the sword from its stone-buried place in these caverns, had already drawn it with the ease with which I drew up this object.

The cauldron did not feel heavy until I brought it to the surface, but with some effort, I dragged it along with me to the shore and soon had taken it up with me onto my horse. The cauldron was the size of a large cooking bowl, the kind that we might make stews in for several guests at the table. Yet it was not beautiful, nor did it have jewels around its silver rim. The mask of the goddess called Coventina was within the bowl, that goddess of the underworld whom the Romans called Proserpine; and on the outer edge of the bowl were images of the Lord of the Dead, Arawn, his sacred boars and adders entwined about it. On its underside was the great Dragon of Life, which slept beneath the cauldron of Rebirth.

I rode again through the black night as if knowing the way to the grotto of Namtareth by heart.

8

The least hideous of the three sisters met me at the grotto and gasped when she saw the bowl. Her mouth moved as if speaking, but no words came from her, such was her delight at seeing the gift I'd stolen for them. I would only learn later that these sisters had been on the verge of death themselves, and the last of their shared soul had been used to its last moments before I brought the sacred cauldron to them.

Her other sisters crawled to the lip of the doorway, and when they finally spoke, it was with one small raspy voice, as of one who has need of drink. "Leave the cauldron," she said.

"Take your mother."

"Morgan le Fay lives again."

"She breathes."

"She lays now beside the Poisoned Well."

"Arawn be praised, he has brought her back."

"From the brink of death, which is a blessing though folk do not believe it."

"Though her blade was poison-tipped, still she lives," they said.

"Take her that she may live again."

"Long life to Queen Morgana," they said.

"Queen of the Faerie, she is."

"And of the Wastelands."

"And North-galis as well, and Cornwall."

"Lover of Arthur."

"Mother of Mordred."

"Sister of Queen Morgause of the Orkneys."

"Daughter of Ygraine."

And still these women did not stop their whispering and echoes of each other's phrases.

I went over to the well, and there beside it, upon a cloak of dried flowers, Morgan le Fay lay, the twin blades removed from her breast but a thick dark stain there. I knelt down beside my mother, slipping my arms beneath her shoulders, keeping a hand at her scalp to support her head. She shuddered slightly, and her breath quickened. I lifted her up, and took her out of that dreadful place.

9

When I reached the caverns with her, I took her immediately to Morgause, awakening her. "I have done something terrible," I said.

Morgause glanced at my face and then at my mother's body.

"She's alive," I said. "But barely. The witches of the well brought her to this."

"She breathes?" Morgause asked, looking at her sister's face and then back to mine.

"She needs a great healing," I said. "Everything that can be done."

"You must go call Viviane," Morgause said. "Go now. Call the wise women and the priests. We will do everything we can, but time cannot be wasted, Mordred. Go!"

10

In life, there are moments of great crisis, and when we are faced with them, we often act better than we might at any other time. Or we act like the worst of criminals and double-dealers, for fear that we might be sucked into the maw of that horrible circumstance and never escape.

What I had done that night would ring forever after in my ears, for I had fulfilled one vow and promise and paid one price but had not ever asked of the price others would pay because of this.

But I would soon find out: For when the goddess is angered, she does not wait years for her retribution.

She does not wait hours.

I had stolen one of the hallowed treasures of our people, for a selfish act that had seemed selfless to me when I performed it. I could mull over all the had-I-nots, but I could take no comfort in that game.

For when the healing circle had begun around my mother, who began to die a slow death, surrounded by all who had ever loved her, Morgause came to me, for she knew what must be done, absolutely, to save the life of Morgan le Fay.

"Mordred," she said. "You must fetch the cauldron of Rebirth from the waters."

I gave her a look that felt within me like a lie.

When I said nothing, she said, "Hurry. Go. It may be used once or twice in a generation, and has not been used for many. But we may speak with Arawn through it and bathe your mother in its healing. You must fetch it now, for each second is precious for my sister's life, and I will not have her die like this."

I began to turn away from her, as if to go, but could not. I faced her again.

"You know where it lies. You touched it once," she said. "Your fingers had burned from it, when the funerary games had begun, and…"

She watched my face, confusion spreading upon her own, mixed with the panic she must have felt. And then she looked at my arms and grabbed them, lifting them up so as to see them better in the firelight.

They were blistered and red, and she did not say a word at first but only let go of my arms and then slapped me as hard as I'd ever been hit on the face, so much so that I nearly fell backward.

"*Whatever you have done,*" Morgause said, snarling nearly like the Anthea, "undo it. *Unmake this wickedness.* Your mother's life hangs in the balance, and her soul has been eaten at by this poison as her flesh was pierced by the blades. Do not let the Queen of Cornwall die because of your evil."

11

This was the night that became known as the Lamentation of Glamour, for those who were there and sat among the forest saw the green phantom lights of the marshes at a great distance and knew that the soul of one of the royal queens of the people of the sea, the Mor or Mir as we were called, that was passing, though had not yet entered the realm of Arawn. A glistening mist came up from those lower regions of the Lake, and many would later say they saw spirits of the dead rise in that mist to come pay respect to the dying queen. The Druids had gone to the grove, and among the thick oaks, they went to the foot of the oldest, called the Ram Oak for the fleece that was laid upon its branches in remembrance of ancestors of healing and wisdom. Here they sang the great song of life and creation in the hidden language that sounded like the call of beautiful birds blended with the hymns of the Romans. The sound was sad and mysterious, and when I heard it, many wept and were inconsolable, for that was the effect of those Druid voices in their song. The herding people went to their fields and paddocks to pray with the animals who spoke directly to the souls of the dead that Queen Morgan might be returned to the Lake, whether this night or in her new incarnation. The warriors took up their bows and aimed arrows for the deepest of pits that they might awaken Arawn to this trouble; the messengers called out from their hills and trees, like a hundred owls in the hunt; the artisans painted, upon the outside walls of the cliff dwellings, the tale of the Lady of the Lake and Arawn, of the sword called Excalibur, and of the cauldron of Rebirth; and Nimue, that wind-on-water spirit, was invoked through much sorcery, though she did not respond. The call also went to Merlin, and even I called to him through vesseling, though I heard nothing when I first sent out my thoughts upon the air. And though many searched the night sky for the white ravens of the Lady, none were seen, nor the gray doves of the rock, nor the stag of Cernunnos among the emerald depths of the forest.

The wise women would not let me in the healing circle, and Morgause told me that I must not pollute my mother further with "those crimes your father brought to us."

I felt alone and empty, and thought of killing myself that I might go beg Arawn to take my soul in exchange for my mother's.

And as I crouched above the caverns, watching the fires that had been lit and the lamps of the forest with their blue-yellow light, someone with a torch in his hand approached me. I glanced up at him, but the shadows cast by his torch hid his face from me.

He crouched down beside me, and I finally recognized him: the hermit from the woods. He drew his cap down and undid his cloak. He wrapped me into it and put his arms around my shoulder, whispering to me, "All the grove is in sorrow. What great queen dies?"

I could not even answer him, but began sobbing against his shoulder, wishing I would not, wishing I could wash the cup of time until there was no memory of the past two days. When I told him what I had done, he said, "Dry your tears. We will get this grail back from these Anthea. I know them too well and their tricks. They have hunted me many years and haunted my dreams, but they have their own fears."

12

Still, he was then a stranger to me, for he offered no name, nor did I offer mine. I rode on the back of his mottled horse, and we passed the cloaked guardians of the Groves, who seemed as if they had become trees themselves, their arms raised up like branches, and yet they were still, as if turned to stone, so fast did we pass them by.

At last, we came to that grotto, but its waters were dry, and the eels and its fish dead at the silt bottom. He went ahead of me, brandishing a sword and his torch as well, as if expecting these sisters to leap out at us from the dark.

There, in the empty chamber with its rushes laid out upon the floor where my mother had recently fallen, was that cauldron that this hermit called "Grail," but it was broken, as if hewn down its center by the great force of a sword. Blood had also been spattered around it, with strange markings etched upon it.

The Anthea were gone, and the only trace of them were the bones of animals that they'd eaten piled in corners, and dried berries and flowers, which the hermit told me "are some for healing, some for death," and he took many of them, and brought them into his carrying pouch. "These jackal-women only hide tonight. They know that I would take their last soul if I should find them."

13

When we arrived, I ran with the two halves of the cauldron to the wise women and passed them to Viviane. When Morgause saw the hermit with me, she glared at him, and then her venom aimed for me, as she drew me aside and said, "Why do you bring him here? He does not belong."

"He helped me get the cauldron back," I said.

"You have done too much damage, Mordred," she said. "Get him out of our sanctuary. He does not belong with us. Tell him to go back to his kingdoms and his swords. He curses us. He curses your mother with his presence here." Morgause's voice was more horrible than I'd ever heard it, as if she'd hidden a creature of cruelty within her soul and only now let it out. "Did he tell you who he is? What he has done? Did *he* bring you to *this*? Tell him that I curse him. I curse you both, whether it damns my soul or not."

It was again as if she had beat me, and I felt battered more on the inside than the out. I caught a glimpse of my mother laying there and of Viviane cutting her own flesh to spill blood onto my mother's wound; and the smell of thick swamp was in the air; and charred incense that smelled too much like bladderwort and myrrh; my mother's face; her eyes closed, lips slightly parted; and her skin more pale than I had ever seen it.

When I went to that strange hermit who had swiftly become my only rock in this sea-swept night, I asked him, "Who are you that Morgause hates you?"

"I am your stag. You are my hunter. Can we not remain so?"

"But she knows you. And you, her."

He looked at me with that intensity that I had seen in his face when he first held me in his arms. He put his hands on my shoulders as if he were afraid that I would run from him. "I am a fallen man, accursed of the goddess. Morgause has hated me many years, and had your mother seen me, she too might have wished to poison my cups, for once, many years ago when all of us were younger than you are now, we shared dark days. I should leave you and never look back here. I hope that Morgan, your mother, recovers, for even broken, the bowl has much power in it."

"They will not let me near her," I said. "Stay with me. Tonight. Here."

"You do not understand," he whispered. "My lovely hunter, you do not know what brambles grow between Morgause and I. Even if you did—"

"Then take me with you."

"With me?"

"Where you sleep. Take me there. For I will not find rest here, and I cannot face the dawn thinking of my mother's life, that I failed to save."

"Do not bury her before her time," he said. "The cauldron has brought the dead to live before, and though it is now cracked by the servants of Namtareth, it may yet hold its water-magick."

"Do not leave me alone tonight," I said, "for I fear what I will do to myself."

14

And so I rode with the hermit, the man I had called Stag when I had brought myself into him as the Hunter, the man of whom all I then knew was that Morgause despised him, as she now hated me on sight for what I caused. But I would discover more of him before I returned homeward again. I would learn that he had once born a foundling of the goddess, at the edge of our lake, said to be the son of the Lady herself, as are all abandoned babies at the Lake's far shore. He was mystery in flesh, and I had only begun to delve into his secrets as we rode together.

Yet that night, he was, to me, the stag of the forest, blessed of Cernunnos, sent to me by the gods. I could not deny that as I rode upon his horse, pressed against his back, his great arms around me, I felt I had become the man that I had been meant to become, no matter what storms the gods would bring down around us.

Within his turf-and-thatch house, he laid me down upon the furs of his bed, and we wrapped ourselves in each other's sorrow and longing and there slept, though I had not thought I could close my eyes.

Too soon, before dawn had crept through the cracks and the windows of that hovel, the hide at the doorway had been drawn back. I opened my eyes as I heard the noise, and when my vision came into focus, I saw Morgause standing over me, looking every inch the priestess of the goddess, with her blue robes and her raven-white cloak, reminding me of that Medea of Colchis, of whom I'd read in Merlin's scrolls. Her eyes were bright and sharp and fierce, and her lips were drawn back across her teeth in a beautiful grimace of fury.

In her hands, the double-bladed dagger that my mother had thrust into her own bosom. She held it over my lover's left shoulder, as I lay beside him.

She whispered in my mind, the vesseling of it like the scratching of a wild beast within my head, startling me with sudden, vicious pain, as surely as if she had brought my hand into the mouths of those eels in the sea that set afire the ones who come near them: *If you do not come with me now, this moment, I will send your lover to his next life in the most painful way you could imagine, nearly as painful as the way your own mother's life trickles into the Otherworld as you lie here with the greatest traitor of your tribe.*

Chapter Thirteen

1

I sat up in bed, staring at her, and then the man beside me awoke and turned slightly over, looking at Morgause and the double blades pointed to his flesh.

"Tell him who you are," she snarled. "Tell him. If you don't, I will."

I put my arms across his shoulders. "It doesn't matter who he is."

"He is the man," my aunt said, "who guided your father down into the labyrinth where you but nights ago had your midsummer rites. He was fifteen then, as young as Arthur, when they, together, stole Excalibur from its burial place and stole the kingdom of the Britons from your mother. His name is..."

Before she could say it, the man whose body I didn't want to ever let go of turned to face me. He whispered, "Lancelot."

2

I had heard this name before but could not know what it meant or why it had been rarely said in all my childhood. Lancelot had been a child of the Lady herself, of the Lake, of the isle. And his legend was of the greatest betrayer of the caverns, for he had been most loved and most honored as a child. He had shown blessings of the Lady and had been the best horseman. The best swordsman. A messenger faster than any other and all when he had been but a boy. But these stories were rarely referred to in my childhood, and none had told what had become of this boy who had been the brightest gift of the goddess to the shores of the isle.

As I lay there, thinking of this, he wrapped his arms around me and pressed his mouth against my ear. His warm breath against me, as if about to say something to me, something to make me understand.

But Morgause's voice grew even more harsh as she taunted us. "And there you are, Lancelot, come to do penance for your terrible crimes against the Lady and against that mortal lady to whom you were once wed. And here is where it has brought you. You bed the son of Arthur himself. Is that your way of being close to him? And you, Mordred. You make yourself the *whore* of this traitor as soon as you reach manhood." I had never before heard her speak like this to me, and the shock of it left me feeling cold inside.

Then she nearly barked her orders to me. "Get up. You have much to do. You lay with your whore-knight here while your mother travels to Annwn. You are going to make sure she does not complete that journey, or so help me, both of you will die before nightfall. Say your good-byes. I will wait but a few moments without this dirt hovel, and I expect you to be clothed and prepared for the journey you must now take, Mordred."

3

"I knew you were Arthur's son," Lancelot whispered to me, holding my face close to his lips as if he meant to kiss me, though we remained seconds from it. "I wanted to resist you. I wanted to, but when you came to me…"

"First in dreams," I said.

He watched me as if afraid of what he would have to say next. He bit his lower lip, and I reached up and drew his hair to the side so that I might see his eyes better and watch them as if I could climb through those soul windows into him. "Everything she said of me is true," he whispered. "I did terrible things when I was young. I pay for them now.

A maiden, abandoned by her husband on their wedding day, was given to me to marry. She bore my child though we but shared two nights abed. I could not love her, though I tried. She died of sorrow, too young, while I was at war. When I returned, I found her body floating along the river near my home. And my child had been taken away before I had even known of its life."

"And my father? You are that same knight who was beloved of him?"

He nodded. "We were once like brothers. But the stain upon my soul grew too great."

I had no time to judge him, to judge his past, any more than I would wish my own to be judged. But I thought of my friend Lukat and how I had loved him as if he were like my brother too. And how this man whose arms I could not draw myself away from had loved my father like that—and in such a way that he had even gone against his own tribes for that deep brotherhood.

"Believe one thing only," he whispered tenderly and yet with a kind of force I had not yet known from him. "I saw you, and I knew that I had to hold you. I could not avoid you. Nor could I resist you another night. If the Lady of the Lake has granted me the blessing of your love, I do not mind all else that may happen. What we have done together feels sacred to me, though you may come to feel that we have committed a terrible wrong. But if I were to die today, I would die with the knowledge that I had you in my arms this morning, and I would go into the Otherworld with that shred of joy within me."

I sighed, for I could not help myself. Then I drew back. "I must go. Now. Before she does something terrible."

He sat up in our bed, drawing the furs away from his body. All I wanted to do was sink back into him and stay there, but the thought of my mother's suffering blocked this from my mind. "Will I see you tonight?" he asked, as if he expected pain to suddenly spring forth from his words.

"I cannot say," I spoke truthfully. "Will you wait here for me?"

"For a thousand nights, I would wait," he said. He watched me as I dressed swiftly, as if he wanted to memorize everything about me.

I could not be sure if I would know the warmth of his bed and the touch of his skin upon mine ever again.

4

Morgause barely spoke a word to me, but I could feel her crackling anger in the air like heat lightning. She straddled her mare, her blue robes covering half the horse, looking like the great pagan queens of old drawn upon the scrolls that the Druids kept. In her fury, she had achieved a nearly youthful beauty, and her skin seemed clear and smooth as if she had discarded that Morgause who had swallowed the life of servitude to King Lot and to her sons. She had become fiercely beautiful. "Be swift," she said. "Your mother's life hangs in the balance."

She offered her arm, and I leapt upon the saddle, just behind her. She drew the reins back like an expert horsewoman. I clung to my aunt as she whispered to the horse an enchantment that made it gallop as if half-mad, out along the banks of the stream, through the vale, into the forest along the ferny path. As we came upon a shimmering glade where the bright sun of morning bathed golden light upon a sparkling stream and tall grasses, the horse slowed, and Morgause said, almost as if she were cursing the spot, "This is where your lover brought Arthur to the Lake of Glass. This is where they slept and where Viviane herself came to help them, for they played at being in need of care. Here is where Lancelot told your father of that sacred place beneath the Lake, where the sword Excalibur lay buried in rock with the bones of the kings of our tribe who had once held it in their hands."

I looked at the spot, trying to imagine this, then at the back of her hair, which had begun to shine in the light as if it were dyed a dark red. She turned to look at me. "Do you see what you've brought to us? Do you see how your life has come to this, for you were cursed at birth, Mordred. Cursed by the crime your father pressed into your mother's womb. And now you have sought out that man who should have been cut down at the altar of the Lady and whose blood should have been spilt for his betrayal of her. All this. Your mother's life itself. Her pain that she has held during these years—and for what? To see her son in the arms of the man who engineered the stealing of our kingdoms from us?"

I could say nothing to her, but I felt that ice within me and the confusion of love and pain and the inability to understand what I would have to do to make this right.

Again, she whispered words to her horse, and we were off, racing along a fen and leaping over the weir just beyond the place where the meadows began that edged the upper doorway to the caverns. Once there, she dismounted and drew me down as if I were a boy. She pressed me against the horse's flanks and drew that sword from the thin girdle at her waist. She pointed it to my throat. "She raveled her life into you, this much I know, so that you might see our homeland. And for this, Merlin taught you that Art that is not meant for others, and of which I know nothing though I have much of the Art within me. You must ravel her and unravel into yourself. Viviane has taken the poison from her blood and brought blood into Morgan's body. But it is not enough. You brought us the broken cauldron, and it cannot save her. They say that the raveling may kill, or it may bring back from the dead. Only this may save her, though it may send you into the Otherworld to do so."

I shivered as she said this, for I knew the ordeal that awaited me with the raveling, the pain and ache it would cause. And yet, for my mother's life I would do anything. For the crime of having stolen the cauldron of Rebirth and betrayed the tribes and the Lady of the Lake who had always watched over me, I would do this.

5

Viviane sat at the edge of the rock-ledge shore of the Lake, surrounded by other wise women and priestesses of the tribes. They had entered that trance of communion with the Lady of the Lake that she might intervene in my mother's life and heal the cauldron of Rebirth that it might bring my mother back to life as it had brought others to life in the past.

Morgause wasted no time going to them but, instead drew me quickly to my mother's bedchamber.

Her bed was covered with fern and wildflower and dried mistletoe cut from the oak in the grove the previous winter and held as medicine by the Druids. Candles were lit about her bed, and there was also a large tub full of water scented with sweet summer herbs and mint. I knew what this was, I had seen it before at the deathbeds of elders who had passed into the Otherworld. It was the ritual bath of the dying, for it is through the water of the Lake itself that the soul moves. Preparing the body with this water, cleansing the body, would help the pathway of the soul.

My mother lay there, her body naked but for the gemstones that had been brought to draw the poisons from her. Her arms had been sliced so that the poisons could be bled from her as well, and so that the healing blood of the priestesses might flow within her. She had been bathed, and had an oily sheen upon her skin. The Druids had painted upon her breasts and stomach as well as across one half of her face.

Morgause clutched my shoulder and whispered against my ear. "She is half in the Annwn now. But you must ravel yourself into her and draw her back."

"It is her memory that is raveled," I said, without thinking. "Not her soul."

"The soul and the memory are bound together," Morgause said. "Now, we must do this quickly, Mordred. No one must know. I will not lose her to the weak magick of these wise women. I have learned in my travels of the gods of the northern countries, and those who are forbidden even from Avalon." She turned me about to face her and drew her sleeves back, showing me her bare arms. They were torn at as if by wolves. "I brought myself last night to the brink of death that I might find her, but I was blind to anything but the soul's journey."

I gasped and looked at her eyes. They seemed wild and afire, as if her mind no longer controlled her actions.

"Will you do this?" she asked, though it was not a question.

I glanced at my mother, who seemed to be sleeping peacefully. I would have thought her dead already but for the slight movement at her throat. She was more than half in the arms of death. I did not even believe she would live another hour.

"If I do this, it may kill her," I said.

Morgause grinned. "If the poison that has torn her inside has not yet killed her, your Art will not. She is past pain. She is past sorrow. You must do this, Mordred. Merlin is not here. Few elders know this Art, and those who do will not use it to draw your mother's soul back into its body."

My fear of Morgause grew as she spoke. My throat grew dry, and I could not stop shivering though the chamber was warm. Part of me wondered how in all those years, my mother, having stolen this Art from Merlin, had not taught it to her sister, as she had shown it to me. And yet Morgause absolutely wanted me to ravel, and to try and stop my mother's passing, or else to at least bring her memory into my own that she might live in a different sense.

"Let us not waste time," I said.

I went over to my mother's bed. I removed my clothing, for to ravel when clothed may interrupt the flow of memory.

I lay down beside her, pressing my face near hers as she had once with me when I'd been a boy and she had raveled her past into my mind. My eyes near hers, I matched her slow, nearly imperceptible breaths with my own. I began to feel myself go into that state of being that Merlin had taught me, letting my mind fly as if it were a raven, detaching my thoughts from my flesh, opening myself to the rhythm of my mother's barely felt heartbeats, as if moving beneath water into her.

As I went, I thought I heard Morgause speaking to me, whispering something that I could not quite understand. It was as if I heard her from some distant place. I was going deep into raveling with my mother, and it grew dark as I felt her death approach. I remembered Merlin warning me about the dying, how they tried to draw you in with them as they went, for the soul hated its lonely journey. Then, as if she were upon a mountaintop somewhere in the darkness of my mind, I heard Morgause calling to me, "Forgive me, Mordred! Forgive me!" But I did not understand her, and soon her language seemed foreign to me and sounded like the cries of hawks along a cliff as they hunt. Instead, I began to feel the slowness of my breath and feel the downward pull of my mother's life as it ebbed. I was being drawn into a deep darkness and felt as if I were floating in the Lake itself. I was inside her now, in her mind and her memories—not memories of her past but her current memories—perhaps mere moments after she experienced them. The thudding of her heartbeat was in the dark water all around me, and though I tried to swim for the surface, it was as if my feet were weighted with irons.

Down I went into this dark watery place and suddenly I moved more swiftly; something was tugging me faster than I could resist, and I stepped through a waterfall.

6

I emerged upon a boat, which was nearly like the flatboats used upon the Lake, although these seemed to be of a simple build, with logs bound together by cross-tied ropes. A woman who looked so ancient that her face had begun splitting along its many wrinkles was at the helm, pressing the boat forward by means of a long pole thrust into the silt beneath the water's surface, for it was not a deep lake. I glanced back at where I'd come from: this waterfall was like no other, for it seemed to flow upward from the Lake upon which we navigated. I knew I must be in her dream, in my mother's mind to such an extent that I had crossed from her memory into her vision.

I saw other boats, some like the longboats that crossed the seas, others like this flatboat made so crudely. As I looked at the woman who pushed her pole into the water, I began to see others standing upon the boat with us. They were insubstantial as marsh light, with a green-yellow outline to their forms that seemed like fine mist. I realized then where I was and where my mother's vision took me.

I was on the true Sea of Glass, of which our Lake was a pale reflection only. This glass was of Annwn, the Otherworld, and I had crossed with my mother's mind into the land of the dead.

7

Although hours seemed to pass on this journey, I knew from Merlin's teaching that a year in the Otherworld might be a brief afternoon in our own, or it might be a century. Time twisted and turned in this place, for there was no setting sun or rising moon. It had that dark brilliance of the shadow of the moon as it crossed the sun. My boat seemed to be filled with warriors who had died in battle, for I caught glimpses of armor and swords, although these shone briefly and then became invisible to me. The old woman who guided the boat did not speak, although I heard the whispers of those around me. When I moved closer to the boat's pilot, her eyes were white as Maponus, the guardian of the labyrinth.

I could not see much ahead of us, for a thick fog had come in, low to the water. But finally, we came to the harbor of Annwn. I did not feel the fear I thought I would, and I suppose this might have been because I only traveled as a soul rider, and not as one who would remain in Annwn. I glanced about at the black-sand shore of the harbor, thinking I would catch a glimpse of my mother's soul. I felt her near me but did not find her among the mists that grew from the shades of the dead.

The shores of Annwn were blackened, but soon enough, the sand turned white as it approached a cliffside meadow above. A rock stair had been carved there, and I moved with the others up its steep ascent until I was at the top of the cliff. I felt the watery movements of others around me, moving forward, pressing at me. I saw faces of men and women and children, the hounds that had died with them also, and they came out of the mist and into a physical form, clothed as they had fallen in death.

At a great distance, I saw that legendary citadel of Arawn's kingdom—the black glass towers of Annwn. The sky filled with doves in flight; the air smelled of the fragrant lilies and the overpowering and heart-gladdening scent of the rare yellow lavender flower of which I'd known few in my life, for most had a purplish hue, brought by messengers from southern climes; and fruit trees blossomed and bore a heavy harvest along the road toward the great towers. Those Orphans of Death—children who had died before they had reached the age of eight—considered to be blessed keys of entry into this place, guided the heavily antlered stags upon which royalty rode toward the kingdom. I glanced about at the stags, but did not see my mother.

Then, a great cloud seemed to move along the sky above us, and I was not alone in looking up at it. Down it came, like a gale wind upon the sea and then seemed to me a plague of locusts moving as one along the water's surface. As it came to the cliff, I heard the baying of hounds—this would be King Arawn, for his hounds announced his arrival in all places. As the locusts took form, I saw his great chariot, and a team of stallions drawing him onward. His white hounds, with their distinctive yellow ears, yapped and howled as they ran alongside the horses. Arawn wore the crown of dark stone, and from it, the two great ram's horns curved over his scalp. His body was thickly muscled, and around his waist he wore a girdle of bones. And then, every bit of him, and the chariot, broke apart again, until it was like that dark cloud moving through those of us who stood along the roadside.

In the thick of these locust clouds, I saw those kings and princesses and warriors who had been slain or had died but had deceived and lied and broken the taboos of the gods. They were wrapped from head to foot in thin thorny branches, and from the terror in their eyes I saw the fears of their lives revealed—and their great crimes against the gods themselves in the ways in which they were held captive.

Still, I did not see my mother there, yet I felt her nearby. Finally, I saw her, up ahead, riding upon a thickset stag, drawn by a Death's Orphan. I pushed my way through the other spirits that traveled slowly along the road. When I reached my mother, I called to her. As she turned to look upon me, I was horrified to see that she had been cut as if in two, from her head down her middle, and only one half of her existed in this realm.

I felt as if I had made a mistake: I had gotten lost in my mother's vision-journey into Annwn, but she had not yet died. She was only half-way there, and the raveling had taken me into that part of her memory and not into the part that survived. My mother looked at me as if she did not remember me.

In the land of the dead, we do not know each other. The life in passing is like a dream, one dream among a thousand dreams.

I had been misled somehow. And yet, how could I have raveled with only half her spirit? How could she be there and also in another place?

In the raveling, it is so much like simply watching, without attachment to what is seen, that my mind could not understand why I saw this, or why I did not find that part of her that had not begun the journey to death.

But I took the stag's lead from the Orphan, and began to move back through the throng of the dead, toward the steps down to the harbor at the Sea of Glass.

As I did so, I felt another presence with me. Not my mother's half-soul, and not those who had died who moved against me as I returned to the harbor.

Someone else was there with me. Another watched me and seemed to breathe upon the back of my neck as I guided the stag to the stairs. Once there, I lifted my mother into my arms and began the descent down the steps toward the sands.

8

It was not until I had reached the flatboat that I knew who had been with me while I searched for my mother among the dead. I saw her, there, on the black sands. She also turned to look upon me.

Like my mother, she also had been cut down her center, only a half-soul.

I felt my mind begin to spiral again, as if spinning as it fell down a deep, dark well. It was Morgause. She stood there, across the sands from my mother and me, and looked at us briefly. Then, she continued walking toward the cliffs.

Something had gone terribly wrong, for I could feel the dissonance of it, as if my mind grew queasy and full of a screeching pain.

Morgause had tricked me. She had made me use the raveling for something that was forbidden. I would not understand her full deception—and the horror it would bring—until I unraveled from my mother's mind.

9

I awoke feeling as if I'd been stabbed in the gut, and I came up not from my mother's bed but from the tub of water that had been placed beside it. I gasped for air, and someone had already grabbed my forearm in her hand—it was Morgause.

She lay naked against my mother's body and had held onto me, in that sacred water, so that I would not come up until she had finished with her ritual. I fought against her, for my own life, as she tried to press me back down beneath the water's surface.

To send me back into Annwn.

Back to the land of the dead.

It had all been an elaborate trick. All of it, to use my knowledge of the Art to bring the half-soul of my mother back to her.

Morgause had lied to me about not knowing raveling herself, but she had practiced a darker form of it. She had raveled into both my mother and me, knowing full well that my mother was dying and could not be revived.

As my eyes came into better focus, I saw that her own eyes had changed. One had turned blood-red from her exertion. The other was my mother's beautiful dark brown eye.

As if Morgause's body was now half my mother's as well.

And half of her still remained in the Otherworld.

"You were too late to save her," Morgause whispered. "Too late, Mordred."

"What have you done?" I gasped, feeling horror in my body that had just begun the wracking fevers of one coming out of the raveling. I stared in terror at my mother's lifeless body and then at my aunt's face, which was washed with blood as if she were some vampyric creature.

"Too late to save my sister," Morgause whispered, her voice like the whispering Anthea themselves. Blood washed across her body, and I saw that my mother's wounds had been reopened.

The knowledge of it hit me with the force of a storm: She had drunk my mother's blood, and mingled it with hers.

She had sent half of her own soul into Annwn and drawn back half of my mother's soul into her own flesh.

Somehow, through these terrible acts—these forbidden acts that could not have been performed if Morgause had not also turned to that goddess of howling places, Namtareth—she had drunk in my mother's soul. She had tried to murder me that I would help her, for in raveling, I also had unraveled myself and brought myself to the brink of death.

My aunt had helped that along with the bath she had pressed me into while I had been in that trance of raveling.

"What in the name of the gods have you done?" I asked, but the room began to spin as I rose from the tub of water, much of which had splashed over the edge onto the tiled floor of my mother's bedchamber. "What have you done?" I screamed at her, though my voice seemed weak. "You lied to me! You took me into the Otherworld with her! You were there!"

"With me did I take you," Morgause said, showing me the cuts she'd made at her wrist and forearm. "I drowned you while you raveled, through her, through me, and she unraveled through you into me. I took us all three there, so that she might never die but live within me and share this flesh."

"But that is—" I gasped, yet the pains in my body made me tremble and I had to find balance or else I would fall. I felt as if any strength in my body had been drained by Morgause's unspeakable crime against me and against my mother.

"It is the greatest crime against the goddess," Morgause said. "It is the unpardonable offense against the gods themselves."

I felt terror clutch at my heart as Morgause said these words. She had attained an even greater beauty from that shining black citadel of the dead, and though streaks of white had come into her dark hair, I could no longer distinguish Morgause from my mother, Morgan. It was as if they both were truly in that one flesh, both bodies within the one. She grabbed me around the neck, not strangling, but drawing me close that she could whisper in my ear. "We live within the one flesh now, and we serve none but Namtareth, the Terrible and the Magnificent, that queen of the ancient mysteries of the Canaanite tomb priestesses, that long-forgotten soul-binding, that twin spirit in one body as one soul may occupy three. No one shall say that Morgan or Morgause is dead, nor shall we die—for we are not alive, but dwell in both realms. For we are here—thank that goddess of the blackest night and your Art, brought into you by your mother and taught to you by Merlin, opened that doorway that we might live. The greatest law of the Lady is that nothing shall interrupt the journey of the soul, and we have all three broken that greatest of laws tonight. I could not have done this without your mastery of the Art."

Then, she let go of me.

I felt myself falling downward, the result of rising too fast from that state of raveling. I put my hands forward as I fell to protect myself, but I passed out before I hit the floor.

Chapter Fourteen

1

I dreamed of Lancelot. We rode together upon his horse through a soft twilight. I do not remember much of this dream, other than the heavy sorrow I felt.

I awoke from the dream, freezing and burning, the sound of summer rain beyond my bed. A fever had taken hold of me and wracked my body. I shook so violently I believed that invisible hands held and pushed at me. I awoke with too much knowledge and sorrow. I could think of nothing but my mother. Her face. The last time I had seen her alive, when the drop of her soul had nearly fallen into that great Sea of Glass. My grief, coupled with the pains in my body that were like my bones splitting, overwhelmed me. I wished to die. I did not wish to return to life again, to its losses. I could muster no tears for my mother's life, for all water poured from me in the form of sweat, yet I felt that same crushing of my emotions as if I lay there sobbing for her. I hated everyone in the world in that moment. I hated my father, who forced my mother to his bed and then sent assassins to kill her and stop my birth. I hated Lukat for abandoning me with his sorrow, and for his need to escape the caverns without me. I hated him for not being able to love me as I would have loved him, for we were more than brothers and yet less than lovers. I hated Lancelot, for, as I recalled his crimes and his betrayals of our people, stealing the sword Excalibur's resting place deep in the forbidden labyrinth below the Lake, as well as his making me love him as I had never wanted to love a man before, I only thought of how he had left me too. How I lay upon my bed and had not awakened to his face, to his touch, to the way he laughed when I tried to be serious. I hated the tribes in the Isle of Glass for their taboos and their laws and their rituals. I hated Morgause for her treachery, and for making me believe that she had loved me as her nephew when she had no love in her heart to give. I hated Merlin for ever having taught me that Art of raveling, and the Art of vesseling and the histories of the ancient world, which made me want to love all people and all lands. My hatred reached the goddess of the Lake herself, that Lady of mystery and power, who seemed to have declared before my birth that all of my life should be accursed. That I should love the man who broke his sacred vows to the Lake that had nurtured him; that I too should break my vows that I might try and save my mother's life to no avail. And all this seemed like a great trick, a joke, as I lay there shivering from that icy fire the fever brought, a great laugh upon me from the nameless Lady in whose care I had entrusted my soul and my life.

And of all of these, I hated my mother the most. I hated her for that want she had to leave the earth, to not fight against those forces that sought to destroy her. I hated that she had given into that impulse to hurt herself rather than turn that pain back on those who had hurt her. But above all this, I hated that she'd left me.

In this state of fear and anger and pain, I drifted in and out of sleep. When my fever cooled slightly, I awoke again, aware of someone's presence nearby.

2

I saw her face first: pale and wrinkled but with the bright eyes of a girl, her white hair drawn back and plaited in braids that ran down her shoulders. *Viviane*.

Viviane sat at the edge of my bed, wrapping cool wet cloths upon my forehead. She smelled of anise and the summer-blossoming houndslip flower, which she used to wash her hair so that, even white as snow, it shone with a reddish-dark hue in the candlelight.

When I parted my lips, she brought a warm soup for me to drink. It tasted of lamb and leeks, heavily salted and spiced so that it opened up my breathing and made me gasp with the way it brought life into me at first gulp.

"Do you feel better?" she asked, tenderly. Viviane had seen more of life than any of us, and she had accepted its losses so long that they rarely brought her to sorrow. Yet, she looked now as if the world had taken too much from her.

I could do no more than rasp and wheeze in reply. She brought the bowl to my lips again, lifting my head slightly with her hand to the back of my scalp. "No need to speak now, my child," she whispered, and though I knew I was no longer a boy, I felt like one there, at the mercy of this body that had not recovered well from the raveling. At the mercy of this world that I hated.

"I am sorry for these tragic days," she said. "For you are more than son to me than my own children were. Had I seen what Morgause had planned...well, had I understood..." Her words faltered, and she drew the bowl back. "You need to rest, Mordred. Rest until you feel strength again in your blood. The soup is full of healing properties, with owl's-bane to quicken the blood that your fever might reach its crisis and pass." Then, she told me of what had come to pass, though I had known much of it. "Morgause has gone mad. She believes that she and your mother's soul are entwined, both here, within her body, and in Annwn. I cannot say if this is true, for I have never seen it before. But she has changed, and I fear she has ill-used you to seek this moonless dark of her spirit. I am sorry for your mother's passing." As she said this, her voice broke slightly, and tears came into her eyes. "We cannot stop those who seek death. But we can try. We can...but to stop the soul on its way is an unholy thing to attempt. Morgause has gone mad. She has left us here, and seeks out the places of the restless dead for she no longer thirsts for life, I am afraid."

She drew the damp cloth down along my neck and shoulders, cooling me as she went. "Do not fear anything, child. I will remain here with you as long as you need me. Others come too with offerings and prayers, and the Druids perform ceremonies to appease the gods that this time of trouble might pass swiftly. I have sent ravens to find Merlin that he too might come with what grace he brings."

I nearly did not want to recover but had hoped I might die that I could simply escape all that I hated and feared and wanted but could not reach. I did not believe I would ever see Lancelot again, and I longed for the arms of my mother as if I were, again, a little boy.

I felt as if I had become a man and then lost the best of what life might offer, all within a short span of days.

3

In that month of recovery, I began to feel Morgause within me, as if somehow that terrible raveling at the edge of death had tied us, inextricably, together. I heard her voice in my dreams, and felt haunted by her when I awoke. In some cavernous darkness, I heard the whispers of her voice as if she were the Anthea, as my Morgan's and Morgause's voices growled together. *We are neither dead nor living, my son, my nephew. Our souls are between the worlds, and we have learned many secrets within the black towers of Lord Arawn and his ministers. We have seen the beautiful white shores of Prince Taranis and traveled beneath the sea to Avalon and its groves, though the priestesses there saw us as spirits of the dead. We have found the wandering souls on our journey, those who cannot gain entry into the Otherworld but desire to invade the flesh of the living. They call to us that we might raise them from beneath the stones of the earth.*

The fevered madness within me grew, and I could not tell sometimes when I imagined things, when I dreamed them, or when I saw them clearly.

One late afternoon, my mind seemed to clear, and there was Merlin at my bedside. I was sure that this was a vision as my others had been, a spidery dream that had left its cobweb behind.

"There he is," Merlin said, leaning over my face, glancing back to Viviane. "He's with us."

"I'm glad my message reached you," Viviane said. "I was afraid he had begun slipping back to Annwn."

"It draws us back once we've journeyed there," Merlin said, keeping watch upon me; his large, wide face taking up all I could see above me, like he was the moon itself filling my view. "I have been there many times, and it is both dark and lovely to remain among its clear lakes and great cities," he said, as if speaking to me, though I could not be sure. "But we must return to life, for there is much to be done." Then, he vesseled within my mind,

Mordred, can you understand me?

Yes.

I want you to leave off this despair and illness that draws you into the arms of Arawn. You have survived much, and if you were meant to die this summer, it would already have come to pass. Do you wish to live?

I had not thought to ask myself that question, and I could not answer him.

Again he asked. And then a third time.

I felt some fluttering in my chest, as if my heart were a sparrow, beating its wings against its cage of flesh and bone.

You must not return to life unless you truly desire it, he vesseled. *You must know that you seek life in order to claim it, whelp. There are many who seek life and they deserve to have it and all its blessings. You feel despair at your mother's passage and anger toward that unknown father. You do not understand this ache of love you have felt, briefly, with the outcast of your tribe. You do not feel up for the fight that it takes to live this life. For to truly live, all must be brave and strong, and must give until there is nothing left to give, and must take when the taking is required. The Dragon of the world is all around us, breathing fire or catching us in its claws. And yet that same Dragon carries us when we struggle and* comforts us when we have pain. But the life in this world is a great gift, Mordred. Even that suffering you feel brings blessings that you cannot understand in one lifetime. I remember all my lifetimes, and I know the value of this life. Even those who pass to Anwnn understand this value and are willing to pay its price to return into life again, though Annwn and all who remain there are rich and joyous beyond compare, and the fruit trees always are heavy with their sweet burden, and the stags offer themselves up for the feast, as do the boars, and yet none dies, and none there is in want. And still, those who have passed wish to return, for the value of this life, Mordred, is in having it at all.

Now, tell me once more, do you wish to die? If so, I shall draw out my curved blade, which should only be used for cutting the sacred mistletoe, but I shall use it to slice your throat that you may return now into the Otherworld and enjoy its wonders. There are adventures to be had there, and you will never grow old, for there is no time, there is no want, there is no end to that land once arrived there. You may experience great pleasures without pain. Or, you may choose life, and I will do what I can to lift this fever from you. I will offer some small strength left within me that you might recover. All is not lost, my friend, prince of no country and prince of all countries. You are too important to this life you shall live. I would not have taught you the raveling if I did not know you were destined to greater things than this fever bed. So tell me now, give me the word, and I shall slit your throat and in seconds you will be back on that flatboat with the old woman who will take your soul to that shore, and I will make sure that Death's Orphan is there with a stag that you might ride in grandeur to that great city of Glass. You shall tonight sit at a feast with King Arawn himself, and his wives and husbands, and the children of Death, and you will never have pain again. Or will you live, and see this through, this world that has begun to shiver and quake with its own unmaking, as the creature that Morgause has become—a twin soul—seeks to raise the dead through her necromantic arts that she might hang the skin of the lady Guinevere upon the tallest oak as a warning to all who seek to marry the high-king? Will you die and allow the Lake of Glass to wither and dry up, *with the cauldron of Rebirth broken, its magick not yet restored, while Morgause has stolen its pieces that she might mend it? Do you not wish to see your mother's soul join its half that she might be reborn through Annwn into a new life?*

Will you, who are good in your soul as I know you, take up the gauntlet and play your part among the living and allow the gods themselves to decide when the cup of your life has drained?

My lips, though parched, parted; and I gasped, "I want to live."

Days and hours mingled in my memory, and I drew in and out of fever. Then, one night, the fever seemed to set my skin afire and, suddenly cooled again. I lay in my bed shivering while Viviane drew woolen blankets over me. "It has broken," she said, kissing me upon the forehead. "You will recover."

"Merlin? Where is Merlin?" I murmured, thinking that his voice had simply been one among the many of the fever dreams.

"He will come by soon enough," she said. "For he carries me to my own bed tonight that I might rest." I glanced about my bedchamber, its familiarity a comfort, for it reminded me of my childhood, and saw that Viviane had made a nest of blankets for herself near the arched doorway.

She had slept on the floor during those weeks of my fever and had not gone far from me the entire time.

4

Merlin came to draw my bath late that night after he'd carried Viviane back to her home down the stony stair. He had boiled water to such an extent that it was too hot for me to rest in for a while, so I sat on the edge of my bed, still feeling weak and suffered tremors as if I had drunk too much mead. "Did I dream that you vesseled into me?" I asked.

He offered up that enormous grin that seemed to widen his face and nodded. "Of course. You understand vesseling. It is as easy as speaking when there are two open vessels."

"And yet it felt like I dreamt it."

He paused from his work at stirring cleansing herbs into the bath and looked up at me as if he could not decide whether to tell me something or not. Finally, he said, "Mordred, if I told you that there are no dreams, as you think of them, what would you make of that?"

"No dreams? And yet I have them."

"Of course. Most have dreams. But they are not these sleeping ventures that vanish with morning's first light. All of us live in that other realm, even while we live here. The dreams are the reflection of what we see there."

"I do not understand this," I said and tested the bath again with the tip of my toe.

"I think it's ready," he said, and helped me slip into it. The water was immediately soothing, and yet caused me to sweat again with its herbs and spices. As he rubbed a soapy mixture into my hair, he said, "Your aunt and mother have brought their twin souls into one body. But half of each of their souls remains in Anwnn. You understand that?"

"Yes."

"There is yet another realm, between this world and the Otherworld. And to that third realm, these seem as but dreams. It does not have a name, just as our Lady is nameless to us, just as the winter solstice days have remained nameless. All of us visit this realm in our sleep, in our dreams, though not all remember. If we could remember, we would have greater insight into this life, which is but the dream of that realm."

My head began pounding as he tried to explain this third realm, and yet I could not comprehend it. Finally, I said, "I understand that you speak of this secret realm, my lord. But what of it? Does this not simply mean that we all dream within dreams and therefore all are equal?"

Even as I said it, I understood what he had just taught me.

"You see? You're brighter than you've led yourself to believe," he chuckled, washing my back with a scraping stone that felt as if it would rake my flesh. "Of course all realms are equal. The realm of our flesh.

The realm of death. And that realm of our dreams that few understand yet many visit."

"And if all are equal," I said. And then, it felt like a lightning bolt. I stood up in my bath, splashing water all over him and the floor, and I turned to him and said, "Then what is of dreams may be brought through magick here. In the flesh itself."

"You are more advanced in this Art than either of your parents, Mordred," Merlin said, wiping the sudsy water from his shiny bald head. "And now I will tell you the dream I had when you were born, for I have waited long to mention it but could not do so until I was sure you would understand it."

So, late into the night, over several sweet breads that Merlin had brought that night for us to share, we sat upon my bed, and he told me of a dream he had of me during the Beltane ritual. It was a long tale to listen to, and much of it had little to do with me but with the love he had for my mother that he had never told her of directly but finally revealed to me. "I saw a great orb of the sun crossed in the shadow of the moon as if it were midday in Annwn, as if the Dragon had swallowed the sun god and yet kept light upon the earth. Yet, this light was cast in a glow that was summer-green, and beyond it, I saw a battlefield upon which many warriors lay dead. Wolves gathered at the edge of dense woods, tearing at the dead and dying, and smoke from the fires of burning villages filled that air and changed the light to a sulfurous yellow. The cries of many went up to the heavens, and flocks of birds came from the smoke, and in their talons were the souls of the mist-like souls of the dead. I saw a man in a mask and full armor, though this was of yellow-gold, with the signs of those goddesses of the East, Persephone and Demeter and those Gorgon sisters of Crete, emblazoned on his breastplate. He held high that sword that your father had stolen from the Lake of Glass and brandished above his head. I saw the jewels about its hilt shining in that unearthly sunlight. I saw the blade, clean and sharp, and the inscription upon it in one of the lost languages, which read, 'Him who is meant to rule Caliburn, the sword of destiny, shall bring death to his enemies and peace to his lands, but woe to him who holds it long, for it is power in all its terrible purity; and woe upon him who grasps this sword without the blessing of its creator for it was forged in the mountain of Calib, within its Lake of fire, and was bought with the souls of many men.' This man who wielded it was not your father. Beneath that mask, I saw your eyes, and in the dream I approached him. I reached up to draw the mask from your face, and that is when my dream ended. But I knew it was Mordred, son of Morgan, queen of many lands, and son of Arthur the high-king of the Britons. I knew it was the baby that had returned his soul into this passage of life. And this is why I have brought you into the knowledge of Art, from which many youths and maidens are forbidden. Even your father has not learned of many things that you have been trained in. You are a swordsman and have the knowledge of a young mage within you. All that you know will grow, for you offered the gods your purity while you studied, and you may be a greater man than many might be in this life. I believe you are here as the son of Morgan and of Arthur because the goddess herself wished for you to be born, Mordred. Do not unwish it ever again, no matter how dark your days may become. You are meant for a great destiny, although I fear..." And here Merlin sighed, deeply, bringing his hands to his face as if despairing of his own visions.

"What do you fear?"

He raised his head up and tried to smile but could not. "I cannot tell you all my fears; for, to one who cannot remember the lifetimes, it is pure terror and madness. But it is simply those elementals that tug at us and draw us where the gods wish. But do not refuse the cup of life as long as you may drink it, Mordred, for you are meant for something great though I cannot know what that is, or if it is a terrible greatness or a wonderful magnificence." The gravity of his voice and feature changed suddenly, and his eyes seemed to twinkle like he was a child again. "How is that bread? It was baked by a fetching wench who warmed me at her fire one night."

I looked at the small curved roll in my hands and then back to his face. "Bread does not interest me this night," I said. "If Morgause has taken the cauldron of Rebirth, and yet it holds no magick since breaking, to what purpose does she put it?"

"It may be mended yet," Merlin said. "There is more to the cauldron than the broken shards of a bowl, Mordred. Its waters are all around us, yet we do not see them. Yet I do. I feel myself move through the waters from that Cauldron."

"Like the pull of the elementals," I said.

He shrugged, nodding. "Certainly. But through the Art you have learned, you may change the current of these things. That is how the healing will begin, and even Morgause does not understand it, for she abandoned her Art long ago. Though she has a foot upon this world and the next, she does not understand this water of life that is around us. She sees only the bowl and not what it contains. It cannot truly be broken, ever, though that bowl has cracked. The cauldron is that cup of life—of eternal life—and to heal its breach, one must first know what to ask of it."

"You have always spoken in riddles, like the Druids do," I said.

"To those who understand, there is no riddle to this," he said. "But to you, well, you have much pain, which keeps you from your understanding."

"Why does life bring so much pain?"

"Men rarely ask this question," he said, "because they are too afraid to know its answer."

"That is not an answer."

He laughed aloud. "No, it is not. Pain is the passage itself. When a child is born, both the child and mother feel pain. And yet, would you keep the child unborn within the mother's womb for many years rather than bring that pain that the child may come through and the mother hold him? And so, in death and loss, we bring pain and we swim within it. But it is a sign of the passage, nothing more. Your mother understood this, though your aunt has never grasped the value of the passing of life."

"I must stop Morgause from what she seeks," I said, after thinking a moment. "She means to destroy that maiden Guinevere who travels to my father at harvesttime."

Merlin wagged a finger in my face. "Stopping her will not be simple. You must not attempt it. Morgause has brought back great power—a knowledge of the souls of the dead even I do not possess. She is nothing but fury and power, and I am afraid that it will be nearly impossible to stop her."

"Nearly? So then she may be stopped. My mother's half-soul may find its rest?"

"All power has a flaw," he said. "For she cannot half her soul and have it remain in Annwn without longing for its other half. And the same is true for your mother's half-soul within her. The soul in Annwn cannot find its other half, unless there is innocent blood on the hands."

"If she kills?"

"If she herself, by her own hand, has the stain of the blood of an innocent upon her, that blood will cry out to Arawn, and the echo of the cry will reach her half-soul. That part of her in the land of the dead will draw its other half into Annwn to be joined together at last, for the soul always seeks what it has lost. But Morgause knows of this and will do all she can to keep her own hands clean."

"Then, she is not to be feared," I said.

"Innocent blood," Merlin reminded me. "She may cause others to murder. She may murder one who has the stain of much guilt upon him. But she will do all in her power to keep her half-soul from calling out to its mate. But let us not think of this now," Merlin said. "For I know that your father's wedding feast is not for many weeks. You must rest awhile. Do not punish yourself further with a visit to Morgause. I am sorry that I did not foresee this twin-soul business many years ago when your mother stole raveling from me. Yet I could deny your mother nothing." His eyes glazed over a bit, and he seemed to have, however briefly, gone to another time in his mind. Then, he returned, and rose up from my bed. "You must rest. You may not find much peace here now that your fever has passed, for the tribes have turned against you, whelp. I can do nothing to convince the council otherwise, though I have tried. Viviane defended you as well. But they have the law of the Lady and the Isle, and you did steal that bloody cauldron, and they blame you as well for all else that has come to pass here. No, you must find a place that welcomes you, a warm bed for rest and a soup bowl for strength. I will seek out Morgause, for she sleeps among the standing stones near the grove, and like a beast she snarls at those who come to her. I will deal with her soon enough. You must find your way in the world until such a time as I may bind her from doing further harm, for it is you she will wish to destroy, and your blood on her hands will not call her soul to Annwn."

5

When I finally emerged from my bedchamber the next morning, nearly all who had lived in the Isle of Glass turned their backs upon me. I had been shunned by the tribes of my own people here. My crimes were known: I had stolen the cauldron of Rebirth from its sacred resting place, and I had caused it to break. It had been useless in saving my mother's life; nor could it be placed back within the water for fear of offending the goddess even more.

I had brought shame into the Lake of Glass as it hadn't known since Arthur and Lancelot, barely more than boys, had brought shame to them.

I walked among my people as a ghost, and though Viviane still faced me and spoke to me, and asked me to carry her to the world above when she wished it, I could tell that even she had nothing left to offer me but sorrow.

Finally, I could stand this living death no longer. I took Viviane up into the meadows above, and we sat at the edge of a copse where I had often gone to gather kindling for the winter fires. Viviane brought with her a basket of yellow and red berries, sweet and tart upon the tongue.

She shared them with me, and after too much silence, she said, "I must bring you the saddest news in a summer of sorrow."

I knew before she spoke what this news would be: "I must leave."

She nodded, and tried to muster a warm smile, but could not.

"Merlin told me before he left us," I said. "I understand."

Tears began to glisten at the corners of her eyes. "You may live above, as the messengers do."

"Messengers and hunters and outcasts," I said, knowing the law all too well. "For even outsiders may have the forest of Broceliande, though only the sanctified of the tribes may dwell upon the Isle of Glass itself."

"We cannot go against the council and the will of our people," she said. "No matter how I wish I could keep you here. I have known you since your birth. I have loved your mother and you all these years. I understand why you had to take the Cauldron."

I glanced over at her. "You do?"

She nodded. "I think even the Lady herself understands, Mordred. You have suffered much for this. But I have lived in this world long enough to know that in times of tragedy, it feels like winter. But winter only lasts so long before the sun comes to the forest again and the lakes above us melt. You are a young man, and you must make your way in the world. I am sorry that the law may not be trespassed, for there are no exceptions. But I know that whatever the goddess has in store for you, it is the path you were meant to take. When I lost the use of my legs, do you think I loved life then? That I felt I had not been cursed by the gods? And yet, now, I see that what happened to me set me upon the path that would become my life and there was no other way for me to find that path. I will hope that you will come to understand how the path of life meets us in such dark days. Life chooses us; we do not choose it. And yet, Mordred, if you can learn to grasp this, to come around to the side of seeing your life as the gods themselves see it, you will not only find happiness, but you will also seek out your path."

I felt my heart grow heavy with grief, and the caverns themselves seemed to have taken on the aspect of a tomb for me. Though the place was filled with children playing at the lakeshore, and the huntsmen had dressed a boar recently brought down in the fields, and I watched the maidens who worked near the burning ovens of the forge, mending swords, it was no longer home. They were at the business of the living, yet they did not seem alive to me anymore.

Finally, as I left my home and said good-bye to Viviane for what I thought would be forever, I packed up provisions and some clothes I had. I drew my blankets across my back and took the few weapons I had earned from childhood to manhood: a dirk and a short sword as well as a small axe I could keep at my side. I climbed the steps upward from the cavern at the isle into the paddocks above. The thickset horses of the Eponi were out in the yellow summer fields, grazing. Men and women were about their work, and the grain had grown high for the fall harvest that would come soon enough. Lukat's father, Anyon, met me, for he did not shun me as others did. He had aged a bit much in the past few years, and I wondered if the grief of his son's leaving had hurt him too much.

"Do you hear from Lukat?" I asked.

He shook his head sadly. "I wait every full moon for the messengers from the coast. But none has brought news of my boy. But should you see him, you tell him to come home for Beltane next, will you, lad?"

The fact that he still saw me as a boy made me even sadder, for it reminded me of my happiness here in the hidden Lake that lay beneath the forest slopes. He offered me a bow and a quiver of arrows that he had carved himself that summer. "A man needs to eat when out in the wilderness," he said. "You are a good shot, so you shall have a fine time of it. And do not ever forget, you're welcome to sleep here, in our shelters, though you must share the paddocks with our horses. The Eponi will never shun a son of Morgan le Fay." He smiled as broadly as he could and chucked me slightly in the shoulder in a way that gladdened my heart. "And I have another gift for you, lad. Just back in the paddock."

He pointed off to the many horses that grazed the field that was enclosed by a low stone wall. "See? That one. That white horse? See? A white horse who is a great-grandson of a royal mare that had been left to die by a Roman prince who did not much care for his horses, the scoundrel. Most of the horses we raise are of the dark kind with the thick legs, but you see? He is slender and strong, and like the whitest of rabbits for his coat, that one."

"I can't take such a beautiful animal," I said.

"It is not mine to give," he said. "Nor yours to refuse." He gave me a wink. I did not understand him, and though I asked him more, he simply told me that the horse had been meant for me, and that I must take it, for to refuse a horse from the Eponi was to insult the honor of all Eponi. Perhaps Merlin had brought the horse for me, though Anyon would not tell.

I tried to read his stoic face for any betrayal of what this meant, but he was too much of his tribe: difficult to understand once they'd decided to be mysterious. "Thank you, for I need this horse, though I do not deserve it," I told him. "You have always been like a father to me."

"And you, like my second son," he said. "Now, let us go meet this magickal horse before I convince you to come live with the horsemen rather than take off on your own."

As we walked across the fields to the horse paddocks, I asked, "How is he magickal?"

"It is a secret magick," he said. "A kind even the Druids don't know, although the horse understands their secrets."

In the paddock, he whistled for the horse. I watched the beast's face glance over at us. "See?" he whispered. "He regards us with uncertainty. This breed is not like ours. He has no trust, though he's a fine rider and a gentle spirit." I felt better than I had in many weeks, standing there with him, for the Eponi were a warm and unusual people who believed that horses were their brothers and sisters and not their property at all. For an Eponi to claim one horse as his was a blasphemy to them, for it would be like claiming a brother as a slave. To them, all horses were the masters and, at worst, friends who had to share the burdens of human life.

"Does he have a name?" I asked.

"Caradoc," he said. "His sire is named Druid and lives off in the forest but comes in the spring to mate. Caradoc is his only son."

"Caradoc is the name of one who is dearly loved," I said.

"So I understand. The one who raised him had much love for Caradoc and for the sire. You can see it in the way Caradoc lords it over the other horses," he said.

"And yet I have never seen this horse before."

"He does not live in our paddocks but comes, like his father, to find the mares. But we have him now, and he is for you alone to ride. But when you ride him, you must be careful, for he has a stronger mind than even your aunt Morgause and a wilder temper. Perhaps, like his father, he was a Druid in another life, for he has the look of them. Or like his grandmother, he ruled Roman lands."

"Perhaps," I said.

Then, the horse deigned to come to his whistle. Anyon warned me, "Now, he can be a difficult horse, Mordred, but if you speak in the Old Tongue to him, he will ride as if with wings. It is said of this Caradoc that he knows the heart's desire of his rider and will take him there. Lukat should have a horse like this. If you meet him again, you must let him ride Caradoc so that I might see my boy before too many seasons pass."

I smiled at this, thinking of Lukat upon this horse, and embraced his father, who also passed me some gold coins of the realms to the west "that I meant to give to my son, but he left too soon. You may use them as you wish. They have no worth to me, but where those armies draw near each other, gold speaks as if it were the wisest of men."

"I will bring the coins to Lukat," I told him and slipped the coins into that small leather pouch I kept hidden within my shirt.

Then, I mounted Caradoc, patting him lightly along the neck and crest. I whispered to him, as best I could, in those few words that I knew from the Eponi, which simply said "Let us ride, my friend," or so I thought.

Instead, the horse took off at a gallop, and I lost my hold of him and had to wrap my arms nearly about his throat as we went, for I feared I would be thrown. Yet the horse knew the paths well and rode out across the meadow and through the narrow fern path into the woods that grew thick and verdant. When we came upon a stream, Caradoc made a leap over it, and I flew from his back.

I landed along the muddy bank, and the horse slowed down a bit farther up the path, while I slowly pushed myself up.

I had not been hurt, though my spirit was bruised. "I may be thrown from my home," I said to the horse as I approached it, "but I will not be thrown from my horse. But then, you are not truly my horse. Yet."

I went before the animal and looked at its eyes, which seemed intelligent for one so brutish. "We must come to an understanding, Caradoc. You carry me where I wish, and I shall make sure you have apples before the day is through. Understood?" I then tried to say this in the Eponi tongue, which was so rarely spoken that even Lukat had only known a few phrases.

As I watched the horse's eyes and he watched mine, we both seemed to calm a bit.

We wandered along the path, for I decided it best to walk awhile with my new mount in order to create trust between us.

I grew tired after a while, for I did not yet know where I would settle for the night. I knew I had to find a life somewhere, but I did not know how that would be. Nor did I care. I had reached a moment when I would let fate decide my course, for anything I had ever done to tamper with fate had turned to dust in my hands.

I mounted Caradoc again and this time asked that he take the path slowly. I thought of Lukat's father, telling me how this horse had magick and might carry me to my heart's desire. But I did not have to think long of what was in my heart—buried there, though I had not yet retrieved it—for Caradoc came upon that clearing I knew well, by the Fountain of Bel-Nemeton, and that rudely constructed turf home of the fallen knight called Lancelot.

Hearing the sound of the approaching horse, the man I had loved on sight emerged from behind the hide at the doorway. He stood there, looking at me upon the horse for a long time.

I felt my heart racing within my chest.

"I take it this is your horse," I finally said, breaking the silence.

"The son of my own horse," he said. "But this one is descended from a fine mare once stolen from—"

"From the Romans," I said, interrupting him. "I heard she was an empress of some kind."

"I named him Caradoc, for he is a horse I've loved since he was a colt. And the Eponi have cared for him when I have had to leave these places."

"A magickal horse," I said. "For I was told he leads us to our heart's desire."

Breaking this spell that I felt had come between us, Lancelot said, "I came to you in your fevers. But they would not let me in your chamber."

"I cannot say what has been between us can ever be mended," I said.

"And I cannot say that what has been between us has needed mending," he said.

He came over to me as I remained upon the horse. He stood at the horse's neck and looked up at me. Perhaps the want of him had driven my senses to imagine things, but this man before me seemed even more beautiful than he had when we'd first shared each other by the stream. I knew it was not the physical beauty of him, for much was hidden beneath his trousers and tunic, and his face was clouded with shadow as if he had not slept many nights or eaten enough for want of something missing—it was that beauty we endow those to whom we have brought into our hearts, and that beauty does not lessen if our hearts remain open and yet full.

But I could not then trust my instincts, nor did I want to feel that same pain I had felt with wanting him, with aching for his presence, his touch, the permission I had felt that Midsummer's Night to hold him. I did not seek for that feeling of horror when I was separated from him for so long.

"No," I said. "I cannot return to this. I have no love in my heart."

He looked up at me, his hair falling across his face as it did too often, for it needed cutting. Then, he reached up to draw me off the stallion.

"No, please," I whispered but had no resistance as his arms went around my waist. "No." But I found myself reaching for him as well, and he brought me down from Caradoc, and we embraced even while I murmured to him, "I hate you. I hate you. I hate you more than all men in the world. I hate the world. I hate you. I hate all of it."

"I know," he whispered, holding me tight, the warmth moving as if in the vessels between us, mingling, breaking down my own vessel as I returned the kisses he passed to me.

6

And so, that end of summer and early autumn I spent with the man I had loved once and had begun loving again. We broke those stone walls we had each built between us, though he slept those first few nights upon the floor of his hovel, for he did not wish to share his bed with me until I offered myself to him without question in my heart. Yet my heart had melted, and on the fourth night of my stay, I drew him up beside me and we enjoyed those pleasures that had passed too quickly earlier that summer. They no longer felt like the frivolous lusts of youth but of wanting to truly bind with each other, to wrap ourselves around the other. And yet, my body did the happy work of this with his, and though I would compare it to a wonderful dance, it felt more as if we wished to vessel into each other again and to never leave the other once there.

Yet I could still not open completely to him as lovers are meant to, for I had drunk too much from that cup of sorrow that my mother's death had brought.

We hid much in those months, living as hunters together in the woods, trading some of our catches with the Eponi for the fish they caught in their weirs and for salted mutton when we needed it, as well as woolen blankets as the weather turned to an early chill before the festival of Samhain.

During this time, he did not speak much of his past, nor I of mine, and I remember it years later as an idyll we had there in the forest, away from the caverns of the Isle of Glass, though the shadows of the summer continued to haunt us both.

And yet even this seemed to bring us closer, for what was unspoken between us seemed to grow in the shadows of the woods. We were pretending for a while. Pretending that the world beyond that small home did not hold sway or require anything from us. We pretended that the wars of the Saxons and the Britons were on that other isle, Britannia, while we, in the Little Britannia of Armorica, were safe and removed from it. We lived in that place between waking and dream, and I did not want it to end, although I knew—and he knew—that it would. I could not even bring myself to ask Lancelot of my father, of what he had been like as a boy, of what he had become as a young king. I felt to do this would be to risk losing that game of pretend we shared, that false sense of peace there in that place, in the warmth of our bed.

That dream.

The dream shattered and the idyll ended when the news came to us from a sword-forge named Culain, with whom we traded that the Roman princess Guinevere had begun the journey across Gaul, for she had reached her marriage age, and she would go to meet the high-king before the winter solstice had begun that they might be married at Christ-Mass at the court of Camelot.

But this echo of the past in the present had not startled me from what I had discovered with Lancelot. It was the rumors that had begun about Morgause and why all of us who lived in Broceliande had much to fear from her now. It was said that she had entombed Merlin, alive.

Chapter Fifteen

1

After she had deceived me, nearly to the point of my own death, Morgause had left the Isle of Glass. It was known that she had gone to sleep among the standing stones, those hunters had been turned to rock when quarrying the Stag of Arawn. She had been seen wearing the skins of wild animals and had begun wandering in the night like a madwoman. When one of the charioteers tried to help her in some small way, she had nearly torn the unfortunate soul to pieces as if she were possessed of terrible furies. Her madness as she wandered near the grove had kept even the Druids from their worship, for they had begun to fear her.

But what no one knew we would learn soon enough, which was something that even Viviane had not seen in any scrying of the future.

I could not believe that she could have power over Merlin or that he would not have called to me if he had needed help in any way.

As soon as I heard the news, Lancelot and I prepared the horses. I mounted Caradoc and raced ahead of him to reach the standing stones at the edge of the grove.

2

When I reached that sacred place, I saw the destruction that Morgause had brought about. The graves of those Roman soldiers who had been swallowed by the earth centuries before had been torn up, and their bones thrown about as if wolves had dug them up.

The standing stones themselves had fallen to the ground, some of them smashed into pebbles as if a giant child had kicked them over.

"What magick does she possess?" Lancelot asked, as we stood there among the Druids and the priestesses of the isle who had gathered about and silently watched the area.

"She is of two worlds," I said. "I do not think even Merlin understood the power she had brought with her from Annwn."

When I saw Viviane sitting along a fallen stone, I went to her and got down on one knee. "Where is he?"

She looked at me at first as if she did not recognize me. And then, when she nodded as if confirming my name for herself, she muttered, "A terrible thing has come to pass. A terrible curse upon us. I would believe this of many others but not of Morgause."

Viviane pointed to a pile of the stones with a long, flat stone across the top of it like an altar stone of the ancients. This was the kind of tomb that would have been used before the Romans had come to raid the ancient burial places. The Druids had already drawn the body of Merlin from it, and laid him down upon the stone.

"Alive and yet not alive," Viviane muttered as if she had gone mad. "It is a sleeping death."

Lancelot had pressed his hands above Merlin's heart. "He still lives. I feel the slow beating of his heart." He looked up at me, hope in his face.

She looked up at me again as if she did not recognize me, and for a fleeting moment I wondered what enchantment she was under. "His soul cannot stay too long when the flesh is like this."

3

Merlin had not yet died, though he lay in a deep sleep from which he could not be awakened. For fear of moving him much, we laid furs down upon that stone table and put him upon them, wrapping him for warmth. All around, the Druids made fires within the pits of those emptied graves.

I sat with him all night, next to him, as he had been with me through my fevers. Lancelot covered me with blankets and brought mulled wine, which we shared by the firelight.

I could not leave Merlin's side. I tried to vessel into him, though each time I did, I felt a strange stinging at the back of my head. But I would begin again, simply with the words *Merlin, are you there?*

Before dawn broke, I felt something clutch at my fingers, though when I looked at my hand, no one touched me. And I heard his voice, vesseling back to me. *Yes, whelp. I am still here.*

4

Merlin vesseled through the night, bringing me much comfort. He was no longer in his body but roamed as if dead, and showed me in my dreams that night of what Morgause had done. I saw her, half of her long flowing hair a pure white and the other half dark as midnight. She had used a power unknown to even Merlin to raise up those dead Romans who had been buried alive at this place. *She brought forth several of them, daemon spirits whose souls had charred as if burnt with fire elementals. These are the worst of those ancient warriors,* he whispered to me. *For the graves you see are but the beginnings of deep tunnels of the dead. These are wandering souls who have waited for a priestess of Death, and she calls them. I began the ceremony of unmaking this terrible magick, but to do it, I had to venture to other realms. Using the Arts she learned in the Otherworld, sshe trapped my flesh, so that I might not rise up against her.*

But where are you? I asked him.

I have taught you of the realms—you have seen the Otherworld and this world and the world of dreams. Now I will tell you that each is a lie. There is only one realm, and these divisions are the limits of the mind. I

am here but not here in my body. *I may vessel, for I am within the energies between us.*

Like water from the vessel, I said. The soul itself. The energy of the
soul.

All that flows will flow again, he responded.

What might I do to bring you back into your flesh?

*I am afraid that will take too much time, whelp. The rituals may
take days. You must go, Mordred. You must go and use the Art to keep
Guinevere safe.*

But, I vesseled, *Morgause cannot take life. For if she has blood upon
her hands, she will pass into the Land of the Dead.*

*She is more clever than that, Mordred. She will do no killing. Those who
are dead will possess the soldiers who bring the princess to the high-king.
The very men who are her most trusted servants will do this deed, Mordred.
I have seen this, for Morgause laughed as she bound me in this death sleep
and told me of all that she would do to destroy the kingdoms that Arthur had
united. It is Guinevere's own guards who will accept the stain of blood, for the
spirits who use them know that innocent blood will free them from this slavery. Guinevere may never see the port of Lyonesse or the palace at Camelot.
Though you do not know your father, still you cannot turn your back upon
this lady who is innocent to these storms that Morgause brings.*

Merlin, this Guinevere, *though innocent of all this, will bring with
her the end of Broceliande. Her bride's price, demanded by her father, is
the entire land of Armorica and the southern mountains as well.*

Whelp! He shouted in my mind so that it hurt a bit. *You cannot think
of claims on land when the cup is passed to you. Either you drink from
life—and serve it—or you destroy it as Morgause does. You either serve
Morgause or you serve the Art itself. Which is it to be?*

I did not need to answer.

How can the dead be fought? I asked him but received no reply.
Still, I felt his breath upon my hand and took heart that he had called
me *whelp* through the night. *How can I raise an army this day to fight
the dead?*

The slight beating of his heart was enough to bring me hope.

You do not need an army, Mordred. You have the Art. Do not forget what I told you once of the elementals all around us.

The fey?

The energies of the forest and streams but also of fire and air. These may be channeled as rivers are channeled that they might bring power.

I do not know enough of the Art, Merlin.

You know how to vessel yourself. That is enough. The world around you is a vessel; all life is contained within it.

Please, you must come with me.

I am afraid that the princess would be murdered ere my spirit returned to my flesh, whelp. You must save Guinevere, for she is the key to the door of your father's kingdom, and you are meant to find her. But I warn you of one thing—do not bring the knight Lancelot with you. This is your journey, and as you perform this task and face these spirits, you will begin to heal that cauldron which has been broken.

I asked him again, *How do I stop these daemon spirits?*

You cannot. Only the vessel of life can stop them. All you can do is slay the flesh that they occupy.

How will the vessel of life stop them?

I do not know. I only know that you must awaken the vessel that is around you so that these spirits can be drawn from those they possess. Morgause has invoked spirits of great strength. All you can do, Mordred, is keep them from killing Guinevere. You must trust that the vessel of life will pour from this and protect you. Or you must die.

His vesseling left a ringing in my ears, but at last he was silent.

At dawn, I slept, and when I awoke late in the day, Lancelot stood vigil beside me. When I looked up at him, it was as if I hadn't seen him before. Gone was my feeling of his beauty and striking presence. He was a man who had become a friend to me, and though I felt that love and its connection between us, I feared what I must do that afternoon without him. Without his protection. Without him keeping me from falling. Without him standing over me as I slept.

He crouched beside me, brushing my hair back, as it had flopped over my face. His face, though kind, seemed to be worn and somehow older than I'd remembered it. I saw flaws in it—the slight bump at his nose, as if he'd been in a fight once and had lost—the creases along his eyes, the stubble of beard that he had not yet shaved from his chin and upper lip. Dust had spread across his face in the night, and he was in need of a bath. And yet, I wanted to press my lips to his and take away the task I would face that day and night. "Are you rested?" he asked.

I smiled. "Somewhat."

"I heard the spirits of the dead before dawn," he said. "All around us. Perhaps I half slept and dreamt this, but it felt true. This is a restless place now. There is no peace here."

"Morgause lives in two worlds," I said. "She is a twinned soul and brings with her shadows."

"It is more than that," he said, glancing at the women who had brought the washing to the riverfall beyond the grove. "It is as if the Lady of the Lake no longer protects this place. Do you see? They feel it."

I looked about, at the horse-herd boys and the elders who returned to the caverns below after a day of labor in the fields.

"It is Samhain approaching," he said. "They feel they have been abandoned. The Druids do not sacrifice, nor do the priestesses scry the days to come. They cannot even mourn Merlin, for he is not dead, yet not living. It is this fear in the air. Morgause has brought it." He looked at me, steadily. "We have brought it. We must—"

I interrupted him. "I must leave here. Before dusk."

He looked at me, not understanding. "*We* will leave."

"No," I said. "This is something I must do alone." I did not understand then why Merlin felt it important for me to take no companion on my journey, nor why Lancelot should not meet this young Roman princess. But Merlin had trained me many years in his discipline, and though I had often ignored it as a boy, I could not do this as a man. Part of me even wished to let the princess die rather than risk my life for her, for what would she bring to Broceliande but soldiers and priests from her homelands? We had seen how Broceliande had been made smaller by the centuries of Roman occupation. To have a Roman chieftain become the king of this forest and its treasures seemed to be the worst fate ever brought to us.

But I felt, in my heart, that if I saved this maiden, if I rescued her from terrible trouble, she might grant that Broceliande would remain untouched and that the tribes of our people could remain within its boundaries without fear of Roman rule. It was, perhaps, a naive dream, but I had done so much to hurt those around me who had raised me on the Lake that I wished to make amends in some important way.

But as I spoke, Lancelot's eyes showed both anger and sadness. He shook his head slightly, and turned away for a moment as if gathering his thoughts. Then, he turned back to me, his eyes nearly burning with some inner fire. "All night I have stood watch and through the day. The caverns below us have changed, Mordred. The people here are changed. They fear where they had no fear before. You cannot expect me to remain behind while you pursue this...this *madness* alone. I have fought in battles. I have seen the rough magick of the Anthea and have cut the throat of more than one necromancer in my time. When I brought your father to that sword..." He hesitated, not wishing to tell me more.

"What did you see?" I asked.

"I saw my shame. I saw the light of Annwn itself in that sword. Reflected in it, I saw my own death," he said. "And it is not today, Mordred. It is not tonight that I will die."

When he said this, I felt thunderstruck by the revelation of it. "And my father saw his death as well?"

Lancelot nodded, keeping his eyes on me for my reaction.

"And I am the one who will kill him?" I asked.

"I could not tell from his manner," he said. "Only that he knew that his son would destroy him."

"His bastard," I said. "I know why Merlin does not wish for you to come with me. You are tainted by the sword Excalibur, Lancelot. You are cursed by that reflection you saw." I felt an icy chill in my heart, for I had given myself to the man who had aided my father, who had hunted my mother as if she were a doe running along the fields to be cut down, a child in its belly. My mind raced as a torment ached within me. "There was a knight, beloved of my father, who brought the guard down to search for Morgan le Fay. You were there in Tintagel when my mother and Merlin had to feel like criminals from that castle. You hunted her. You would have cut her throat while I grew inside her."

"It is my shame that I did so," he said, keeping his voice low. "You must believe that."

"You and I both have dishonored the Lady," I said. "You must stay here."

"That would be foolish," he said. His eyes softened slightly, and he whispered, "Do not keep me from this. Though you know the dishonor of my youth, your heart knows of my love for you."

He looked to me, then, like a man who had lost his dreams. Part of me wished to embrace him, and part of me wished to hate him. The alchemy of love is a mingling of confusion with flesh and soul, and I cannot fathom its depths, nor can I do more than journey with it. At that moment, I felt the ice chill of indifference and the resignation I had begun to feel in that idyll we had spent after my mother's passing—a new word to me, for I had heard it but had not understood it: guilt. I felt guilty for our crimes of passion, and for my mother's death and for this world that had begun unmaking itself around us. I had gone to Lancelot with the purity of love and the urgency of lust, but we had to separate now, because of the consequences of that mating. Yet I knew I loved him, for this is the curse of love: that it will bring about terrible things to those who find it, and yet, it is worse to have none at all.

By nightfall, I had mounted Caradoc, whose saddle and pommel had been draped with light provisions so as not to weigh him down. In the flickering shadows of evening torchlight, Lancelot approached me again, and when he saw that I meant to speak, he held his hand up for me to stop.

"I do not come to entreat you," he said. "I will be here waiting for your return, though I do not wish for you to take this dangerous journey alone." Then, he drew a small brooch from his collar. "This was a gift to me from your father. It is too dark to see what is engraved upon it, but it shows the red and white dragons of the pen-Dragon, and upon its curve is written, 'No subject of Arthur pen-Dragon, King of the Seven Kingdoms, shall harm the one who carries this.' It was given to me when I left his service. I give it to you now that it might protect you should you need it."

He passed it to me, and I leaned down, pressing my lips to his forehead. "I will return with it," I said. "If the gods are kind."

"I know," he replied.

I took the small brooch from him. It had a slightly curved hasp and a long, sharp point to its pin. The brooch itself was a metal disc with some inlaid filigree upon it. I carefully thrust it through the cloth at the neck of my cloak.

"And this, if you will accept it," he said. He drew from within the folds of his cloak a torque. The torque was once a symbol of our tribes, a collar made of twisted metal that all but met at its center. These were still worn, though they had become symbols of our slavery to Rome to those who lived before I was born and were out of fashion with many. Yet, this curved and twisted bracelet—for this originally was for his own upper arm—seemed beautiful to me as I held it in my hand.

"It is a symbol of my faith in you," he said. "As once it was given to me as a symbol of my purity, for you are the only pure thing in my life."

I could not see its design or what metal had been used to make it, but it felt light in my hands. "It is too big for my arm," I said. "But here." I slipped it behind my neck and pressed it so that its open end met my throat. It came to rest perfectly, nearly as if it were meant for my neck.

"Are you still my hunter?" he asked.

"As you are my stag," I said.

"May the wind be at your back and the gods in your sword," he said.

He watched me as I brought Caradoc around toward the path at the edge of the grove. I glanced back to him once. He stood there, a shadow among shadows, watching me go.

I leaned forward to the horse and whispered those few Ogham words I knew that might allow the horse to move swiftly along the forest paths. As the horse began to gallop, I passed that altar stone upon which Merlin lay. The Druids had covered his body with sirus branches and the bark of the willow, though his great painted face showed through. Seven priestesses of the Lady performed purification rituals with their cauldrons and prayers, the bright yellow of torches all around reminding me of the Glamour Lamentation of light among the elementals of the forest when my mother had begun her passage to death.

The high, sweet, yet infinitely sad songs of the young children of the Lake, singing the ancient songs for the safety of Merlin soul, seemed to rise above the trees and to move as if with wings along the darkening sky, following me with its pure sorrow.

Do not go yet into that night, I vesseled to Merlin, hoping he could hear me.

5

The Roman roads ran often in straight lines at the high ground through Broceliande. The villas and their growing towns—or those that were long abandoned—were off the roads, in clearings that either had been meadows once or were a result of years of cutting back at the forest. But I could not take these roads, which had begun falling into disrepair in my lifetime. Instead, I stuck to the spiderwebbed narrow paths of the forest and marshes, those thin ways between bogs and along streambeds that I could identify by those markings left by our tribes, for alders and birches often were planted near them, and if in a straight row, I would know the path as one of our forest highways.

These were not as sophisticated as the Roman's brilliantly laid out roads, but they were shortcuts through the endless forest that outsiders had never learned to master.

The crisp chill of an early autumn was in the air, and riding so fast—for Caradoc had wings upon his hooves, it seemed—made it that much colder for me, as if we flew through an icy wind. Caradoc knew these paths by instinct or luck, and though I kept my body low to his neck and shoulders, out of fear of branches, he carried me safely along the way.

And then, suddenly, I felt a sharp stabbing just behind my left ear, and I nearly let go off the reins with the pain of it. But it was Merlin's voice, vesseling at that great distance to me. *It is too late,* his voice seemed feeble and weak. *Guinevere has fallen. The murderous spirits have taken over her most trusted guards. You must hurry. You must use the vessel itself, Mordred. The vessel.*

6

Though my horse kept moving at a swift gallop, it was if things slowed for me in my mind and vision. I could see light in the forest where they hadn't been any, as if moonlight itself were a being that did not come from above but from beneath the ground in a steam from the bogs. Merlin continued to vessel into me. *This is the final lesson of that Art called vesseling, whelp. You must heed this, for I may not speak within you long. The soul within my body longs for its journey, and I cannot hold it for many more hours. The cauldron of Rebirth is the physical vessel of making and unmaking. But the vessel of the goddess is all around you, and as your flesh gives of this halo that become the vessel, all sentient creatures do as well. The water, the rocks, those elementals, it is the source of life itself, within the greatest vessel. Imagine you are in a river, and you must divert its flow with your body. You raise your arms. You push with your legs. You create new channels for that river to flow. So the vessel is there, and it is only to be used with the Art. You may not use this as if you are a sorcerer from Ravenna. Even I have only tapped into the vessel's power once or twice in this current lifetime. But it is important that the maiden you seek reach the shores of Britain unharmed. Men have grown drunk with the invisible flow of the vessel, Mordred. You must resist its pull, for once you feel it, you will wish for more of it.*

While he spoke, I saw evidence all around me of this vessel in this slowness of time that made it seem as if Caradoc's hooves only touched the ground every few moments, and the world around us froze and yet moved slowly. I saw light as I had never seen it in the night: colors of yellow and green and blue and a deep violet haze, all of it flowing like a watery mist, almost as if I were riding that horse slowly through the bottom of the Lake of Glass and all else moved in a stream around us.

Life, Merlin told me, *is painted upon the vessel, and its source flows from within it. The vessel and the cauldron are one, and the Art is there to control the flow of the vessel in times of great trouble. Though it does not seem it, this is one of those dangerous times, whelp, and I wish you were not the one to drink at its cup. But you must, for I cannot, and you are a greater student of this Art than any youth I have ever known. Morgause has damaged my final soul, and I allow it to flee this body, for I am bound and settled here. Do not ever forget that though you will be faced with trials and dangers, the flow of life is meant to be protected from those who do not trust the gods themselves.*

And then his voice went silent, and the world returned to what it had been moments before: the light faded into darkness, and I rode upon my horse that moved swiftly as time resumed its normal pace. As if guided by Merlin himself, Caradoc began to slow as we reached a northeastern edge of the woods that encircled a generous sward, a circle of grassland that had been a perfect camp for the future queen's retinue.

And then I saw one of the most terrifying things I have ever before seen. I knew the stories of Roman punishments from my teachings, but never imagined that I would see this: Torches nearly as tall as men lit the clearing, as if to display the handiwork of those servants of Morgause. Each torch had bounded to it at its base a soldier bounded to it, blackened with pitch, so that when the torch burned down the staff, it would continue burning the flesh of the dead man beneath it.

From the edge of the sward to its center, along any low trees there, soldiers had been stripped to a cloth that was wound about their loins and were crucified along crossed branches of the trees. Great spikes had been nailed at their wrists, and their arms and legs were bound with thick cords. Some of them had been used as a kind of dagger practice; others had spears piercing their sides and chests and faces; still others had been burnt by torches. They had many stab wounds in their bodies, and the surrounding trees were spattered crimson black with blood, and the roots soaked with it.

It was the old Roman punishment, done in a way that shocked me from the level of innocence I had before seeing it. I had not been able to imagine absolute evil, nor did I believe it existed. I had been taught by the elders that all in nature was good, but it was obvious to me that evil existed as well, for these acts against these dead men evoked horror and pity within me. My life before this moment, for whatever trouble there had been, whatever tragic sorrow I had felt in my mother's death, was a pale flickering from a candle when compared to the enormity of this unspeakable act before me. It was like a pageant of human savagery.

The enormity of it—of seeing twenty-five men thus bound and wounded, all of them dead from arrows shot into them as they hung there—took my breath away.

Merlin had been right. I was too late for Guinevere.

The remnants of a camp had been torn down as if by savage beasts, and scaffolding had been erected at the center of the ring of the crucified. I did not recognize immediately what this small stage might be, but I could guess it: those spirits who had invaded the flesh of Guinevere's guardians intended to torture her in some way, if they had not already finished with her.

I tried to remember all Merlin had taught me of the Arts—whether of vesseling or raveling; or of that summer in my childhood when he taught me the forms of using the sword with that "dragon memory," which was of the earth and its power, and of the prayer of calling wind, though this might not be answered; or the whistle one might make to call wolves of the forest, though these might bring danger to one's side as well as to the enemy.

I hoped to hear Merlin's voice reassuring me, but I had begun to fear that he had left the world. I had no time for grief. No time for reflection any longer.

There was a gathering about the stage, and the men there held something high above their heads, something wrapped in linens and fur. I could only guess what this might be.

It was Guinevere herself, bound.

As I dismounted Caradoc, leading him off the path through the tangle of dried vines, I moved closer to the edge of the trees to see what these creatures had planned. Yet, it was eerily silent, as if they could not speak at all and as if the feet of the men they'd possessed did not make a sound when touching the dried leaves that had begun to fall along the meadow.

Though I say "creatures," these were men who had the thin, beaky looks of the Gallic races. They wore the armor of guards, and I counted nearly twenty-three of them gathered around that stage that was no stage but a funeral pyre.

I guessed what they planned: They would tie her to that bed of thorns and brambles they had gathered, and set her ablaze while she lived.

Merlin, I vesseled. *Merlin, come to me.*

I waited but seconds, completely alone with my horse and needing to face twenty-three men possessed by the wandering spirits, who are the hungriest of ghosts, for they eat the souls of others for sustenance.

I remembered what Merlin had told me before his voice had died away:

The vessel of the goddess is all around you, and as your flesh gives of this halo that become the vessel, all sentient creatures do as well. The water, the rocks, those elementals, it is the source of life itself, within the

*greatest vessel. Imagine you are in a river, and you must divert its flow
with your body. You raise your arms. You push with your legs. You create
new channels for that river to flow.*

So, I thought: *Imagine you are in a river. Imagine this. Imagine the
elementals themselves.*

I glanced among the trees—the oaks that twisted and grew from
great rock, the rowans, the crack willow, the alders, the hawthorn along
the sedge of the bog not far away, the ash trees that clumped together
on the other side of the meadow, even the blackthorn brambles along
the periphery of the camp—all of them sacred to the Druids, sacred of
the grove. These had the vesseling within them, as did the fern and ivy
that grew thick and that bog cabbage that had reached its peak not a
month earlier. The rocks themselves and the water of the bog and of the
rill and stream over which we'd passed along the forest path.

The elementals are of fire, air, water, and earth.

I did not know how I would do this, but I knew I must try. I slowly
unsheathed my sword, raising it up first to the sky above and then
thrusting it into the moss at my feet. I called with my mind to that great
dragon which slept within the earth that it might bless my blade. I whispered aloud, "I am Mordred, son of the high-king Arthur pen-Dragon,
whose line descends from your brethren. I am here to protect Arthur's
bride. Bless this sword that it might protect her."

Then, I raised the sword again into the air and whispered, "I am
Mordred, son of Morgan of the Fay, who lives as a twinned soul in the
flesh with her sister Morgause. You spirits of the air who lamented my
mother's passing, I ask you to bless this blade that it will protect me."

I felt nothing then, and wondered if such prayers were foolish rituals
that might make one feel strong and yet confer nothing of magick.

Life itself is a vessel.

Merlin had once said to me when I was a boy, "*Somewhere
between where I sit and where you sit, our essence has been poured into
a vessel.*"

I glanced at the trees, at the bog, at the moss and vines near my feet.

There was no time for this.

"Caradoc," I patted my horse, whispering in his ear. "We must do this now."

At the pyre, they had unwrapped the princess, and she lay upon the brambles. The men began wrapping rope about her as she struggled against them. She wore a white gown that caught the torchlight as if it were made of jewels, and I could see what might have been dark blood mixed across her golden hair.

I mounted Caradoc, holding my sword up, and just as I was about to give him a tap with my heels, I felt the change around me.

I felt the vessel.

Again the world slowed. The strange lights came up as if emanating from the trees themselves, as if each had a soul of light within that radiated outward. The bog seemed to be a sunburst that lay upon the earth, and the rocks nearby of that violet color shifted as if alive.

In that slowness of time, I began moving forward, and though I went slowly and the Caradoc moved as if against a quicksand of air, I felt those elementals follow me, as if the light from the oaks outstretched like hands from the branches, as if a thousand cords made of color moved with me.

Even those monstrous torches that encircled the sward emitted light that stretched and discolored into a black light, for the fire elementals could not be held back by Morgause's enchantments.

For a moment, I looked back, and instead of mere light, it seemed as if a great creature, taller than the trees, rose up behind me. Its wings spread outward, its claws gleaming in the moonlight, the twisted horns upon its head like brambles themselves.

I saw for that moment the Dragon that had been seen by the ancients. The Dragon that protected us. The Dragon that was our earth.

And then, I saw only the darkening trees.

Time had begun moving more swiftly, and I was flung forward into it. Caradoc charged onto the grass, his hoofbeats thunderous. I could not be certain, but it was as if my horse were possessed of those elemental spirits that had reached for us. My ears only heard the booming of some distant night surf, but my mouth was open in a war cry though I had never heard one before.

The demon-guards had turned to look at me and did not at first know what to make of this attack upon them. They drew their swords, and two of them leapt as if they were lizards upon the bier where Guinevere struggled against her ropes.

Still others came running at me with sword and spear, and yet I did not feel fear at that moment. I did not think death would take me, for I knew that prophecy of my father's own death: if his bastard son were to take his life one day, and if I were his only bastard, then surely this would not be the night I was meant to die.

The first of the guards reached me, and I slashed my sword downward, hacking deep into the shoulder of one. Caradoc turned, nearly spinning, as if born to battles such as this; I brought the sword back from the man I'd cut down and rammed it into the throat of the other as he came at me, nearly leaping to my horse to take me. Still others came to me, and my mind did not seem to work anymore, but my limbs knew what to do and I thought I really was underwater for it was as if some channel brushed against me, and I felt an energy greater than my own direct my arm as I thrust my blade deep into a man's chest and then tore up to his chin. As I did this, Caradoc moved easily and did not rear up as I thought he might. In the faces of these guards, I saw that green-yellow of marsh light I had seen in Annwn on my raveled journey. These wandering spirits were clinging to the flesh of these guards, who were already dead when I cut them down.

All but two of the guards had abandoned the pyre, and it felt to me as if they multiplied before me. They made no sound, though their mouths opened in what seemed like shrieks of agony, and those I had cut down rose up again, though some were hacked through with my sword. I had not noticed my own wounds, for something did protect me there, some amulet that I did not know I possessed, but one of these demon-spirits had pressed a blade deep beneath my right arm, another had slashed at my left leg.

Finally, I had to leap from Caradoc or risk the horse being swarmed by these creatures whom death did not seem to take. When I reached the ground, I jabbed upward with my sword into oncoming flesh. As I rose up, I saw that there would be little hope.

I had no time to marshal my ability to vessel, nor was I still clear about how this might come about, though I did not doubt the power of it. And then, I heard the sound of a distant horn, as of the kind used for battle. The daemon spirits drew back from me, and with me turned in the direction of the sound.

There, coming from the forest, the light of torches with them, was what seemed an army of fifteen or so men on horseback.

J

As they charged into the light within the sward, I recognized them, for they did not wear armor or carry shield. These were young Eponi horsemen, wearing only the traditional trouser of the Eponi warrior, their chests bare and gleaming with the oil they used for their war ceremonies. I knew many of these young men from childhood, and I could not fathom how they had found me. And leading them, upon his mottled horse, Druid, in full armor, brandishing a long sword before him to lead the charge, was Lancelot, his helmet drawn back, an axe in his other hand, as his knees pressed into Druid's flanks so that he could fight with both hands.

I thrust my sword deep into the gut of a demon-spirit near me, and soon my countrymen were with me, slaughtering the demons, though they nearly flew at us. I soon found that by severing the head from the body would stop the demon-spirits from reviving and so shouted man to man, "Take their heads and they will perish!"

I cannot speak too much of this carnage, for it was bloody and long as we fought them, and soaked as I was with the blood of the flesh, I sent six of the demon-spirits back to their darkness.

Still, none had reached the pyre, and I saw that one of the creatures crouched upon Guinevere's stomach and leaned forward over her face as if taunting her. In his hand, a twisted and thorny bramble for kindling, burning at its uppermost tip.

I raced toward him but did not think I could make it in time for the fire to be put out.

As I ran, I vesseled as best I could, and the slowness of things began again, and the light of the elementals came up for me. This light sliced between the bodies of men in their fight, with a sword thrust into a shoulder or a spear cutting into a leg, and it was like a holy light from the Lady herself, for it seemed the light of the sun cutting through the waters of the Lake of Glass.

I vesseled all that I could, and what words formed from me were *Fire, free yourself from the hand that holds you.*

Again, time moved swiftly; that unearthly light gone. I had nearly reached that stage upon which the princess lay, when the kindling branch's fire caught to bright and seemed to burst and jump to the demon-spirit's face, and burning, it fell backward, into the kindling that had been laid for Guinevere herself.

I had nearly reached her when one of the Eponi youth, a dark-haired man whose name was Malon, leapt forward, and in his face, I saw yet another green-yellow aura of the demon-spirit.

They were not passing out of the flesh of those guards at death. They were jumping. Jumping into our own men.

Malon brought up a bloodied spear that still held the skeins of flesh of those he had killed. He grinned as if he were a wolf, and his eyes gleamed a sickly yellow. He seemed to be speaking to me yet was mute. I felt sick in the pit of my stomach that I would have to fight and kill one of my own tribe. Behind him, I saw the burning body of the demon-spirit as it lit the lower kindling that lay in circles of brambles just beneath the maiden I had come to rescue from this fate.

I had a sword in one hand and a dagger in the other. As I stared at my opponent, who had been fighting with me seconds before, I knew that I had to kill him. And even in killing him, that yellow-green spirit within him would leap into the body of another. Was this man already dead before me? I could not be sure, and I felt that trembling fear that I would cut down my brethren for this foreign woman's life. I would cut down a comrade-at-arms who had been willing to ignore the law of the tribes and lay down his life for my own and for this future queen of a distant and indifferent high-king.

And worse, if I did not kill him, he would surely run his spear through me until his hands, curved in tight fists at the base of the spear, were close to my heart.

"You are commanded by Morgause of Orkney," I snarled at him. "But she has led you into another hell."

Malon's grin broadened, and I saw blood along his teeth. He snapped his jaws open, and I saw that spirit light come from within his mouth like the mist of a bog in winter. He jabbed his spear toward me, and I leapt backward. I glanced quickly to my left and saw Lancelot also facing three of our own Eponi horsemen.

The vessel of life is the only thing that can stop these demon-spirits.

What is the vessel of life?

I thrust my sword and hacked against his shoulder blade, but Malon dodged this blow, again giving me that feeling that this was a lizard and not a man, for his bones did not seem to crack and his movements were fluid and snakelike.

I began to hear the cries of the Eponi as they were cut down by their own, possessed now by these spirits. And then, a new light came up at the edge of the treetops. It was not unearthly at all, but it moved more swiftly than I could recall that it had ever moved before. It was the sunlight itself, and its violet rays passed like a warm hand across the darkening sky of dawn—yes, dawn, though it seemed hours early for it.

As I ducked and rolled to the earth to avoid Malon's spear, I felt that vessel of life, that flow of water that was not water at all. This was the vessel that Merlin had spoken of. The sunlight itself had been born too early that day and had been called not by any Art I knew to draw it from its resting place. These were creatures of night who feared that great sunlight, for their power would be much diminished; and though they might return at dawn, they had no power with the coming of the disc of the sun.

The slowing of time returned to me, and I felt that surge of power from those elementals around us: from the fire of torches, from the breeze, from those strange and wonderful colors that grew out from the trees and the grass and the earth itself.

For just a moment, I saw these terrible swarms of things, buzzing and moving as if with one mind between them, dodging the light of the elementals as they reached for them. And for just a moment I saw her there, within the light.

8

I saw the vague form of that nameless goddess whose painting had adorned the cavern walls at the far shore of the Lake of Glass, that Lady whose cauldron of Rebirth I had stolen, whose people I had betrayed through this. And yet I felt her presence though her face was invisible to me. And yet, this was her face: the forest light and the fire and the wind and the rain that began falling.

Her face was all.

Time returned swiftly, as it had earlier, but I felt her there, the Lady of the Lake, come to me, perhaps called by Merlin to aid me in this or perhaps called by my own vesseling.

As soon as I moved again in real time, I felt I had lost something with the returning darkness. Perhaps that ability to tap into the vessel of life. I could not be sure. But the surge of power within me had abandoned me, as if I had asked too much of the vessel this night.

9

Malon fell before me, and as he touched the ground, I saw that spirit of corruption rise out of his flesh, its vulpine jaws spreading wide as if in a scream of agony, and then it broke into a thousand tiny bits, like locusts, swarming as it rose to meet the other swarms rising from the bodies of the men who had become possessed.

Malon's eyes opened, though he did not seem to be well revived.

But there was no time left. The pyre had begun burning, and the white shining dress of that princess had already caught the flame.

10

I leapt upon that bier and, using my dagger, sliced through the ropes binding that fair lady for whom many had risked—and lost—their lives. Though her mouth was bound with strips of cloth, her eyes, full of terror, were opened wide and pleading with me.

The fires were around her, and I called again to the fire to leap away, but whatever of the Art I had possessed no longer seemed to work. Magick would not put out these flames. I dropped my sword and dagger, and drew her up, her long dress burning. With her in my arms, I jumped to the earth, and rolled with her in that dirt and grass until the edges of her dress were ash and it had torn along her legs and shoulders, though she did not have burns upon her skin.

I drew off those cloths that had gagged her, and saw in that instant her delicate beauty that was so unlike that of the Britons.

She looked up at me and whispered in the frail voice of one who has spent a night in the camp of terror, "I owe you my life. Who are you?"

"Mordred, my lady," I said but did not wish to mention my parentage for fear of exposure.

"I am in your service, Mordred, and all that is mine shall be yours." Her voice faltered as she spoke. "I will never forget that it was you who brought me from the fire."

As I lifted her into my arms for her comfort, I saw in the sky above us that there had been no sunrise at all. Darkness surrounded the torches.

What sunlight I had seen had been illusion. Had this been Merlin's last gift to me through the Art? I did not know. Had this been the vessel itself?

The vessel of life had brought us the illusion of the sun that the demon-spirits might flee this place. I had seen them in that false dawn, rising from the bodies of our men, becoming like a swarm of locusts in the sky, moving ever upward, drawn away from this place and the illusion of the sun's rays that reached for them.

I felt an overwhelming sense of the sacred here, at this place, and it brought tears to my eyes as if a great loss had taken place. A loss beyond any I had known or felt and yet in that loss, a lightening of my own spirit within me.

It was as if, for a moment, the mask of the goddess had been removed, and I had felt a touch of the source of existence that drew my thoughts from this battle, from this maiden, from this clearing within the forest.

Chapter Sixteen

1

After I had made sure that two of the Eponi protected Guinevere,
I searched among the wounded and dead for Lancelot. When I found
him, sheathing his sword and turning about as if searching for someone
himself, he gasped when he saw me. His armor was half-torn from him,
for the demon-spirits had attacked him with great ferocity, but he was
unharmed. He looked over at me, and I at him. At a distance of several
feet, I said, "I asked you to stay."

"I stayed," he said. "With you."

"Those spirits will return if they can," I said, putting aside my other
concerns. "It is the dawn they fear."

"The dawn will come soon," he said. "And your wounds need binding. Viviane sent me away with salves for those wounded here."

2

Even as Lancelot rubbed the salve across my back and shoulders,
wrapping my wounds with thin strips of cloth that had been soaked by
Viviane and the priestesses in hawk-leaf, which sped up the healing
process and rarely allowed the wound to fester, I felt an uncomfortable
distance between us, as if we were thousands of leagues apart rather
than close enough to reach the other with just a few steps forward.

"Morgause will not rest with this princess alive here," I said, when he was done and the last of the salve had been rubbed along my thighs, where they'd been slashed only slightly. The soreness went away as soon as he had smeared the healing grease over my skin.

"We must hurry then," he said. "Come here. Help me with my armor, for I have no need of it if we are to fly."

I went to him and began to help remove the breastplate that had received blows to it, though it had not been penetrated.

He took my hand in his and brought it to his lips. He looked at me carefully and said, "I am sorry that I did not listen to you."

I turned my palm upward as he kissed it and reached beneath his chin to draw his face up to mine. "I would be sorry if you had," I said.

2

Fearing Morgause and the spirits she commanded, I mounted my horse and slid the princess on behind me. "Hold tight to me," I said. "For we must ride as if chased by the sunrise itself."

"What of these men?" she asked, glancing at the Eponi, some of whom still tended to the wounded among them.

"They know the way to their home," I said. "But you are in danger still. We must fly."

Lancelot had been checking on the Eponi, some of whom had died in this battle, most of whom were wounded. Then, he mounted his horse, Druid, and joined us. "We ride for the coast, my lady," he said, a sidelong glance to Guinevere.

I heard her sweet voice against my ear as she said, "The knight who is your lover is a beautiful man. You are lucky, sir."

I took this in stride and glanced over at Lancelot, nodding to him as our horses began galloping toward the forest path again that we might make it to the sea before the next nightfall.

We rode hard that day and did not stop at the Isle of Glass and its caverns, though I longed to find out if Merlin had survived the night. But Guinevere would not be well received by the tribes, and Morgause might bring her fury down upon those we loved there if she knew they hid the princess.

We reached the marshes by the Dragon's Mount too late to hire a boatman; however, Guinevere had jewels, which she passed to a fisherman, and so bought a small boat that was barely serviceable with two oars, no sail, and of a size that would not balance should one of us stand.

The channel seemed calm that night, so we hoped for the best.

3

And so, my lover Lancelot and I carried that fair maiden Guinevere across the marshes, hooking our hands together beneath her that she might ride without her beautiful feet touching the waters. Over the rise of the Dragon's Mount, the fires had been lit to signal our boat's safe passage from the coast. Twilight had descended into a shadowy night.

She laughed and whispered to me as I set her down in the small boat well beneath her means and station, "I owe you so much. When I am queen, I will make sure that your every wish is granted."

"You do not need to make such promises," I said.

"Do not question the gift," she said tenderly. "For you have done more for me in one night than any have done for me in my lifetime."

I kissed her lightly on her cheek as she said this. As I did so, I glanced over at Lancelot, who watched me as if he did not like anything I had begun doing since finding the princess.

"Is it wise to leave tonight?" she asked as we pushed off from the strand through the tidal pools.

"If you wish to stay and see if the darkness brings more of what we saw last night, then be my guest, my lady," Lancelot said. He glanced at me, a look that seemed irritated, and turned, reaching for an oar. We were all three exhausted from lack of sleep, and he and I knew we'd be up most of the night, rowing.

"We might find another boat by dawn," she said sweetly. "You need rest. Both of you."

"We will rest when we reach the far shore," I said, although I longed for a few hours of rest.

"I'm sure those horrible devils won't find us." She fingered the small pendant at her throat, an amulet of her religion. "I am sure I will be safe."

I leaned over toward Lancelot and touched his shoulder that he might know how I longed for that simpler day when we could ride our horses along the path. Yet our lives had changed so rapidly, in such a short season. He shot me a glance that was half a flash of anger and half of what seemed to me longing, though this might have been my imagination. In my mind, I wished we could be back at that thatched-roof house by the fountain, not knowing each other's name, not knowing the places we'd come from that had brought us into that knot of destiny.

I looked over at Guinevere, with her soft-rounded eyes, and that sweetness that maidens possessed—that no doubt my mother and Morgause had once had when innocent hopes were still theirs. She was not yet eighteen, and she would marry my father though she did not know of my relation to him. My deceit did not seem so terrible to me then as I rowed, for I could comfort myself with the knowledge that I was helping my father. I would bring him his betrothed in safety. I would bring him his lost friend, Lancelot, who had lived in sorrow for many years, separated from his beloved king and in anguish from the part he'd played in bringing Arthur into the secrets of the labyrinth itself.

My past seemed one of sorrow, and I could not remember the intense happiness I had once felt for the Lake of Glass or its nameless Lady. When my mother's face passed across my mind like a cloud across the sun, I remembered her tragedy too easily and not her life. When I thought of Morgause, all I saw was the vengeful fury of her face and not the kindness and gentleness she'd brought to my childhood.

The past was a place that I could no longer visit; the future, ahead of us, lay across the narrow sea from Armorica to Britannia.

I had great hope then, watching this maiden with her happy expectation for the future as well as her fear of what marriage to a Briton king might mean seeing my beloved beside me, both of us turning the oars as if we had always been boatmen, though I had never manned a boat except on the Lake of Glass itself. I felt as if my boyhood friend Lukat were there beside me and Guinevere his beloved, Melisse, and it was some long-ago day of summer when we rowed to the far shore of the Lake to look at the ancient paintings. I offered a smile to Guinevere as she passed me a waterskin for drinking.

"When you grow tired, try and sleep so that when we arrive tomorrow, you will look as radiant as you do at this moment," I told her.

"Will it be so long? All night?" she asked.

Lancelot grumbled, "Perhaps longer. We have no sail, and should the sea turn rough, we cannot know if we will even make it."

Out in that channel, the water seemed unnaturally calm. "A storm may come," Lancelot said, glancing at the sky. "Though I do not see other signs of it."

"The sea is like a lake," Guinevere said. "It is beautiful."

"When it grows calm like this, my lady," Lancelot said, "It sometimes heralds an approaching gale."

"You both are too kind to me," she said. She had won me over with her person, for she was not the pretentious Roman royal lady I had half expected, nor was she a spoiled little girl whose father had sold her for land. I quite liked her, and the touch of her hand brought a strange and wonderful thrill to me.

Warmth came into her face, that same tenderness that had won me over when we found her. She offered to take Lancelot's oar that she might row the night rather than make him suffer that pain. He grumbled at her touch upon his hand and looked off to the northern sky, pretending to gauge the weather by the drifting dark clouds across the star-strewn heavens.

"You ask much of us, my lady," he said.

"I will ensure that any wrong done against you, sir, will be redressed. I promise you that any past charges of crimes brought against you shall be pardoned and you both shall be paid handsomely for having saved me from those phantoms of the dark wood."

He did not look at her as she spoke but kept watch of the sky. "See?" he said, pointing to starboard. "The taranis crows gather in those clouds. A storm will come, whether at sea or inland. But if you wish, we will go forward rather than back."

"We cannot go back," I reminded him.

As I rowed, my muscles sore but my spirit hopeful, I glanced back at the now-distant fires along the Dragon's Mount, where my mother had first come with me in her belly, running from the very kingdom and man to whom we now journeyed.

I wondered when I would next return to Broceliande and when if ever I would see Viviane or Merlin again; if I would ever return to find Lukat, a soldier in the service of King Hoel, whose armies patrolled the coast of Armorica; if I would ride the Eponi horses, or hunt the boars of Moccus, or visit that terrible Well of Poison that brought so much darkness with it into my life. I thought most about that broken cauldron, and about my mother, whose soul could not rest so long as Morgause lived.

Lancelot, across from me, remained sullen, though both the lady and I tried to cheer him with joke and song as our weary toil across the water continued. "You must save your strength," he muttered, glancing at me as I shared some old rhyme I'd been taught by Merlin. Then, with some tenderness, he let his oar rest for a moment, and reached up to touch the back of my scalp, just at the nape of my neck, so that his fingers slipped beneath the cool metal of the torque he'd given me. He whispered, "I am thinking of that first night. Of the two of us upon a flat rock. Strangers who could not resist each other, bewitched by the summer solstice."

I grinned, happy suddenly, as if I could handle anything that the gods threw at me—at us—and I rowed harder and glanced over at him often through the long night, catching the edge of his smile when he cared to look my way.

We first felt a warm wind, damp against our faces sometime past midnight. Guinevere had long before fallen asleep, covered in fur and sheepskin, turned about in such a way that all I could see was her golden hair in the shimmering moonlight. My shoulders ached from fighting the current, and my stomach had turned sour from the slapping waves that had begun hours before.

"It is coming," Lancelot said, quietly. I looked to the dark, swift gusts of cloud that veiled the moon as they moved across the curve of sky. "You can smell the worst of the storm an hour before it comes," he said. "Take a deep breath."

I inhaled deeply, and felt as if I could smell that fragrance of storm that often did come well before the lightning bolts themselves would strike.

"Do not be afraid." He kept his voice low so as not to wake the princess. "We will need to lash ourselves to the boat."

"But if the boat breaks…" I said.

"The boat will not break," he shook his head, grinning. "You lived too long in those caves. The boat will ride this out, but should the waves grow too high, we may each of us be cast off. Here, draw that rope from the mooring hook."

I set my oar down lengthwise in the boat, and leaned forward, reaching for the rope. When I had it, he directed me with hand motions to loop it about Guinevere's waist. I had to reach beneath her coverings, and I felt for her hips. When I found them, she stirred slightly in sleep. I brought the rope gently around her, tightening it.

"Through the oarlock," he said, nodding.

I did as I was told, and then wrapped it around my right hand and he wrapped it around his left, and then through his oarlock. Finally, he knotted it tightly.

I glanced at our wrists, bound as they were to each other. "We have hand-fasted," I said.

He laughed. "Yes, I suppose we have."

And then the first of the rain began. I looked up to it, opening my mouth from thirst, tasting its sweetness.

"Enjoy it now." He shook his head at me as if I were mad. "For soon enough, the worst of it will be upon us." His eyes scanned the dark horizon ahead of us.

"Nothing but storms in life," I said.

"Storms make things interesting."

"How far do you think we are from land?"

"We'll know by the fires at Lyonesse, unless we've drifted more to the north than I believe."

"Where would that take us?"

"We might end up in the Saxon ports if we've gone too far. But if I've followed the stars—"

"You read the stars?"

"In some fashion," he nodded. "The winds that are heading toward us may take us at some distance from the White Raven's Mount."

"Are you scared?" I asked, glancing at the sleeping maiden, at the sky, and at the face of the man I loved from the first moment I saw him.

"Of the wind?" His eyes gleamed even in that moonlit dark, with the rain spitting down on us. "Of rain? These are nothing to be afraid of. I cannot say, Mordred, what will become of us when we reach shore. She may not protect me from the charges that I will surely face, for I once deserted my king. You are the son of Morgan le Fay, and I understand what that means as well. We may be heading toward our doom. What is a storm compared to that? I have done terrible things in my youth for which I will surely pay, whether at the hand of the king or at the hand of the goddess herself. You know of my past, of that Lady of Astolat who took her life for grief that her husband had abandoned her. Of the shame I bore and of my lost child, hidden from me for too many years. You know of my terrible betrayal of our people as well. And yet, knowing this, none of these crimes of my past brings great fear to me. I am here. With you. Now. What is a storm against us? And what of the world itself, should it rise up against us?"

He lifted his bound wrist wrapped with the rope that hung loose, connecting the two of us, though also the sleeping maiden, a princess of another land. "We are tied by more than rope, Mordred. And whether we go to that Otherworld tonight or in some future day of reckoning, I have faith that you will be here, as you are now."

"I shall," I said.

"And so shall I," he whispered in that gruff way he did when embarrassed by a shared tenderness. After a moment, his thoughts wandering, he shook his head slightly. "Look at her, sleeping like she has no cares. Who is she that she should take men's lives? We may drown tonight to bring her to those rocks."

I glanced over at the sleeping maiden, her hair nearly white against the dark of night; her small hand with its jeweled fingers peeking out beneath blankets. I had a slight memory of Merlin telling me that Lancelot should never meet her, and I hoped it wasn't because she would betray him to the king. I could not bear it if I had been the instrument of anything that harmed him. Yet she seemed so innocent and kind, and watching her sleep kept my thoughts from straying into darker territory. "I like her," I said. "She's not what I thought a Roman princess would be."

"She's precisely what I expected," he said sullenly. He glanced over at me and gave me a quick wink. "We could always throw her over the side."

I liked seeing his good humor again and felt a bit of warmth as I watched him. I did not know what to expect in the coming day, nor did I even understand why it had been so important to Merlin that we ensure Guinevere's safety into the arms of my father, but I felt Lancelot and I were on the path of life, together, and though sorrow followed us from the past, I did not believe it could be ahead of us even if danger lurked.

And so, I took up the oar again, thinking of our connection that ran deep in such a short time, as if the Lady of the Lake and the Lord of the Forest had indeed blessed us despite our crimes against them.

The wind rose, and soon enough would beat against us. I had no doubt we would have a terrible battle with the taranis crows, which are the storm clouds of the gods sent to vex us.

I thought of my mother, young, running from my father, with Merlin beside her in a long boat but on a similar journey. All these were the connections of existence, which brought the soul's journey to completion.

I had all that I needed within that small boat. Ahead of me, the future, which no one could predict to my satisfaction; perhaps my father would embrace me, once he knew my identity or perhaps he would seek to have me murdered. My mother's castle of Tintagel, with its arched doorways and small windows and rough-hewn steps, of which I'd heard much and seen through her visions, might wait. Or perhaps Morgause's prediction, which had been Merlin's prophecy before my birth, that I would be the instrument of the great unmaking, the greatest unraveling of all, would be my future. My childhood and youth and those crimes of such innocence and ignorance were behind me. But here, within this boat, with the approaching storm sweeping down upon us, wasmy present, as Lancelot himself had whispered to me: *Here, now.*

In this humble boat, with a princess who would soon be queen, with a hermit who had been a knight, and with that third soul, the one that he and I shared between us. Not a half-soul of shadow, but that soul made by the binding of our two souls.

I did not even know if the morrow would bring our separation. I did not even know this man beyond my experience with him and my sense of him. We had been through much in a short period of time, and I would lay down my life for him now if it was asked of me.

And yet, these were my thoughts as the storm descended upon us: *No fear, no sorrow.*

For we were bound in some way, beyond rope itself.

I cannot ask more from the world than this moment, I thought. *It is a sacred moment, a flickering candle to be protected from the wind.*

The debt of love. It was that overwhelming sense of binding with another soul and the obligation to protect that flickering candle of it.

From storms. From armies. Even from self. I owed this love all that I had to offer.

Even then, in my innocence, I could not have predicted what awaited us within a few short hours. I could not know that, sometimes, even the one you love and trust has shadows that cannot be swept back with the hand of love nor that all promises made might not be kept.

Still, I had no fear when the storm came. As the waves lifted our boat up, we fought against the will of the universe to toss and drown us, that vessel of life that protects and destroys, with our backs to the past and our muscles taxed to their limits from the fight.

Bound together, we moved toward dawn.

Epilogue

1

In that cell within the monastery, many years after, Mordred finished the telling of his early life for the evening; he no longer was in that boat, crossing with Lancelot and Guinevere, many years before. He lay upon the straw of his gaol, worn from a night of memories.

The young monk of fair face stared at him as if not recognizing the man who had begun the tale. "It was as if—"

"I spoke in your mind," Mordred said. "Do you not think I had perfected that Art learned in childhood?"

"But this is not the end of your tale," the monk said. "For I know of events that have come to pass since this. Of Guinevere and of Lancelot. I have heard of Morgan's fury at its greatest moment like a pillar of fire."

"That half-soul within Morgause, yes," Mordred nodded. "She did not rest, having lost her first battle for Guinevere. You demand so much from me. Why is that, little brother monk? What incites this burning interest in the life of these folk that I knew in my life?"

"You have known great knights, and kings and queens. You have known sorcery and magick," the monk said. "All I have known are within these walls."

"You may hear these rumors from field hands about the terrible and powerful Mordred. Why do you risk your own life here? For surely the night is half done, and your brethren might wonder why you spend a night alone in a cell with the traitor, Mordred, bastard son of Arthur and of that Witch-Queen Morgan."

The monk grew pale but did not speak for several moments. Then, he said tenderly, "I do not believe everything said by those who did not bear witness. But you must be tired. You should sleep."

But Mordred's curiosity had been raised. "Though you are young, did you play some part in my life that I did not know? Why this keen interest?"

"I have sworn a vow to never speak of these things," the monk said.

"And yet, I must speak of them, fair monk."

"If you have this great Art, surely you have already sifted my thoughts."

"I am a knave in many things," Mordred said. "But I would not penetrate a mind against the will of its owner. You promised me freedom if I told you all that I know."

"And I shall hold you to that," the young monk said. "As you will hold me to it as well."

"And yet, in the morning, that deceitful knight, Sir Bedevere, who craved that sacred sword from the moment he saw it and now wields it as if he were king, will come to behead me with its sharp blade."

"Do not worry about the knights who come for you," the monk said. "They cannot pass into this monastery if we do not wish it, even with that pagan sword."

Mordred chuckled. "These are knights, youth. They are not priests of your churchyards. I have heard of knights who have slaughtered women and their children at mass. Bedevere will not stop at your wooden gate to say his prayers."

"You underestimate us here," the monk said. "For we have had many soldiers who arrived here to burn us from this place. But they cannot, and for reasons I may not reveal yet. But perhaps you will learn of this." Then he stretched his arms out and yawned. "But it is late, and dawn is not far off in coming. Will you tell me more tomorrow when the sun has set? For I may come then and sit with you."

"You hide much, little monk," Mordred said, arching an eyebrow. "Who are you that you and your fellows hold back armies from this place?"

But the monk ignored his question, rising up and taking the nearly dark torch up. "I will bring a good supper for you tomorrow. But I wish to know more of Arthur and your lover, Lancelot, and if you know the fate of your cousin Sir Gawain and of that Prince of Lyonesse, called Tristan—"

"As I can, so I shall," Mordred said but felt the pull of sleep take him over. He lay back in the straw, closing his eyes, trying not to dream.

2

The young monk stepped outside the cell, shutting and locking the door behind him. He glanced through the small square window, barely large enough for a man's fist, and watched as the captive turned onto his side and fell fast asleep upon his straw bed.

He stood there awhile longer, watching Mordred in his sleep, wondering if he dreamed of Lancelot even then, of the great King Arthur and the knights of the round table, and of the palace at Camelot, with its towers that went nearly to the sun.

The monk then returned to his own sleeping quarters, and as he lay down upon his hard bed, he thought of those two men on the boat, tied by rope, the storm all around them.

He closed his eyes, feeling a terrible longing for that which he had not yet learned.

That night, he dreamed of Mordred and Lancelot, on the boat with the sleeping maiden, facing the storm of life that was to come.

The Mordred Trilogy will be continued.